Barking at
Butterflies

and Other Stories

Barking at
Butterflies

and Other Stories

Evan Hunter
a.k.a. Ed McBain

Five Star
Unity, Maine

Five Star First Edition Mystery Series.
Published in 2000 in conjunction with Tekno-Books and Ed Gorman.

First Edition, Second Printing

Cover photograph by Dragica Dimitrijevic-Hunter

Set in 11 pt. Plantin by Al Chase.

Printed in the United States on permanent paper.

Library of Congress Cataloging in Publication Data

Hunter, Evan, 1926–
    Barking at butterflies, and other stories / by Evan Hunter
a.k.a. Ed McBain. — 1st ed.
        p. cm.
    ISBN 0-7862-2536-X (HC : alk. paper)
    1. Detective and mystery stories, American. I. Title.
PS3515.U585 B37   2000
    813'.54—dc21
                                                    00-025939

Table of Contents

First Offense

He sat in the police van with the collar of his leather jacket turned up, the bright silver studs sharp against the otherwise unrelieved black. He was seventeen years old and he wore his hair in a high black crown. He carried his head high and erect because he knew he had a good profile, and he carried his mouth like a switch knife, ready to spring open at the slightest provocation. His hands were thrust deep into his jacket pockets, and his gray eyes reflected the walls of the van. There was excitement in his eyes, too, an almost holiday excitement. He tried to tell himself he was in trouble, but he couldn't quite believe it. His gradual descent to disbelief had been a spiral that had spun dizzily through the range of his emotions. Terror when the cop's flash had picked him out; blind panic when he'd started to run; rebellion when the cop's firm hand had closed around the leather sleeve of his jacket; sullen resignation when the cop had thrown him into the RMP car; and then cocky stubbornness when they'd booked him at the local precinct.

The desk sergeant had looked him over curiously, with a strange aloofness in his Irish eyes.

"What's the matter, Fatty?" he asked.

The sergeant stared at him implacably. "Put him away for the night," the sergeant said.

He'd slept overnight in the precinct cell block, and he'd awakened with this strange excitement pulsing through his narrow body, and it was the excitement that had caused his disbelief. Trouble, hell! He'd been in trouble before, but it had never felt like this. This was different. This was a ball, man. This was like being initiated into a secret society some place. His contempt for the police had grown when they refused him the opportunity to shave after breakfast. He was only seventeen, but he had a fairly decent beard, and a man should be allowed to shave in the morning, what the hell! But even the beard had somehow lent to the unreality of the situation, made him appear—in his own eyes—somehow more desperate, more sinister-looking. He knew he was in trouble, but the trouble was glamorous, and he surrounded it with the gossamer lie of make-believe. He was living the storybook legend. He was big time now. They'd caught him and booked him, and he should have been scared but he was excited instead.

There was one other person in the van with him, a guy who'd spent the night in the cell block, too. The guy was an obvious bum, and his breath stank of cheap wine, but he was better than nobody to talk to.

"Hey!" he said.

The bum looked up. "You talking to me?"

"Yeah. Where we going?"

"The line-up, kid," the bum said. "This your first offense?"

"This's the first time I got caught," he answered cockily.

"All felonies go to the line-up," the bum told him. "And also some special types of misdemeanors. You commit a felony?"

"Yeah," he said, hoping he sounded nonchalant. What'd they have this bum in for anyway? Sleeping on a park bench?

"Well, that's why you're going to the line-up. They have guys from every detective squad in the city there, to look you over. So they'll remember you next time. They put you on a stage, and they read off the offense, and the Chief of Detectives starts firing questions at you. What's your name, kid?"

"What's it to you?"

8

"Don't get smart, punk, or I'll break your arm," the bum said.

He looked at the bum curiously. He was a pretty big guy, with a heavy growth of beard, and powerful shoulders.

"My name's Stevie," he said.

"I'm Jim Skinner," the bum said. "When somebody's trying to give you advice, don't go hip on him."

"Yeah, well what's your advice?" he asked, not wanting to back down completely.

"When they get you up there, you don't have to answer anything. They'll throw questions, but you don't have to answer. Did you make a statement at the scene?"

"No," he answered.

"Good. Then don't make no statement now, either. They can't force you to. Just keep your mouth shut, and don't tell them nothing."

"I ain't afraid. They know all about it anyway," Stevie said.

The bum shrugged and gathered around him the sullen pearls of his scattered wisdom. Stevie sat in the van whistling, listening to the accompanying hum of the tires, hearing the secret hum of his blood beneath the other louder sound. He sat at the core of a self-imposed importance, basking in its warm glow, whistling contentedly, secretly happy. Beside him, Skinner leaned back against the wall of the van.

When they arrived at the Centre Street Headquarters, they put them in detention cells, awaiting the line-up which began at nine. At ten minutes to nine, they led him out of his cell, and the cop who'd arrested him originally took him into the special prisoner's elevator.

"How's it feel being an elevator boy?" he asked the cop.

The cop didn't answer him. They went upstairs to the big room where the line-up was being held. A detective in front of them was pinning on his shield so he could get past the cop at the desk. They crossed the large gymnasium-like compartment, walking past the men sitting on folded chairs before the stage.

"Get a nice turnout, don't you?" Stevie said.

"You ever tried vaudeville?" the cop answered.

The blinds in the room had not been drawn yet, and Stevie could see everything clearly. The stage itself with the permanently fixed microphone hanging from a narrow metal tube above; the height markers—four feet, five feet, six feet—behind the mike on the wide white wall. The men in the seats, he knew, were all detectives and his sense of importance suddenly flared again when he realized these bulls had come from all over the city just to look at him. Behind the bulls was a raised platform with a sort of lecturer's stand on it. A microphone rested on the stand, and a chair was behind it, and he assumed this was where the Chief bull would sit. There were uniformed cops stationed here and there around the room, and there was one man in civilian clothing who sat at a desk in front of the stage.

"Who's that?" Stevie asked the cop.

"Police stenographer," the cop answered. "He's going to take down your words for posterity."

They walked behind the stage, and Stevie watched as other felony offenders from all over the city joined them. There was one woman, but all the rest were men, and he studied their faces carefully, hoping to pick up some tricks from them, hoping to learn the subtlety of their expressions. They didn't look like much. He was better-looking than all of them, and the knowledge pleased him. He'd be the star of this little shindig. The cop who'd been with him moved over to talk to a big broad who was obviously a policewoman. Stevie looked around, spotted Skinner and walked over to him.

"What happens now?" he asked.

"They're gonna pull the shades in a few minutes," Skinner said. "Then they'll turn on the spots and start the line-up. The spots won't blind you, but you won't be able to see the faces of any of the bulls out there."

"Who wants to see them mugs?" Stevie asked.

Skinner shrugged. "When your case is called, your arresting officer goes back and stands near the Chief of Detectives, just in case the Chief needs more dope from him. The Chief'll read off your name and the borough where you was pinched. A number'll follow the borough. Like he'll say 'Manhattan one' or 'Manhattan two.' That's just the number of the case from that borough. You're first, you get number one, you follow?"

"Yeah," Stevie said.

"He'll tell the bulls what they got you on, and then he'll say either 'Statement' or 'No statement.' If you made a statement, chances are he won't ask many questions 'cause he won't want you to contradict anything damaging you already said. If there's no statement, he'll fire questions like a machine gun. But you won't have to answer nothing."

"Then what?"

"When he's through, you go downstairs to get mugged and printed. Then they take you over to the Criminal Courts Building for arraignment."

"They're gonna take my picture, huh?" Stevie asked.

"Yeah."

"You think there'll be reporters here?"

"Huh?"

"Reporters."

"Oh. Maybe. All the wire services hang out in a room across the street from where the vans pulled up. They got their own police radio in there, and they get the straight dope

11

as soon as it's happening, in case they want to roll with it. There may be some reporters." Skinner paused. "Why? What'd you do?"

"It ain't so much what I done," Stevie said. "I was just wonderin' if we'd make the papers."

Skinner stared at him curiously. "You're all charged up, ain't you, Stevie?"

"Hell, no. Don't you think I know I'm in trouble?"

"Maybe you don't know just how much trouble," Skinner said.

"What the hell are you talking about?"

"This ain't as exciting as you think, kid. Take my word for it."

"Sure, you know all about it."

"I been around a little," Skinner said dryly.

"Sure, on park benches all over the country. I know I'm in trouble, don't worry."

"You kill anybody?"

"No," Stevie said.

"Assault?"

Stevie didn't answer.

"Whatever you done," Skinner advised, "and no matter how long you been doin' it before they caught you, make like it's your first time. Tell them you done it, and then say you don't know why you done it, but you'll never do it again. It might help you, kid. You might get off with a suspended sentence."

"Yeah?"

"Sure. And then keep your nose clean afterwards, and you'll be okay."

"Keep my nose clean! Don't make me laugh, pal."

Skinner clutched Stevie's arm in a tight grip. "Kid, don't be a damn fool. If you can get out, get out now! I coulda got out a hundred times; and I'm still with it, and it's no picnic. Get out before you get started."

Stevie shook off Skinner's hand. "Come on, willya?" he said, annoyed.

"Knock it off there," the cop said. "We're ready to start."

"Take a look at your neighbors, kid," Skinner whispered. "Take a hard look. And then get out of it while you still can."

Stevie grimaced and turned away from Skinner. Skinner whirled him around to face him again, and there was a pleading desperation on the unshaven face, a mute reaching in the red-rimmed eyes before he spoke again. "Kid," he said, "listen to me. Take my advice. I've been . . ."

"Knock it off!" the cop warned again.

He was suddenly aware of the fact that the shades had been drawn and the room was dim. It was very quiet out there, and he hoped they would take him first. The excitement had risen to an almost fever pitch inside him, and he couldn't wait to get on that stage. What the hell was Skinner talking about anyway? "Take a look at your neighbors, kid." The poor jerk probably had a wet brain. What the hell did the police bother with old drunks for, anyway?

A uniformed cop led one of the men from behind the stage, and Stevie moved a little to his left, so that he could see the stage, hoping none of the cops would shove him back where he wouldn't have a good view. His cop and the police-woman were still talking, paying no attention to him. He smiled, unaware that the smile developed as a smirk, and watched the first man mounting the steps to the stage.

The man's eyes were very small, and he kept blinking them, blinking them. He was bald at the back of his head, and he was wearing a Navy peacoat and dark tweed trousers, and his eyes were red-rimmed and sleepy-looking. He reached to the five-foot-six-inches marker on the wall behind him, and he stared out at the bulls, blinking.

"Assisi," the Chief of Detectives said, "Augustus, Manhattan one. Thirty-three years old. Picked up in a bar on 43rd and Broadway, carrying a .45 Colt automatic. No statement. How about it, Gus?"

"How about what?" Assisi asked.

"Were you carrying a gun?"

"Yes, I was carrying a gun." Assisi seemed to realize his shoulders were slumped. He pulled them back suddenly, standing erect.

"Where, Gus?"

"In my pocket."

"What were you doing with the gun, Gus?"

"I was just carrying it."

"Why?"

"Listen, I'm not going to answer any questions," Assisi said. "You're gonna put me through a third-degree, I ain't answering nothing. I want a lawyer."

"You'll get plenty opportunity to have a lawyer," the Chief of Detectives said. "And nobody's giving you a third-degree. We just want to know what you were doing with a gun. You know that's against the law, don't you?"

"I've got a permit for the gun," Assisi said.

"We checked with Pistol Permits, and they say no. This is a Navy gun, isn't it?"

"Yeah."

"What?"

"I said yeah, it's a Navy gun."

"What were you doing with it? Why were you carrying it around?"

"I like guns."

"Why?"

"Why what? Why do I like guns? Because . . ."

"Why were you carrying it around?"

"I don't know."

"Well, you must have a reason for carrying a loaded .45. The gun *was* loaded, wasn't it?"

"Yeah, it was loaded."

"You have any other guns?"

"No."

"We found a .38 in your room. How about that one?"

"It's no good."

"What?"

"The .38."

"What do you mean, no good?"

"The firin' mechanism is busted."

"You want a gun that works, is that it?"

"I didn't say that."

"You said the .38's no good because it won't fire, didn't you?"

"Well, what good's a gun that won't fire?"

"Why do you need a gun that fires?"

"I was just carrying it. I didn't shoot anybody, did I?"

"No, you didn't. Were you planning on shooting somebody?"

"Sure," Assisi said. "That's just what I was planning."

"Who?"

"I don't know," Assisi said sarcastically. "Anybody. The first guy I saw, all right? Everybody, all right? I was planning on wholesale murder."

"Not murder, maybe, but a little larceny, huh?"

"Murder," Assisi insisted, in his stride now. "I was just going to shoot up the whole town. Okay? You happy now?"

"Where'd you get the gun?"

"In the Navy."

"Where?"

"From my ship."

"It's a stolen gun?"

"No, I found it."

"You stole government property, is that it?"

"I found it."

"When'd you get out of the Navy?"

"Three months ago."

"You worked since?"

"No."

"Where were you discharged?"

"Pensacola."

"Is that where you stole the gun?"

"I didn't steal it."

"Why'd you leave the Navy?"

Assisi hesitated for a long time.

"Why'd you leave the Navy?" the Chief of Detectives asked again.

"They kicked me out!" Assisi snapped.

"Why?"

"I was undesirable!" he shouted.

"Why?"

Assisi did not answer.

"Why?"

There was silence in the darkened room. Stevie watched Assisi's face, the twitching mouth, the blinking eyelids.

"Next case," the Chief of Detectives said.

Stevie watched as Assisi walked across the stage and down the steps on the other side, where the uniformed cop met him. He'd handled himself well, Assisi had. They'd rattled him a little at the end there, but on the whole he'd done a good job. So the guy was lugging a gun around, so what? He was right, wasn't he? He didn't shoot nobody, so what was all the fuss about? Cops! They had nothing else to do, they went around hauling in guys who were carrying guns. Poor bastard was a veteran, too, that was really rubbing it in. But he did a good job up there, even though he was nervous, you could see he was very nervous.

A man and a woman walked past him and onto the stage. The man was very tall, topping the six-foot marker. The woman was shorter, a bleached blonde turning to fat.

"They picked them up together," Skinner whispered. "So they show them together. They figure a pair'll always work as a pair, usually."

"How'd you like that Assisi?" Stevie whispered back. "He really had them bulls on the run, didn't he?"

Skinner didn't answer. The Chief of Detectives cleared his throat.

"MacGregor, Peter, aged forty-five, and Anderson, Marcia, aged forty-two, Bronx one. Got them in a parked car on the Grand Concourse. Back seat of the car was loaded with goods including luggage, a typewriter, a portable sewing machine, and a fur coat. No statements. What about all that stuff, Pete?"

"It's mine."

"The fur coat, too?"

"No, that's Marcia's."

"You're not married, are you?"

"No."

"Living together?"

"Well, you know," Pete said.

"What about the stuff?" the Chief of Detectives said again.

"I told you," Pete said. "It's ours."

"What was it doing in the car?"

"Oh. Well, we were . . . uh . . ." The man paused for a long time. "We were going on a trip."

"Where to?"

17

"Where? Oh. To . . . uh . . ."

Again he paused, frowning, and Stevie smiled, thinking what a clown this guy was. This guy was better than a side-show at Coney. This guy couldn't tell a lie without having to think about it for an hour. And the dumpy broad with him was a hot sketch, too. This act alone was worth the price of admission.

"Uh . . ." Pete said, still fumbling for words. "Uh . . . we were going to . . . uh . . . Denver."

"What for?"

"Oh, just a little pleasure trip, you know," he said, attempting a smile.

"How much money were you carrying when we picked you up?"

"Forty dollars."

"You were going to Denver on forty dollars?"

"Well, it was fifty dollars. Yeah, it was more like fifty dollars."

"Come on, Pete, what were you doing with all that stuff in the car?"

"I told you. We were taking a trip."

"With a sewing machine, huh? You do a lot of sewing, Pete?"

"Marcia does."

"That right, Marcia?"

The blonde spoke in a high reedy voice. "Yeah, I do a lot of sewing."

"That fur coat, Marcia. Is it yours?"

"Sure."

"It has the initials G.D. on the lining. Those aren't your initials, are they, Marcia?"

"No."

"Whose are they?"

18

"Search me. We bought that coat in a hock shop."

"Where?"

"Myrtle Avenue, Brooklyn. You know where that is?"

"Yes, I know where it is. What about that luggage? It had initials on it, too. And they weren't yours or Pete's. How about it?"

"We got that in a hock shop, too."

"And the typewriter?"

"That's Pete's."

"Are you a typist, Pete?"

"Well, I fool around a little, you know."

"We're going to check all this stuff against our Stolen Goods list, you know that, don't you?"

"We got all that stuff in hock shops," Pete said. "If it's stolen, we don't know nothing about it."

"Were you going to Denver with him, Marcia?"

"Oh, sure."

"When did you both decide to go? A few minutes ago?"

"We decided last week sometime."

"Were you going to Denver by way of the Grand Concourse?"

"Huh?" Pete said.

"Your car was parked on the Grand Concourse. What were you doing there with a carload of stolen goods?"

"It wasn't stolen," Pete said.

"We were on our way to Yonkers," the woman said.

"I thought you were going to Denver."

"Yeah, but we had to get the car fixed first. There was something wrong with the . . ." She paused, turning to Pete. "What was it, Pete? That thing that was wrong?"

Pete waited a long time before answering. "Uh . . . the . . . uh . . . the flywheel, yeah. There's a garage up in Yonkers fixes them good, we heard. Flywheels, I mean."

"If you were going to Yonkers, why were you parked on the Concourse?"

"Well, we were having an argument."

"What kind of an argument?"

"Not an argument, really. Just a discussion, sort of."

"About what?"

"About what to eat."

"What!"

"About what to eat. I wanted to eat Chink's, but Marcia wanted a glass of milk and a piece of pie. So we were trying to decide whether we should go to the Chink's or the cafeteria. That's why we were parked on the Concourse."

"We found a wallet in your coat, Pete. It wasn't yours, was it?"

"No."

"Whose was it?"

"I don't know." He paused, then added hastily, "There wasn't no money in it."

"No, but there was identification. A Mr. Simon Granger. Where'd you get it, Pete?"

"I found it in the subway. There wasn't no money in it."

"Did you find all that other stuff in the subway, too?"

"No, sir, I bought that." He paused. "I was going to return the wallet, but I forgot to stick it in the mail."

"Too busy planning for the Denver trip, huh?"

"Yeah, I guess so."

"When's the last time you earned an honest dollar, Pete?"

Pete grinned. "Oh, about two, three years ago, I guess."

"Here's their records," the Chief of Detectives said. "Marcia, 1938, Sullivan Law; 1939, Concealing Birth of Issue; 1940, Possession of Narcotics—you still on the stuff, Marcia?"

"No."

"1942, dis cond; 1943, Narcotics again; 1947—you had enough, Marcia?"

Marcia didn't answer.

"Pete," the Chief of Detectives said, "1940, Attempted Rape; 1941, Selective Service Act; 1942, dis cond; 1943, Attempted Burglary; 1945, Living on Proceeds of Prostitution; 1947, Assault and Battery, did two years at Ossining."

"I never done no time," Pete said.

"According to this, you did."

"I never done no time," he insisted.

"1950," the Chief of Detectives went on, "Carnal Abuse of a Child." He paused. "Want to tell us about that one, Pete?"

"I . . . uh . . ." Pete swallowed. "I got nothing to say."

"You're ashamed of *some* things, that it?"

Pete didn't answer.

"Get them out of here," the Chief of Detectives said.

"See how long he kept them up there?" Skinner whispered. "He knows what they are, wants every bull in the city to recognize them if they . . ."

"Come on," a detective said, taking Skinner's arm.

Stevie watched as Skinner climbed the steps to the stage. Those two had really been something, all right. And just looking at them, you'd never know they were such operators. You'd never know they . . .

"Skinner, James, Manhattan two. Aged fifty-one. Threw a garbage can through the plate glass window of a clothing store on Third Avenue. Arresting officer found him inside the store with a bundle of overcoats. No statement. That right, James?"

"I don't remember," Skinner said.

"Is it, or isn't it?"

"All I remember is waking up in jail this morning."

21

"You don't remember throwing that ash can through the window?"

"No, sir."

"You don't remember taking those overcoats?"

"No, sir."

"Well, you must have done it, don't you think? The off-duty detective found you inside the store with the coats in your arms."

"I got only his word for that, sir."

"Well, his word is pretty good. Especially since he found you inside the store with your arms full of merchandise."

"I don't remember, sir."

"You've been here before, haven't you?"

"I don't remember, sir."

"What do you do for a living, James?"

"I'm unemployed, sir."

"When's the last time you worked?"

"I don't remember, sir."

"You don't remember much of anything, do you?"

"I have a poor memory, sir."

"Maybe the record has a better memory than you, James," the Chief of Detectives said.

"Maybe so, sir. I couldn't say."

"I hardly know where to start, James. You haven't been exactly an ideal citizen."

"Haven't I, sir?"

"Here's as good a place as any. 1948, Assault and Robbery; 1949, Indecent Exposure; 1951, Burglary; 1952, Assault and Robbery again. You're quite a guy, aren't you, James?"

"If you say so, sir."

"I say so. Now how about that store?"

"I don't remember anything about a store, sir."

"Why'd you break into it?"

"I don't remember breaking into any store, sir."

"Hey, what's this?" the Chief of Detectives said suddenly.

"Sir?"

"Maybe we should've started back a little further, huh, James? Here, on your record. 1938, convicted of first degree murder, sentenced to execution."

The assembled bulls began murmuring among themselves. Stevie leaned forward eagerly, anxious to get a better look at this bum who'd offered him advice.

"What happened there, James?"

"What happened where, sir?"

"You were sentenced to death? How come you're still with us?"

"The case was appealed."

"And never retried?"

"No, sir."

"You're pretty lucky, aren't you?"

"I'm pretty unlucky, sir, if you ask me."

"Is that right? You cheat the chair, and you call that unlucky. Well, the law won't slip up this time."

"I don't know anything about law, sir."

"You don't, huh?"

"No, sir. I only know that if you want to get a police station into action, all you have to do is buy a cheap bottle of wine and drink it quiet, minding your own business."

"And that's what you did, huh, James?"

"That's what I did, sir."

"And you don't remember breaking into that store?"

"I don't remember anything."

"All right, next case."

Skinner turned his head slowly, and his eyes met Stevie's squarely. Again, there was the same mute pleading in his eyes, and then he turned his head away and shuffled off the stage and down the steps into the darkness.

The cop's hand closed around Stevie's biceps. For an instant he didn't know what was happening, and then he realized his case was the next one. He shook off the cop's hand, squared his shoulders, lifted his head, and began climbing the steps.

He felt taller all at once. He felt like an actor coming on after his cue. There was an aura of unreality about the stage and the darkened room beyond it, the bulls sitting in that room.

The Chief of Detectives was reading off the information about him, but he didn't hear it. He kept looking at the lights, which weren't really so bright, they didn't blind him at all. Didn't they have brighter lights? Couldn't they put more lights on him, so they could see him when he told his story?

He tried to make out the faces of the detectives, but he couldn't see them clearly, and he was aware of the Chief of Detectives' voice droning on and on, but he didn't hear what the man was saying, he heard only the hum of his voice. He glanced over his shoulder, trying to see how tall he was against the markers, and then he stood erect, his shoulders back, moving closer to the hanging microphone, wanting to be sure his voice was heard when he began speaking.

". . . no statement," the Chief of Detectives concluded. There was a long pause, and Stevie waited, holding his breath. "This your first offense, Steve?" the Chief of Detectives asked.

"Don't you know?" Stevie answered.

"I'm asking you."

"Yeah, it's my first offense."

"You want to tell us all about it?"

"There's nothing to tell. You know the whole story, anyway."

"Sure, but do you?"

"What are you talking about?"

"Tell us the story, Steve."

"Whatya makin' a big federal case out of a lousy stick-up for? Ain't you got nothing better to do with your time?"

"We've got plenty of time, Steve."

"Well, I'm in a hurry."

"You're not going anyplace, kid. Tell us about it."

"What's there to tell? There was a candy store stuck up, that's all."

"Did you stick it up?"

"That's for me to know and you to find out."

"We know you did."

"Then don't ask me stupid questions."

"Why'd you do it?"

"I ran out of butts."

"Come on, kid."

"I done it 'cause I wanted to."

"Why?"

"Look, you caught me cold, so let's get this over with, huh? Whatya wastin' time with me for?"

"We want to hear what you've got to say. Why'd you pick this particular candy store?"

"I just picked it. I put slips in a hat and picked this one out."

"You didn't really, did you, Steve?"

"No, I didn't really. I picked it 'cause there's an old crumb who runs it, and I figured it was a pushover."

"What time did you enter the store, Steve?"

"The old guy told you all this already, didn't he? Look, I know I'm up here so you can get a good look at me. All right, take your good look, and let's get it over with."

"What time, Steve?"

"I don't have to tell you nothing."

"Except that we know it already."

"Then why do you want to hear it again? Ten o'clock, all right? How does that fit?"

"A little early, isn't it?"

"How's eleven? Try that one for size."

"Let's make it twelve, and we'll be closer."

"Make it whatever you want to," Stevie said, pleased with the way he was handling this. They knew all about it, anyway, so he might as well have himself a ball, show them they couldn't shove him around.

"You went into the store at twelve, is that right?"

"If you say so, Chief."

"Did you have a gun?"

"No."

"What then?"

"Nothing."

"Nothing at all?"

"Just me, I scared him with a dirty look, that's all."

"You had a switch knife, didn't you?"

"You found one on me, so why ask?"

"Did you use the knife?"

"No."

"You didn't tell the old man to open the cash register or you'd cut him up? Isn't that what you said?"

"I didn't make a tape recording of what I said."

"But you did threaten him with the knife. You did force him to open the cash register, holding the knife on him."

"I suppose so."

"How much money did you get?"

"You've got the dough. Why don't you count it?"

"We already have. Twelve dollars, is that right?"

"I didn't get a chance to count it. The Law showed."

"When did the Law show?"

"When I was leaving. Ask the cop who pinched me. He knows when."

"Something happened before you left, though."

"Nothing happened. I cleaned out the register and then blew. Period."

"Your knife had blood on it."

"Yeah? I was cleaning chickens last night."

"You stabbed the owner of that store, didn't you?"

"Me? I never stabbed nobody in my whole life."

"Why'd you stab him?"

"I didn't."

"Where'd you stab him?"

"I didn't stab him."

"Did he start yelling?"

"I don't know what you're talking about."

"You stabbed him, Steve. We know you did."

"You're full of crap."

"Don't get smart, Steve."

"Ain't you had your look yet? What the hell more do you want?"

"We want you to tell us why you stabbed the owner of that store."

"And I told you I didn't stab him."

"He was taken to the hospital last night with six knife wounds in his chest and abdomen. Now how about that, Steve?"

"Save your questioning for the detective squadroom. I ain't saying another word."

"You had your money. Why'd you stab him?"

Stevie did not answer.

"Were you afraid?"

"Afraid of what?" Stevie answered defiantly.

"I don't know. Afraid he'd tell who held him up? Afraid

he'd start yelling? What were you afraid of, kid?"

"I wasn't afraid of nothing. I told the old crumb to keep his mouth shut. He shoulda listened to me."

"He didn't keep his mouth shut?"

"Ask him."

"I'm asking you!"

"No, he didn't keep his mouth shut. He started yelling. Right after I'd cleaned out the drawer. The damn jerk, for a lousy twelve bucks he starts yelling."

"What'd you do?"

"I told him to shut up."

"And he didn't."

"No, he didn't. So I hit him, and he still kept yelling. So— so I gave him the knife."

"Six times?"

"I don't know how many times. I just—gave it to him. He shouldn't have yelled. You ask him if I did any harm to him before that. Go ahead, ask him. He'll tell you. I didn't even touch the crumb before he started yelling. Go to the hospital and ask him if I touched him. Go ahead, ask him."

"We can't, Steve."

"Wh . . ."

"He died this morning."

"He . . ." for a moment, Stevie could not think clearly. Died? Is that what he'd said? The room was curiously still now. It had been silently attentive before, but this was something else, something different, and the stillness suddenly chilled him, and he looked down at his shoes.

"I . . . I didn't mean him to pass away," he mumbled.

The police stenographer looked up. "To what?"

"To pass away," a uniformed cop repeated, whispering.

"What?" the stenographer asked again.

"He didn't mean him to pass away!" the cop shouted.

The cop's voice echoed in the silent room. The stenographer bent his head and began scribbling in his pad.

"Next case," the Chief of Detectives said.

Stevie walked off the stage, his mind curiously blank, his feet strangely leaden. He followed the cop to the door, and then walked with him to the elevator. They were both silent as the doors closed.

"You picked an important one for your first one," the cop said.

"He shouldn't have died on me," Stevie answered.

"You shouldn't have stabbed him," the cop said.

He tried to remember what Skinner had said to him before the line-up, but the noise of the elevator was loud in his ears, and he couldn't think clearly. He could only remember the word "neighbors" as the elevator dropped to the basement to join them.

Uncle Jimbo's Marbles

Last summer they quarantined the camp two weeks after we'd arrived.

Uncle Marvin called all us counselors into the dining room one July night and announced briefly that there was a polio scare at a nearby camp. He went on to say that whereas all of *our* campers had of course been vaccinated, he nonetheless felt it would be in the best interests of public safety if we voluntarily agreed not to leave the campgrounds until the threat had subsided. The words "public safety" were Uncle Marvin's own. He was the principal of a junior high school in the Bronx, and he also happened to own Camp Marvin, which is why it was called Camp Marvin and not Camp Chippewa or Manetoga or Hiawatha. He could have called it "Camp Levine," I suppose, Levine being his last name, but I somehow feel his choice was judicious. Besides, the name Marvin seemed to fit a camp whose owner was a man given to saying things like "public safety," especially when he became *Uncle* Marvin for the summer.

I was Uncle Don for the summer.

The kids in my bunk had never heard of Uncle Don on the radio, so they never made any jokes about my name. To tell the truth, I'd barely heard of him myself. Besides, they were a nice bunch of kids, and we were getting along fine until the voluntary quarantine in the best interests of public safety was declared by Marvin, and then things got a little strained and eventually led to a sort of hysteria.

Marvin's wife was named Lydia, and so the girls' camp

across the lake from Camp Marvin was called Camp Lydia, and the entire complex was called Camp Lydia-Marvin, which was possibly one of the most exciting names in the annals of American camp history. I was Uncle Don last summer, and I was nineteen years old. Across the lake in Camp Lydia was a girl named Aunt Rebecca, who was also nineteen years old and whom I loved ferociously. When the quarantine began, I started writing notes to her, and I would have them smuggled across the lake, tied to the handles of the big milk cans. *I love you, Aunt Rebecca,* my notes would say. And I would look across the still waters of the lake and try to imagine Becky opening my note, her dark eyes lowered as she read the words, her quick smile flashing over her face. I imagined she would look up hastily, she moved hastily, her eyes would dart, the smile would widen, she would stare into the distance at the pine trees towering over the boys' cabins, and maybe her heart would skip a beat, and maybe she would murmur softly under her breath, *I love you, too, Uncle Don.*

I hated Camp Marvin.

I will tell you what I loved.

I loved Rebecca Goldblatt, that's all. I had loved Rebecca Goldblatt long before I met her. I had loved her, to tell the truth, from the day I was twelve years old and was allowed to join the adult section of the public library. I had clutched my new card in my hand that bright October day, the card unmarked, every space on it empty, and wandered among the shelves. It was very warm inside the library, warm and hushed, and as I walked past the big windows I could hear the wind outside, and I could see the huge tree out front with its leaves shaking loose every time there was a new gust, and beyond that on the other side of the street some smaller trees, bare already, bending a little in the wind. It was very cold outside, but I was warm as I walked through the aisles with a smile on my face, holding my new library card, and wondering if everyone could tell I was an adult now, it said so on my card.

I found the book on one of the open shelves. The cover was red, tooled in gold. The title was *Ivanhoe*.

And that night I fell in love with Rebecca, not Rebecca Goldblatt, but the girl in *Ivanhoe*. And then when they re-released the movie, I fell in love with her all over again, not Elizabeth Taylor, but Rebecca, the girl in *Ivanhoe*. I can still remember one of the lines in the movie. It had nothing to do with either Ivanhoe's Rebecca or my own Rebecca Goldblatt, but I will never forget it anyway. It was when Robert Taylor was standing horseless, without a shield, trying to fend off the mace blows of the mounted Norman knight. And the judge or the referee, or whatever he was called in those days, looked at Robert Taylor, who had almost hit the Norman's horse with his sword, and shouted, "Beware, Saxon, lest you strike horse!" That was a rule, you see. You weren't allowed to strike the horse.

Oh, how I loved Rebecca Goldblatt!

I loved everything about her, her eyes, her nose, her mouth, her eyes. Her eyes were black. I know a lot of girls claim to have really black eyes, but Rebecca is the only person I have ever known in my entire life whose eyes were truly black and not simply a very dark brown. Sometimes, when she was in a sulky, brooding mood, her eyes got so mysterious and menacing they scared me half to death. Girls' eyes always do that to me when they're in that very dramatic solitary mood, as if they're pondering all the female secrets of the world. But usually her eyes were very bright and glowing, like a black purey. I shouldn't talk about marbles, I suppose, since marbles started all the trouble that summer—but that was how her eyes looked, the way a black purey looks when you hold it up to the sun.

I loved her eyes and I loved her smile, which was fast and open and yet somehow secretive, as if she'd been amused by something for a very long time before allowing it to burst onto her mouth. And I loved her figure which was very slender with sort of small breasts and very long legs that carried her in a strange sort of lope, especially when she was wearing a trenchcoat, don't ask me why. I loved her name and the way she looked. I loved her walk, and I loved the way she talked, too, a sort of combination of middle-class Bronx Jewish girl with a touch of City College Speech One thrown in, which is where she went to school and which is where I met her.

I think I should tell you now that I'm Italian.

That's how I happened to be at Camp Marvin in Stockbridge, Massachusetts, with a girl named Rebecca Goldblatt across the lake in Camp Lydia.

I know that's not much of a problem these days, what with new nations clamoring for freedom, and Federal troops crawling all over the South, and discrimination of all sorts every place you look. It's not much of a problem unless you happen to be nineteen years old and involved in it, and then it seems like a pretty big problem. I'm too young to have seen *Abie's Irish Rose*, but I honestly don't think I will ever understand what was so funny about *that* situation, believe me. I didn't think it was so funny last summer, and I still don't think it's funny, but maybe what happened with Uncle Jimbo's marbles had something to do with that. I don't really know. I just know for certain now that you can get so involved in something you don't really see the truth of it anymore. And the simple truth of Becky and me was that we loved each other. The rest of it was all hysteria, like with the marbles.

I have to tell you that I didn't want to go to Camp Marvin in the first place. It was all Becky's idea, and she presented it with that straightforward solemn look she always gets on her face when she discusses things like sending food to the starving people in China or disarmament or thalidomide or pesticides. She gets so deep and so involved sometimes that I feel like kissing her. Anyway, it was her idea, and I didn't like it because I said it sounded to me like hiding.

"It's not hiding," Becky said.

"Then what is it if not hiding?" I answered. "I don't *want* to be a counselor this summer. I want to go to the beach and listen to records and hold your hand."

"They have a beach at Camp Marvin," Becky said.

"And I don't like the name of the camp."

"Why not?"

"It's unimaginative. Anybody who would name a place Camp Marvin must be a very unimaginative person."

"He's a junior high school principal," Becky said.

"That only proves my point." She was looking very very solemn just about then, the way she gets when we discuss the Cuban situation, so I said, "Give me one good reason why we should go to Stockbridge, Massachusetts, to a camp named *Marvin,* of all things, would you please?"

"Yes."

"Well, go ahead."

"We would be together all summer," Becky said simply, "and we wouldn't have to hide from my father."

"That's the craziest thing I ever heard in my life," I said. "You want to go away and hide from him just so we won't have to hide from him."

"That's not what I'm saying," Becky said.

"Then what is it, if not hiding from him?"

"It's not my fault he's a bigoted jerk!" Becky said angrily, and I didn't realize how much this meant to her until that minute, because tears suddenly sprang into her eyes. I never

34

know what to do when a girl starts crying, especially someone you love.

"Becky," I said, "if we run away this summer, we're only confirming his . . ."

"He doesn't even know you, Donald," she said. "He doesn't know how sweet you are."

"Yes, but if we hide from him . . ."

"If he'd only meet you, if he'd only talk to you . . ."

"Yes, but if we run away to hide, then all we're doing is joining in with his lunacy, honey. Can't you see that?"

"My father is not a lunatic," Becky said. "My father is a dentist and a prejudiced ass, but he's not a lunatic. And anyway, you have to remember that *his* father can still remember pogroms in Russia."

"All right, but this isn't Russia," I said.

"I know."

"And I'm not about to ride into the town and rape all the women and kill all the men."

"You don't even know *how* to ride," Becky said.

"That's right," I said, "but even if I *did* know how to ride, I wouldn't do it."

"I know, you're so sweet," Becky said.

"Okay. Now if your father believes that I'm some kind of assassin with a stiletto, that's *his* fantasy, you see, Beck? And if I sneak away with you this summer, then I'm *joining* his fantasy, I'm becoming as crazy as he is. How can you ask me to do that?"

"I can ask you because I love you and I want to be alone with you without having to sneak and skulk all the time. It isn't fair."

"What isn't fair?"

"Sneaking and skulking all the time."

"That's right."

"When I love you so much."

"I love you, too, Beck," I said. "But . . ."

"Well, if you love me so much, it seems like a very simple thing to do to simply say you'll come with me to Camp Lydia-Marvin this summer."

I didn't say anything.

"Donald?" Becky said.

"This is a mistake," I said, shaking my head.

"We'll be alone."

"We'll be surrounded by eight thousand screaming kids!"

"The kids go to sleep early."

"We'll be hiding, we'll be—"

"We'll be alone."

"Damn it, Becky, sometimes . . ."

"Will you come, Donald?"

"Well, what else can I do? Let you go alone?"

"I think that's what scares my father," Becky said, the smile coming onto her mouth, her black eyes glowing.

"What are you talking about?"

"That fiery Italian temper."

"Yeah, go to hell, you *and* your father," I said smiling, and then I kissed her because what else can you do with a girl like that whom you love so terribly much?

That's how we came to be at Camp Lydia-Marvin last summer.

The quarantine was very ironic in an O. Henry way because we had gone to camp to be *together*, you see, and when Uncle Marvin had his bright quarantine idea, he really meant *quarantine*, the girls with the girls and the boys with the boys. So there was Rebecca clear the hell over on the other side of the lake, and here was I with a bunch of counselors named Uncle Bud and Uncle Jimbo and Uncle Dave and Uncle Ronnie and even Uncle Emil, who was a gym teacher at

Benjamin Franklin High School in Manhattan. All the uncles took the quarantine in high good spirits for the first week, I guess. I must admit that even I found a sense of adventure in tying my love notes to the handles of the milk cans. I never once questioned the validity of a quarantine that allowed milk to be passed from one side of the lake to the other. In fact, if it hadn't been for the milk cans, I would have gone out of my mind immediately. As it was, I *almost* went out of my mind, but not until much later. And by that time everybody was a little nutty.

I think it all started with the kids. Everything usually starts with kids. I once read a Ray Bradbury story called "Invasion" or something, about these Martians, or aliens, anyway, I don't remember which planet, who are planning an invasion of Earth, and they're doing it through the kids. Boy, that story scared me, I can tell you, since I have a kid brother who gets a very fanatical gleam in his eye every now and then. I wouldn't be at all surprised.

The thing that started with the kids was the marbles. Now every kid who goes to camp for the summer takes marbles with him. There's usually what they call Free Play or Unassigned, and that's when the kids go to ping pong or tether ball or marbles. Marbles were very big at Camp Marvin, especially after the quarantine started, though I'm still not sure whether the quarantine really had anything to do with the craze. Maybe there was just an unusual number of marbles at camp that summer, I don't know. At the end there, it sure *seemed* like a lot of marbles. The most marbles I had ever seen in my life before that was when I was eight years old and still living in Manhattan, before we moved up to the Bronx. My mother and father gave me a *hundred* marbles for my birthday, and they also gave me a leather pouch with drawstrings to put the marbles in. I went downstairs with the hundred marbles, and I lost them all in a two-hour game. I almost lost the pouch, too, because a kid on the block wanted to trade me forty immies and a steelie for it, but I had the wisdom to refuse the offer. I'll never forget my mother's face when I went upstairs and told her I'd been wiped out.

"You lost *all* the marbles?" she asked incredulously.

"Yeah, all the immies," I said.

"How?"

"Just playing immies," I said.

They didn't play immies at Camp Marvin; they played marbles. They used to draw a circle in the dirt, and each kid would put five or six marbles in the circle and try to hit them out with his shooter. I didn't know how to play marbles because all I played as a kid was immies, which is played by the curb, in the gutter. In fact, it was best to play immies after a rainstorm because then there would be puddles all over the street, and you never knew where the other guy's immie was. You just shot and prayed and felt around in the dirty water with your hand spread, trying to span the immies. It used to be fun when I was a kid. A city street is something like a summer camp all year round, you see. There are always a thousand kids on the block and a hundred games to choose from: stickball, stoopball, skullies, Johnny-on-a-Pony, Kick the Can, Statues, Salugi, Ring-a-Leavio, hundreds of games. I sometimes wonder why the *Herald Tribune* sends slum kids to the country. I think somebody ought to start sending country kids to the slums. In a way, when the marble craze started at Camp Marvin, it was very much like a craze starting on a city street, where one day a kid will come down with his roller skates, and the next day the roller-skating season has started. It was the same thing with the marbles at Camp Marvin. A couple of kids started a game, and before any of us were really completely aware of it, there were marble games being played all over the camp.

It would have been all right if the craze had restricted itself to the kids. But you have to remember that we were quarantined, which meant that we worked with the kids all day long, and then were not permitted to leave the grounds at night, on our time off. Children are very nice and all that, and someday I hope to have a dozen of my own, but that summer it was important to get away from them every now and then. I mean, physically and geographically *away* from them. It was important to have other interests. It was important to have an emotional and mental respite. What it was important to do, in fact, was to hold Becky in my arms and kiss her, but Marvin of course had made that impossible with his stupid quarantine. The funny thing was he didn't seem to miss his wife Lydia at all. Maybe that's because they'd been married for fourteen years. But most of the rest of us began to feel the strain of the quarantine by the end of the second week, and I think it was then that Uncle Jimbo ventured into his first game of marbles.

Jimbo, like the rest of us, was beginning to crave a little action. He was a very tall man who taught science at a high school someplace in Brooklyn. His real name was James McFarland, but in the family structure of Camp Marvin he immediately became Uncle Jim. And then, because it is fatal to have a name like Jim at any camp, he was naturally renamed Jimbo. He seemed like a very serious fellow, this Jimbo, about thirty-eight years old, with a wife and two kids at home. He wore eyeglasses, and he had sandy-colored hair that was always falling onto his forehead. The forehead itself bore a perpetual frown, even when he was playing marbles, as if he were constantly trying to figure out one of Einstein's theories. He always wore sneakers and Bermuda shorts that had been made by cutting down a pair of dungarees. When the quarantine started, one of the kids in his bunk painted a big PW on Jimbo's dungaree Bermuda shorts, the PW standing for prisoner of war—a joke Jimbo didn't think was very comical. I knew how he felt. I wasn't married, of course, but I knew what it was like to be separated from someone you loved, and Jimbo's wife and kids were away the hell out there in Brooklyn while we were locked up in Stockbridge.

I happened to be there the day he joined one of the games, thereby starting the madness that followed. He had found a single marble near the tennis courts and then had gone foraging on his free time until he'd come up with half a dozen more. It was just after dinner, and three kids were playing in front of my bunk when Jimbo strolled over and asked if he could get in the game. If there's one thing a kid can spot at fifty paces, it's a sucker. They took one look at the tall science teacher from Brooklyn and fairly leaped on him in their anxiety to get him in the game. Well, that was the last leaping any of them did for the rest of the evening. Jimbo had seven marbles. He put six of them in the ring, and he kept the biggest one for his shooter. The kids, bowing graciously to their guest, allowed him to shoot first. Standing ten feet from the circle in the dust, Jimbo took careful aim and let his shooter go. It sprang out of his hand with the speed of sound, almost cracking a marble in the dead center of the ring and sending it flying out onto the surrounding dirt.

The kids weren't terribly impressed because they were very hip and knew all about beginner's luck. They didn't begin to realize they were playing with a pro until they saw Jimbo squat down on one knee and proceed to knock every single marble out of the ring without missing a shot. Then, because there's no sucker like a sucker who thinks he knows one, the kids decided they could take Jimbo *anyway*, and they spent the rest of the evening disproving the theory by losing marble after marble to him. Jimbo told me later that he'd been raised in Plainfield, New Jersey, and had played marbles practically every day of his childhood. But the kids didn't know that at the time, and by the end of that first evening Jimbo had won perhaps two hundred marbles.

I wasn't sure I liked what Jimbo had done. He was, after all, a grown man, and he was playing with kids, and one of the kids he'd beaten happened to be a kid in my bunk. I watched that kid walk away from the game after Jimbo collected all the marbles. His name was Max, which is a funny name for a kid anyway, and he was walking with his head bent, his hands in the pockets of his shorts, his sneakers scuffing the ground.

"What's the matter, Max?" I asked.

"Nothing," he said.

"Come here, sit down," I said. He came over and sat on the bunk steps with me. I knew better than to talk about the marbles he had lost. I talked about the baseball game that afternoon and about the volleyball tournament, and all the while I was thinking of those hundred marbles I had got for my eighth birthday, and the leather pouch, and the look on my mother's face when I climbed to the third floor and told her I'd lost them all. It was getting on about dusk, and I said to Max, "Something very important is going to happen in just a few minutes, Max. Do you know what it is?"

"No," Max said.

"Well, can you guess?"

"I don't know. Is it the boxing matches tonight?" he asked.

"No, this is before the boxing matches."

"Well, what is it?" he asked.

"It happens every day at about this time," I said, "and we hardly ever stop to look at it." Max turned his puzzled face up to mine. "Look out there, Max," I said. "Look out there over the lake."

Together, Max and I sat and serenely watched the sunset.

The madness started the next day.

It started when Uncle Emil, the gym teacher from Benjamin Franklin, decided that marbles was essentially a game of athletic skill. Being a gym teacher and also being in charge of the camp's entire sports program, he naturally decided that in order to uphold his honor and his title, he would have to defeat Uncle Jimbo. He didn't declare a formal match or anything like that. He simply wandered up to Jimbo during the noon rest hour and said, "Hey, Jimbo, want to shoot some marbles?"

Jimbo looked at him with the slow steady gaze of a renowned gunslick and then said, "Sure. Why not?" Lazily he went back to his own bunk. In a few minutes he returned with a cigar box containing his winnings of the night before. They drew a circle in the dust, and each put twelve marbles in the circle. I was only sitting there writing a letter to Becky, and I guess they decided I wasn't doing anything important, so they made me referee. Jimbo was wearing a yellow short-sleeved sports shirt and his sawed-off dungarees. Emil was wearing spotless white shorts and a spotless white T shirt, as if he were about to settle the Davis Cup at Wimbledon or someplace. They flipped a coin to see who would shoot first. Emil won the toss.

Standing behind the line they had drawn in the dust some ten feet from the ring, Emil held his shooter out and sighted along the length of his arm. Jimbo stood watching him with a faintly amused look on his face. I looked up from my letter because I was supposed to be referee, even though I'd been in the middle of telling Becky I loved her, which I always seemed to be in the middle of doing whenever I got the chance. Emil licked his lips with his tongue, cocked his thumb against the big marble in his fist, and then triggered his shot. The marble leaped from his hand, spinning across the open air in a direct, unwavering, deadly accurate line toward the middle of the circle. It collided with one of the marbles in the ring, which richocheted off onto another marble, which struck two more marbles, which knocked out yet another marble for a total of five marbles knocked out of the circle on the first shot. I must admit I felt a slight thrill of pleasure. I can remember thinking, *All right, Jimbo, this time you're not playing with kids.* But I can also remember looking over at Jimbo and noticing that he didn't seem at all disturbed, that he was still wearing that same faintly amused expression on his long face.

Emil walked to the ring and, grinning, turned to Jimbo and said, "Want to forfeit?"

"Shoot," Jimbo said.

Emil grinned again, crouched in the dust, picked up his big marble, and shot. He knocked two more marbles out of the ring in succession and then missed the third by a hair, and that was the end of the game. I say that was the end of the game only because Jimbo then shot and knocked out all the remaining marbles in the circle. And then, because he had won this round, it was his turn to shoot first in the next round. He shot first, and he knocked four marbles out with his opening blast, and then proceeded to clean up the ring again. And then, because he'd won this round as well, he shot first again, and again cleaned up the ring, and he kept doing that all through the rest period until he'd won seventy-five marbles from Uncle Emil.

Uncle Emil muttered something about having a little rheumatism in his fingers, throwing his game off, and Jimbo listened sympathetically while he added the seventy-five marbles to the collection in his bulging cigar box. That afternoon Emil came back with a hundred marbles he had scrounged from the kids, and Jimbo won them all in a matter of a half hour. That evening Jimbo went to the mess hall to pick up a cardboard carton for his marble winnings. And, also that evening, he became a celebrity.

I guess I was the only person, man or boy, in that camp who didn't want to try beating Uncle Jimbo in the hectic weeks that followed. To begin with, I am not a very competitive fellow, and besides, I only knew how to play immies, not marbles. Marbles required a strong thumb and a fast eye, Jimbo explained to me. My thumbs were pretty weak and my eyes were tired from staring across the lake trying to catch a glimpse of a distant figure I could identify as Becky. But everyone else in camp seemed to possess powerful thumbs and 20/20 vision, and they were all anxious to pit these assets against the champion. When you come to think of it, I suppose, champions exist *only* to be challenged, anyway. The challengers in this case included *everybody*, and all for different reasons.

Uncle Ronnie was a counselor whom everyone, including the kids, called Horizontal Ronnie because his two favorite pursuits both required a bed and a horizontal position. He wanted to beat Jimbo because the quarantine had deprived him of the satisfying company of a girl named Laura in Camp Lydia. Jimbo won two hundred marbles from Ronnie in an hour of play.

Uncle Dave taught mathematics at Evander Childs High School, and he thought he had figured out a foolproof system that he wanted to try in practice. The system worked for fifteen minutes, at the end of which time Jimbo blasted the game from its hinges and then barged on through to win a hundred and fifty marbles.

Uncle Marvin, too, had his own reason for wanting to beat Jimbo. Before the season had begun, when Marvin was still hiring counselors, he had offered Jimbo twelve hundred dollars for the job. Jimbo had held out for thirteen hundred, which Marvin eventually and grudgingly paid him. But the extra hundred dollars rankled, and Marvin was determined to get it back somehow.

You may think it odd that he decided to get back his hundred dollars by winning *marbles* from Jimbo. After all, marbles are marbles, and money is money. But a very strange thing had happened in the second week of the madness. Marbles, which up to that time had only been round pieces of colored glass, suddenly became the hottest item of currency in the camp's vast and complicated trading system. Before then, dimes were very hot property because the Coke machine in the counselors' shack took only dimes. The kids weren't allowed to enter the counselors' shack, nor were they allowed to drink Cokes, all of which made it absolutely necessary for them to have dimes so they could sneak into the counselors' shack and drink Cokes. Almost every letter home, before the marble madness began, started with the words, "Dear Mom and Dad, I am fine. Please send me some dimes." But suddenly, because Jimbo kept winning marbles with such frequency, there was a shortage of marbles in the camp. Marbles became a precious commodity, like gold or silver, and the basis of the camp economy. If you had marbles, you could trade them for all the dimes you needed. You could, in fact, get almost anything you wanted, if you only had marbles. Uncle Jimbo had a lot of marbles. Uncle Jimbo had a whole damn suitcase full of them, which he kept locked and on a shelf over his bed. He was surely the richest man in camp.

He became even richer the afternoon he played Uncle Marvin and won five hundred marbles from him, a blow from which Marvin never recovered. By this time, beating Jimbo had become an obsession. Jimbo was the sole topic of camp discussion, overshadowing the approaching Color War, eclipsing the visit of a famous football player who talked about the ways and means of forward passing while nobody listened. The counselors, the kids, even the camp doctor, were interested only in the ways and means of amassing more marbles to pit against Jimbo's growing empire. They discussed shooting techniques, and whether or not they should play with the sun facing them or behind their backs. They discussed the potency of the mass shot as against a slow deliberate one-at-a-time sort of game. They discussed different kinds of shooters, the illegality of using steelies, the current exchange rate of pureys. The kids loved every minute of it. They awoke each morning brimming with plans for Jimbo's ultimate downfall. To them, beating him was important only because it would give them an opportunity to prove that adults, especially adult counselors, were all a bunch of no-good finks.

On Monday of the third week of the madness, the smart money entered the marbles business—and the gambling element began taking over.

But before that, on Sunday night, I broke quarantine.

I am usually a law-abiding fellow, and I might never have broken quarantine were it not for Horizontal Ronnie, who, I later came to learn, had very definite criminal leanings.

"Look," he said to me, "what's to stop us from taking one of the canoes and paddling over to the other side?"

"Well," I said, "there's a polio scare."

"Don't you want to see What's-her-name?"

"Rebecca."

"Yeah, don't you want to see her?"

"Sure I do."

"Has every kid in this camp and also in Camp Lydia, by

46

Marvin's own admission, in his very own words, been inoculated against polio?"

"Well, yes," I said.

"Then would you mind telling me how there is a polio scare?"

"I don't know," I said.

"Fine. I'll meet you at the boat dock tonight at nine o'clock. I'll take care of getting word to the girls."

I guess I didn't trust him even then, because I took care of getting word to Becky myself that afternoon, by sending over one of my notes tied to an empty milk can. That night, at nine o'clock on the dot, Ronnie and I met at the boat dock and silently slipped one of the canoes into the water. We didn't talk at all until we were in the middle of the lake, and then Ronnie said, "We'll come back around eleven. Is that all right with you?"

"Sure," I said.

"Boy, that Laura," he said, and fell silent again, apparently contemplating what was ahead. Laura, whom I had only seen once or twice before the quarantine, was a very pretty blond girl who always wore white sweaters and tight white shorts. She also wore a perfume that was very hard to avoid smelling, and the few times I had seen her was in the counselors' shack where she kept playing the "Malaguena" over and over again on the piano. She was a very mysterious girl, what with her sweater and shorts and her perfume and her "Malaguena." She was eighteen years old.

"I think I know how to beat him," Ronnie said suddenly.

"Huh?"

"Jimbo. I think I know how to beat the bastard."

"How?" I asked.

"Never mind," Ronnie said, and then he fell silent again, but it seemed to me he was paddling more furiously.

I met Rebecca under the pines bordering the lake. She was wearing black slacks and a black bulky sweater, and she rushed into my arms and didn't say anything for the longest time, just held herself close to me, and then lifted her head and stared into my face, and then smiled that fast-breaking smile, and fleetingly kissed me on the cheek, and pulled away and looked into my face again.

We skirted the edge of the pine forest, the night was still, I could feel her hand tight in my own. We sat with our backs to one of the huge boulders overlooking the lake, and I held her in my arms and told her how miserable I'd been without her, and she kept kissing my closed eyes as I spoke, tiny little punctuating kisses that made me weak.

The night was very dark. Somewhere across the lake a dog began barking, and then the barking stopped and the night was still again.

"I can barely see you, Becky," I whispered.

I held her close, I held her slender body close to mine. She was Becky, she was trembling, she was joy and sadness together, echoing inside me. If I held her a moment longer my heart would burst, I knew my heart would burst and shower trailing sparks on the night. And yet I held her, wanting to cry in my happiness, dizzy with the smell of her hair, loving everything about her in that timeless, brimming moment, still knowing my heart would burst, loving her closed eyes and the whispery touch of her lashes, and the rough wool of her sweater, and the delicate motion of her hands on my face. I kissed her, I died, I smiled, I listened to thunder, for oh, the kiss of Rebecca Goldblatt, the kiss, the heart-stopping kiss of my girl.

The world was dark and still.

"I love you," she said.

"I love you," I said.

And then she threw her arms around my neck and put her face against mine, tight, I could feel her cheekbone hard against mine, and suddenly she was crying.

"Hey," I said. "What . . . honey, what is it?"

"Oh, Donald," she said, "what are we going to do? I love you so much."

"I think we ought to tell him," I said, "when we get back."

"How can we do that?" Becky said.

"I can go to him. I can say we're in love with each other."

"Oh yes, *yes*," Becky said breathlessly. "I *do* love you, Donald."

"Then that's what we'll do."

"He . . ." She shook her head in the darkness. I knew that her eyes were very solemn, even though I couldn't see them. "He won't listen," Becky said. "He'll try to break us up."

"Nobody will ever break us up," I said. "Ever."

"What—what will you tell him?"

"That we love each other. That when we finish school we're going to get married."

"He won't let us."

"The hell with him."

"He doesn't *know* you. He thinks Italians are terrible."

"I can't help what he thinks," I said.

"Donald . . ." She paused. She was shaking her head again, and she began to tremble. "Donald, you can't do it."

"Why not?"

"Because he *believes* it, don't you see? He really believes you *are* some—some terrible sort of person."

"I know, but that doesn't make it true. And simply because *he* believes it is no reason for me to behave as if *I* believe it." I nodded my head in the darkness. I felt pretty convinced by what I was saying, but at the same time I was scared to death of facing her father. "I'll tell him when we get back," I said.

49

Becky was quiet for a long long time.

Then she said, "If only I was Italian."

I held her very close to me, and I kissed the top of her head very gently. Right then I knew everything was going to be all right. I knew it because Becky had said, "If only I was Italian," when she could just as easily have said, "If only you were Jewish."

Horizontal Ronnie swung into action the very next day.

He had been inordinately silent the night before on the trip back across the lake, and I hadn't disturbed his thoughts because I assumed he was working out his system for beating Jimbo. Besides, I was working out what I would tell Becky's father when we got back to the city.

The course of action Ronnie decided upon was really the only one that offered the slightest opportunity of defeating Jimbo and destroying his empire. He had correctly concluded that Jimbo was the best marble player in camp, if not in the entire world, and had further reasoned it would be impossible to beat him through skill alone. So, discounting skill, Ronnie had decided to try his hand at luck. At eight o'clock that Monday morning, as the kids lined up for muster, Ronnie came over with his fist clenched. He held out his hand to one of the senior boys and said, "Odds or evens?"

"Huh?" the senior said. The senior boys at Camp Marvin weren't exactly the brightest kids in the world. In fact, the junior boys had written a song about them which went something like "We've got seen-yuh boys, dumpy, lumpy seen-yuh boys, we've got seen-yuh boys, the worst!" Besides, it was only eight o'clock in the morning, and when someone thrusts his fist in your face at eight o'clock in the morning and says, "Odds or evens?" what else can you reply but "Huh?"

"My fist is full of marbles," Ronnie explained.

"Yeah?" the senior boy said. Mention of marbles seemed to have awakened him suddenly. His eyes gleamed.

"They're either an odd number of marbles or an even number," Ronnie went on. "You guess odds or evens. If you're right, I give you the marbles in my hand. If you're wrong, you match the marbles in my hand."

"You mean if I'm wrong I give you the number of marbles you're holding?"

"That's right."

The senior boy thought this over carefully for a moment, then nodded and said, "Odds."

Ronnie opened his fist. There were four marbles in his hand.

"You pay me," he said, and that was the beginning of the Las Vegas phase of the marble madness.

If Uncle Marvin saw what was going on, he made no comment upon it. The common opinion was that he was still smarting from his loss of five hundred marbles to Jimbo and deliberately avoided contact with everyone in the camp. It is doubtful that he could have stopped the frenzy even if he'd wanted to. The kids, presented with a new and exciting activity, took to it immediately. Here was a sport that required no skill. Here was a game that promised and delivered immediate action: the closed fist, the simple question, the guess, the payoff. Kids who were hopeless washouts on the baseball diamond suddenly discovered a sport in which they could excel. Kids who couldn't sing a note in a camp musical set the grounds reverberating with their shouted "Odds or evens?" A large shipment of marbles from home to a kid named Irwin in bunk nine only increased the feverish tempo of the gambling activity. The simple guessing game started at reveille each morning, before a kid's feet had barely touched the wooden floor of his bunk. It did not end until lights out, and even after

that there were the whispered familiar words, and the surreptitious glow of flashlights.

Uncle Jimbo, startled by this new development, stayed
fastidiously away from the gambling in the first few days.
Ronnie, meanwhile, exhibiting his true gambler's instincts,
began by slowly winning a handful of marbles from every kid
he could challenge, and then became more and more reckless
with his bets, clenching his fists around as many marbles as
they could hold. Before too long, a bookie system became
necessary, with counselors and campers writing down a
number on a slip of paper and then folding the slip, so that a
challenger had only to guess odds or evens on a written figure
rather than on an actual fistful of marbles. That week, Ronnie
successfully and infallibly called bets ranging from a low of
three marbles to a high of a hundred and fifty-two marbles. It
became clear almost immediately that if Jimbo were to defend
his title, he would have to enter this new phase of the sport or
lose by default.

I think he was beginning to like his title by then. Or perhaps he was only beginning to like his wealth. Whatever it
was, he could not afford to drop out of the race. He studied
the new rules, and learned them. They were really quite
simple. If someone challenged you, you could either accept
or decline the challenge. But once you had accepted, once the
question "Odds or evens?" was asked in earnest, you either
called immediately or lost the bet by default. In the beginning, Jimbo took no chances. He deliberately sought out only
those campers whose luck had been running incredibly bad.
His bets were small, four marbles, seven marbles, a dozen
marbles. If he won a bet, he immediately pocketed a portion
of his initial investment and then began playing on his winnings alone. And then, because he thought of himself as a
blood-smelling champion closing in for the kill, he began to

bet more heavily, taking on all comers, swinging freely through the camp, challenging campers and counselors alike. Eventually he wrote a bookie slip for five hundred and seven marbles and won the bet from a kid in bunk seven, knocking him completely out of the competition. Jimbo's luck was turning out to be almost as incredible as his skill had been. He lost occasionally, oh yes, but his winnings kept mounting, and marble after marble poured into the locked suitcase on the shelf over his bed. It was becoming apparent to almost everyone in the camp—except Uncle Marvin, who still didn't know what the hell was going on—that an elimination match was taking place, and that the chief contenders for Jimbo's as yet unchallenged title were Ronnie and the *nouveau riche* kid in bunk nine, who had parlayed his shipment from home into a sizable fortune.

Irwin, the kid in bunk nine, was a tiny little kid whom everybody called Irwin the Vermin. He wore glasses, and he always had a runny nose and a disposition to match. Ronnie, correctly figuring he would have to collar every loose marble in the camp before a showdown with Jimbo, went over to bunk nine one afternoon and promptly challenged Irwin the Vermin. The number of marbles being wagered on a single bet had by this time reached fairly astronomical proportions. It was rumored that Irwin owned one thousand seven hundred and fifty marbles. Ronnie, whose number of marbles now totaled nine hundred and four, sat on the edge of Irwin's bed and wrote out a slip of paper with the number 903 on it.

He folded the slip of paper and then looked Irwin directly in the eye.

"Odds or evens?" he said.

Irwin blinked behind his glasses, grinned maliciously, licked his lips with his tongue and said, "Odds."

Ronnie swallowed. "What?"

"Odds," Irwin repeated.

"Yeah," Ronnie said. He unfolded the slip, and together they walked back to his bunk where he made payment. "I've got a few marbles left," he lied; he had only one marble to his name. "Do you want to play some more?"

Irwin looked at him steadily and then, true to his nature, said, "Find yourself another sucker, jerk."

Ronnie watched Irwin as he left the bunk loaded down with his winnings. He must have seen in that tiny figure retreating across the grounds a symbol of all his frustration, the quarantine that kept him from the mysterious Laura, the defeat of his system to beat Jimbo. It was late afternoon, and the cries of the boys at Free Play sounded from the ball diamonds and the basketball courts far off in the camp hills. Ronnie must have watched little Irwin walking away with his shattered hopes and dreams in a brown cardboard carton, and it must have been then that he made his final decision, the decision that brought the marble madness to its peak of insanity.

I was coming back from the tennis courts, where I was trying to help little Max with his backhand, when I saw Ronnie striding across the grounds towards Jimbo's bunk. He was carrying an old battered suitcase, and there was something odd about his walk, a purposeful, angry stride which was at the same time somewhat surreptitious. I looked at him curiously and then followed him past the flagpole and watched as he entered the bunk. I stood outside for a few minutes, wondering, and then I quietly climbed the front steps.

Ronnie was in the middle of forcing the lock on Jimbo's suitcase. He looked up when I entered the bunk and then went right back to work.

"What are you doing?" I said.

"What does it look like I'm doing?" he answered.

"It looks like you're trying to break open Jimbo's suitcase."

"That's right," Ronnie said, and in that moment he broke the lock and opened the lid. "Give me a hand here," he said.

"No."

"Come on, don't be a jerk."

"You're stealing his marbles," I said.

"That's just what I'm doing. It's a gag. Come on, give me a hand here."

The next second was when I almost lost my own sanity because I said, I actually heard myself say, "You can go to jail for that!" as if even *I* had begun to believe there was a fortune in that suitcase instead of hunks of colored glass.

"For stealing marbles?" Ronnie asked incredulously. "Don't be a jackass."

His answer startled me back to reality, but at the same time it puzzled me. Because here he was, a grown man, twenty years old, and he was telling me these were only marbles, and yet he was thoroughly involved in all this frantic nuttiness, so involved that he was in Jimbo's bunk actually *stealing* marbles which he claimed he *knew* were only marbles. He opened his own suitcase and then, seeing I was staring at him with a dumfounded expression, and knowing I wasn't about to help him, he lifted Jimbo's bag himself and tilted it. The marbles spilled from one bag to the other, bright shining marbles, yellow and red and striped and black and green; glass marbles and steelies and glistening pureys, marbles of every size and hue, thousands and thousands of marbles, spilling from Jimbo's bag to Ronnie's in a dazzling, glittering heap.

I shook my head and said, "I think you're all nuts," and then I walked out of the bunk. Ronnie came out after me a minute later, carrying his own full suitcase, bending over with the weight of it. I watched him as he struggled across to the flagpole in the center of the camp. He put the bag down at his feet and then, his eyes gleaming, he cupped his hands to his mouth and shouted, "Where's Jimbo McFarland?"

There was no answer.

"Where's Jimbo McFarland?" he shouted again.

"Stop yelling," I called from the steps of the bunk. "He's up at the handball courts."

"Jimbo McFarland!" Ronnie screamed. "Jimbo McFarland!" and the camp voice-telephone system picked up the name, shouting it across behind the bunks and down by the gully and through the nature shack, "Jimbo McFarland!" and over to the lake where some kids were taking their Red Cross tests, and then up into the hills by the mess hall, and across the upper-camp baseball diamond, and the volleyball court, and finally reaching Jimbo where he was playing handball with one of the counselors.

Jimbo came striding down into the camp proper. He walked out of the hills like the gunslick he was, his back to the sun, crossing the dusty grounds for a final showdown, stopping some twenty feet from where Ronnie stood near the flagpole.

"You calling me?" he said.

"You want to play marbles?" Ronnie answered.

"Have you *got* any marbles?" Jimbo said.

"Will you match whatever I've got?"

Jimbo hesitated a moment, weighing his luck, and then said, "Sure," tentatively accepting the challenge.

"Whatever's in this bag?" Ronnie asked.

Again Jimbo hesitated. A crowd of kids had begun to gather, some of whom had followed Jimbo down out of the hills, the rest of whom had felt an excitement in the air, had felt that the moment of truth had finally arrived. They milled around the flagpole, waiting for Jimbo's decision. The gauntlet was in the dust, the challenge had been delivered, and now they waited for the undisputed champion to decide whether or not he would defend his title. Jimbo nodded.

"However much you want to bet," he said slowly, "is all right with me." He had irrevocably accepted the challenge. He now had to call or lose the bet by default.

"Okay, then," Ronnie said. He stooped down beside his suitcase. Slowly, nonchalantly, he unclasped the latches on either side. He put one hand gently on the lid, and then he looked up at Jimbo, grinned, quietly said, "Odds or evens, Jimbo?" and snapped open the lid of the bag.

From where I sat, I saw Jimbo's face go white. I don't know what crossed his mind in those few terrible moments as he stared into the bag at those thousands and thousands of marbles. I don't know whether or not he even made a mental stab at calculating the number of glistening spheres in the suitcase. I only know that he staggered back a pace and his jaw fell slack. The kids were silent now, watching him. Ronnie kept squatting beside the suitcase, his hand resting on the opened lid, the sun glowing on the marbles.

"Well, Jimbo?" he said. "Odds or evens?"

"I . . ."

"Odds or evens, Jimbo?"

Perhaps Jimbo was feverishly calculating in those breathless moments. Perhaps he was realizing he had walked into a trap from which there was no return: he would either call correctly and become the marble king of the entire world; or he would call incorrectly or not at all, and lose his fortune and his fame.

"Odds or evens?" Ronnie demanded.

Odds or evens, but how to call? How many thousands of

marbles were in that suitcase, and really what difference did it make when it all narrowed down to a single marble, the real difference between odds and evens, one solitary marble, call wrong and the empire would come crashing down. Jimbo took a deep breath. The sweat was standing out on his face, his eyes were blinking. The kids around the flagpole stood silently awaiting his decision. Ronnie squatted by the suitcase with his hand on the lid.

"Odds or evens?" he asked again.

Jimbo shrugged. Honestly, because it was what he was really thinking, he said, "I . . . I don't know."

"Did you hear him?" Ronnie said immediately. "He loses by default!"

"Wait a minute, I . . ."

"You refused to call, you said you didn't know! I win by default!" Ronnie said, and he snapped the lid of the bag shut, latched it and immediately lifted it from the ground.

"Now just a second," Jimbo protested, but Ronnie was already walking away from him.

He stopped some five paces from the flagpole, turned abruptly, put the bag down, grinned, and said, "You stupid jerk! They were your own marbles!"

For a moment, his announcement hung on the dust-laden air. Jimbo blinked, not understanding him at first. The kids were silent and puzzled in the circle around the flagpole. Ronnie picked up the bag of marbles again and began walking toward his bunk with it, a triumphant grin on his face. And then the meaning of what he had said registered on Jimbo's face, his eyes first, intelligence sparking there, his nose next, the nostrils flaring, his mouth then, the lips pulling back to show his teeth, and then his voice, bursting from his mouth in a wounded roar.

"You thief!"

His words, too, hung on the silent air, and then one of the kids said, "Did he steal them from you, Uncle Jimbo?" and another kid shouted, "He's a crook!" and then suddenly the word "Thief!" was shouted by one of the senior boys and picked up by a junior, "Thief!" and the air rang with the word, "Thief!" and then it was shouted in unison, "Thief! Thief!" and all at once there was a bloodthirsty mob. A kid who had come down from the ball diamond waved his bat in the air and began running after Ronnie. Another kid seized a fallen branch and rushed past the flagpole with it. The others bellowed screams of anger and rage, hysterically racing toward Ronnie, who had dropped the suitcase and turned to face them. There was a pale, sickly smile on his mouth, as though he hadn't expected this kind of backfire. "Look," he said, but his voice was drowned out in the roar of the kids as they rushed forward with Jimbo. Ronnie turned and tried to run for his bunk, but Jimbo caught his collar from behind, and pulled him backward to the ground. I saw the kid raise his baseball bat and I leaped to my feet and yelled, "Stop it! Goddamn you, stop it!"

The bat hung in midair. Slowly they turned toward me.

"It's only marbles," I said.

The camp was silent.

"It's only marbles," I repeated. "Don't you see?"

And then, because I had intruded upon a fantasy and threatened to shatter it, because the entire spiraling marbles structure was suddenly in danger, they turned from Ronnie, who was lying on the ground, and they ran toward me, shouting and screaming. Jimbo, the champion, struck me on the jaw with his fist, and when I fell to the ground, the kids began kicking me and pummeling me. There was more than anger in their blows and their whispered curses. There was conviction and an overriding necessity to convince the unbeliever as well. I refused to be convinced. I felt each deliberate blow, yes, each fierce kick, but I would not be convinced because I knew, even if they didn't, that it was only marbles.

I quit Camp Marvin early the next morning. Not because of the beating. That wasn't important. I carried my two suitcases all around the lake to Camp Lydia. It was raining, and I got soaking wet. I waited at the gate while one of the girl campers ran to get Rebecca. She came walking through the rain wearing her dirty trenchcoat, walking with that peculiar sideward lope, her hair wet and clinging to her face.

"Come on, Beck," I said. "We're going home."

She looked at me for a long time, searching my face with her dark solemn eyes while the rain came down around us. I knew that word of the beating had traveled across the lake, but I didn't know whether she was looking for cuts and bruises or for something else.

"Are you all right?" she said at last.

"Yes, I'm fine," I said. "Becky, please go pack your things." And then, as she turned to go, I said, "Becky?"

She stopped in the center of the road with the rain streaming on her face and she looked at me curiously, her eyebrows raised, waiting.

"As soon as we get back," I said, "today, this afternoon, I'm going to talk to your father."

She stared at me a moment longer, her eyes very serious, and then she gave a small nod, and a smile began forming on her face, not the usual fast-breaking smile, but a slow steady smile that was somehow very sad and very old, even though she was only nineteen.

"All right, Donald," she said.

That afternoon I went to see her father at his dental office on Fordham Road in the Bronx. It was still raining. When he heard who was calling, he told his receptionist he didn't want to see me, so I marched right in and stood beside his chair while he was working on a patient, and I said, "Dr. Goldblatt, you had better see me, because you're going to see a lot of me from now on."

He didn't want to make a very big fuss because a patient was sitting in the chair with her mouth open, so he walked over to his receptionist and quietly asked her to get the police, but I just kept standing by the chair very calmly. He didn't know it, but I had been through the hysteria bit before, in spades, and this mild case didn't faze me at all. Finally, when he realized I wasn't going to leave, he again left his patient sitting in the chair, and he told his receptionist to never mind the police, and he led me to a private little office where we sat on opposite sides of a desk.

He looked at me with dark solemn eyes, almost as black as Rebecca's, and he said, "What the hell do you want from my life?"

"Dr. Goldblatt," I said, "I don't want anything from your life."

"Except my daughter," he said sourly.

"Yes, but that's not from *your* life, that's from *hers.*"

"No," Dr. Goldblatt said.

"Dr. Goldblatt," I said politely, "I didn't come here to ask your permission to see her. I came here to tell you that we're getting engaged, and as soon as we graduate we're going to get married."

"No," Dr. Goldblatt said. "You're a Gentile, she's a Jewish girl, it would never work. Don't you know the trouble you're asking for? Different religions, different cultures, how will you raise the children, what will you . . . ?"

"Dr. Goldblatt," I said, "that's only marbles."

"What?"

"I said it's only marbles."

The office went very silent, just the way the camp had when I'd shouted those words the day before. Dr. Goldblatt looked at me for a long time, his face expressionless. Then, all he said was "Marbles."

"Yes," I said, "marbles. Dr. Goldblatt, I'm going to pick up Becky at the house tonight at eight o'clock. At the *house,* Dr. Goldblatt. I'm not going to meet her in some dark alley any more."

Dr. Goldblatt said nothing.

"Because she's too nice to be meeting in dark alleys," I said, "and I love her."

Dr. Goldblatt still said nothing.

"Well," I said, "it was nice talking to you."

I got up and offered my hand to him, which he refused. I shrugged and started for the door. I had my hand on the knob when I heard him say behind me, "Marbles. *This* is what my daughter picked. Marbles."

I didn't let him see me smile. I walked downstairs to the street. The rain had tapered off to a fine drizzle. The gutters ran with water, and large puddles had formed in the hollows near the curb. I could remember sticking my hand into puddles just like those long ago when I was a kid, when the loss of a hundred immies had meant a great deal to me.

I called Becky from a telephone booth in the corner drugstore.

The nut—she cried.

To Break the Wall

The door to Room 206 was locked when Richard Dadier reached it for his fifth period English class. He tried the knob several times, peered in through the glass panel, and motioned for Serubi to open the door. Serubi, sitting in the seat closest the door, shrugged his shoulders innocently and grinned. Richard felt again the mixed revulsion and fear he felt before every class.

Easy, he told himself. Easy does it.

He reached into his pocket and slipped the large key into the keyhole. Swinging the door open, he slapped it fast against the prongs that jutted out from the wall, and then walked briskly to his desk.

A falsetto voice somewhere in the back of the room rapidly squeaked, "Daddy-oh!" Richard busied himself with his Delaney book, not looking up at the class. He still remembered that first day, when he had told them his name.

"Mr. Dadier," he had said, and he'd pronounced it carefully. One of the boys had yelled, "Daddy-oh," and the class had roared approval. The name had stuck since then.

Quickly, he glanced around the room, flipping cards over as he took the attendance. Half were absent as usual. He was secretly glad. They were easier to handle in small groups.

He turned over the last card, and waited for them to quiet down. They never would, he knew, never.

Reaching down, he pulled a heavy book from his briefcase and rested it on the palm of his hand. Without warning, he slammed it onto the desk.

"Shut up!" he bellowed.

The class groaned into silence, startled by the outburst.

Now, he thought. Now, I'll press it home. Surprise plus advantage plus seize your advantage. Just like waging war. All day long I wage war. Some fun.

"Assignment for tomorrow," Richard said flatly.

A moan escaped from the group. Gregory Miller, a large boy of seventeen, dark-haired, with a lazy sneer and hard, bright eyes said, "You work too hard, Mr. Daddy-oh."

The name twisted deep inside Richard, and he felt the tiny needles of apprehension start at the base of his spine.

"Quiet, Mueller," Richard said, feeling pleasure at mispronouncing the boy's name. "Assignment for tomorrow. In *New Horizons* . . ."

"In what?" Ganigan asked.

I should have known better, Richard reminded himself. We've only been using the book two months now. I can't expect them to remember the title. No.

"In *New Horizons*," he repeated impatiently, "the blue book, the one we've been using, all term." He paused, gaining control of himself. "In the blue book," he continued softly, "read the first ten pages of *Army Ants in the Jungle*."

"Here in class?" Hennesy asked.

"No. At home."

"Christ," Hennesy mumbled.

"It's on page two seventy-five," Richard said.

"What page?" Antoro called out.

"Two seventy-five."

"What page?" Levy asked.

"Two seventy-five," Richard said. "My God, what's the matter with you?" He turned rapidly and wrote the figures on the board in a large hand, repeating the numerals slowly. "Two, seven-ty-five." He heard a chuckle spread maliciously behind him, and he whirled quickly. Every boy in the class wore a deadpan.

"There will be a short test on the homework tomorrow," he announced grimly.

"Another one?" Miller asked lazily.

"Yes, Mailler," Richard said, "another one." He glared at the boy heatedly, but Miller only grinned in return.

"And now," Richard said, "the test I promised you yesterday."

A hush fell over the class.

Quick, Richard thought. Press the advantage. Strike again and again. Don't wait for them. Keep one step ahead always. Move fast and they won't know what's going on. Keep them too busy to get into mischief.

Richard began chalking the test on the board. He turned his head and barked over his shoulder, "All books away. Finley, hand out the paper."

This is the way to do it, he realized. I've figured it out. The way to control these monsters is to give them a test every day of the week. Write their fingers off.

"Begin immediately," Richard said in a businesslike voice. "Don't forget your heading."

"What's that, that heading?" Busco asked.

"Name, official class, subject class, subject teacher," Richard said wearily.

Seventy-two, he thought. I've said it seventy-two times since I started teaching here two months ago. Seventy-two times.

"Who's our subject teacher?" Busco asked. His face expressed complete bewilderment.

"Mr. Daddy-oh," Vota said quite plainly. Vota was big and rawboned, a muscular, rangy, seventeen-year-old. Stringy blond hair hung over his pimply forehead. There was something mannishly sinister about his eyes, something boyishly innocent about his smile. And he was Miller's friend. Richard never forgot that for a moment.

"Mr. Dadier is the subject teacher," Richard said to Busco. "And incidentally, Vito," he glared at Vota, "anyone misspelling my name in the heading will lose ten points."

"What!" Vota complained, outraged.

"You heard me, Vota," Richard snapped.

"Well, how do you spell Daddy-oh?" Vota asked, the innocent smile curling his lips again.

"You figure it out, Vota. I don't need the ten points."

Richard bitterly pressed the chalk into the board. It snapped in two, and he picked up another piece from the runner. With the chalk squeaking wildly, he wrote out the rest of the test.

"No talking," he ordered. He sat down behind the desk and eyed the class suspiciously.

A puzzled frown crossed Miller's face. "I don't understand the first question, teach'," he called out.

Richard leaned back in his chair and looked at the board. "It's very simple, Miltzer," he said. "There are ten words on the board. Some are spelled correctly, and some are wrong. If they're wrong, you correct them. If they're right, spell them just the way they're written."

"Mmmmm," Miller said thoughtfully, his eyes glowing. "How do you spell the second word?"

Richard leaned back again, looked at the second word, and began, "D-I-S . . ." He caught himself and faced Miller squarely. "Just the way you want to. You're taking the test, not me."

Miller grinned widely. "Oh. I didn't know that, teach'."

"You'll know when you see your mark, Miller."

Richard cursed himself for having pronounced the boy's name correctly. He made himself comfortable at the desk and looked out over the class.

Di Pasco will cheat, he thought. He will cheat and I won't catch him. He's uncanny that way. God, how I wish I could catch him. How does he? On his cuff? Where? He probably has it stuffed in his ear. Should I search him? No, what's the use? He'd cheat his own mother. An inborn crook. A louse.

Louse, Richard mused. Even I call them that now. All louses. I must tell Helen that I've succumbed. Or should I wait until after the baby is born? Perhaps it would be best not to disillusion her yet. Perhaps I should let her think I'm still trying to reach them, still trying. What was it Solly Klein had said?

"This is the garbage can of the educational system."

He had stood in the teachers' lunchroom, near the bulletin, pointing his stubby forefinger at Richard.

"And it's our job to sit on the lid and make sure none of this garbage spills over into the street."

Richard had smiled then. He was new, and he still thought he could teach them something, still felt he could mold the clay.

Lou Savoldi, an electrical wiring teacher, had smiled too and said, "Solly's a great philosopher."

"Yeah, yeah, philosopher." Solly smiled. "All I know is I've been teaching machine shop here for twelve years now, and only once did I find anything valuable in the garbage." He had nodded his head emphatically then. "Nobody knowingly throws anything valuable in with the garbage."

Then why should I bother? Richard wondered now. Why should I teach? Why should I get ulcers?

"Keep your eyes on your own paper, Busco," he cautioned.

Everyone is a cheat, a potential thief. Solly was right. We have to keep them off the streets. They should really hire a

67

policeman. It would be funny, he thought, if it weren't so damned serious. How long can you handle garbage without beginning to stink yourself? Already, I stink.

"All right, Busco, bring your paper up. I'm subtracting five points from it," Richard suddenly said.

"Why? What the hell did I do?"

"Bring me your paper."

Busco reluctantly slouched to the front of the room and tossed his paper onto the desk. He stood with his thumbs looped in the tops of his dungarees as Richard marked a large -5 on the paper in bright red.

"What's that for?" Busco asked.

"For having loose eyes."

Busco snatched the paper from the desk and examined it with disgust. He wrinkled his face into a grimace and slowly started back to his seat.

As he passed Miller, Miller looked to the front of the room. His eyes met Richard's, and he sneered, "Chicken!"

"What?" Richard asked.

Miller looked surprised. "You talking to me, teach'?"

"Yes, Miller. What did you just say?"

"I didn't say nothing, teach'." Miller smiled.

"Bring me your paper, Miller."

"What for?"

"Bring it up!"

"What for, I said."

"I heard what you said, Miller. And *I* said bring me your paper. Now. Right this minute."

"I don't see why," Miller persisted, the smile beginning to vanish from his face.

"Because I say so, that's why."

Miller's answer came slowly, pointedly. "And supposing I don't feel like?" A frown was twisting his forehead.

The other boys in the room were suddenly interested. Heads that were bent over papers snapped upright. Richard felt every eye in the class focus on him.

They were rooting for Miller, of course. They wanted Miller to win. They wanted Miller to defy him. He couldn't let that happen.

He walked crisply up the aisle and stood beside Miller. The boy looked up.

"Get up." Richard said, trying to control the modulation of his voice.

My voice is shaking, he told himself. I can feel it shaking. He knows it, too. He's mocking me with those little, hard eyes of his. I must control my voice. This is really funny. My voice is shaking.

"Get up, Miller."

"I don't see, Mr. Daddy-oh, just why I should," Miller answered. He pronounced the name with great care.

"Get up, Miller. Get up and say my name correctly."

"Don't you know your own name, Mr. Daddy-oh?"

Richard's hand snapped out and grasped Miller by the collar of his shirt. He pulled him to his feet, almost tearing the collar. Miller stood a scant two inches shorter than Richard, squirming to release himself. Richard's hand crushed tighter on the collar. He heard the slight rasp of material ripping. He peered into the hateful eyes and spoke quietly. "Pronounce my name correctly, Miller."

The class had grown terribly quiet. There was no sound in the room now. Richard heard only the grate of his own shallow breathing. I should let him loose, he thought. What can come of this? How far can I go? *Let him loose!*

"You want me to pronounce your name, sir?" Miller asked.

"You heard me."

"Go to hell, Mr. Daddy . . ."

Richard's fist lashed out, catching the boy squarely across the mouth. He felt his knuckles scrape against hard teeth, saw the blood leap across the upper lip in a thin crimson slash, saw the eyes widen with surprise and then narrow immediately with deep, dark hatred. And then the knife snapped into view, sudden and terrifying. Long and shining, it caught the pale sunlight that slanted through the long schoolroom windows. Richard backed away involuntarily, eyeing the sharp blade with respect.

Now what, he thought? Now the garbage can turns into a coffin. Now the garbage overflows. Now I lie dead and bleeding on a schoolroom floor while a moron slashes me to ribbons. Now.

"What do you intend doing with that, Miller?"

My voice is exceptionally calm, he mused. I think I'm frightened, but my voice is calm. Exceptionally.

"Just come a little closer and you'll see," Miller snarled, the blood in his mouth staining his teeth.

"Give me that knife, Miller."

I'm kidding, a voice persisted in Richard's mind. I must be kidding. This is all a big, hilarious joke. I'll die laughing in the morning. I'll die . . .

"Come and get it, Daddy-oh!"

Richard took a step closer to Miller and watched his arm swing back and forth in a threatening arc. Miller's eyes were hard and unforgiving.

And suddenly, Richard caught a flash of color out of the corner of his eye. Someone was behind him! He whirled instinctively, his fist smashing into a boy's stomach. As the boy fell to the floor Richard realized it was Miller's friend Vota. Vota cramped into a tight little ball that writhed and moaned on the floor, and Richard knew that any danger he might have presented was past. He turned quickly to Miller, a satisfied smile clinging to his lips.

"Give me that knife, Miller, and give it to me now."

He stared into the boy's eyes. Miller looked big and dangerous. Perspiration stood out on his forehead. His breath was coming in hurried gasps. "Give it to me now, Miller, or I'm going to take it from you and beat you black and blue."

He was advancing slowly on the boy.

"Give it to me, Miller. Hand it over," his voice rolled on hypnotically, charged with an undercurrent of threat.

The class seemed to catch its breath together. No one moved to help Vota who lay in a heap on the floor, his arms hugging his waist. He moaned occasionally, squirming violently. But no one moved to help him.

I've got to keep one eye on Vota, Richard figured. He may be playing possum. I have to be careful.

"Hand it over, Miller. Hand it over."

Miller stopped retreating, realizing that he was the one who held the weapon. He stuck the spring-action knife out in front of him, probing the air with it. His back curved into a large C as he crouched over, head low, the knife always moving in front of him as he advanced. Richard held his ground and waited. Miller advanced cautiously, his eyes fastened on Richard's throat, the knife hand moving constantly, murderously, in a swinging arc. He grinned terribly, a redstained, white smile on his face.

The chair, Richard suddenly remembered. There's a chair. I'll take the chair and swing. Under the chin. No. Across the chest. Fast though. It'll have to be fast, one movement. Wait. Not yet, wait. Come on, Miller. Come on. *Come on!*

Miller paused and searched Richard's face. He grinned again and began speaking softly as he advanced, almost in a whisper, almost as if he were thinking aloud.

"See the knife, Mr. Daddy-oh? See the pretty knife? I'm gonna slash you up real good, Mr. Daddy-oh. I'm gonna slash you, and then I'm gonna slash you some more. I'm gonna cut you up real fine. I'm gonna cut you up so nobody'll know you any more, Mr. Daddy-oh."

All the while moving closer, closer, swinging the knife.

"Ever get cut, Mr. Daddy-oh? Ever get sliced with a sharp knife? This one is sharp, Mr. Daddy-oh, and you're gonna get cut with it. I'm gonna cut you now, and you're never gonna bother us no more. No more."

Richard backed away down the aisle.

Thoughts tumbled into his mind with blinding rapidity. I'll make him think I'm retreating. I'll give him confidence. The empty seat in the third now. Next to Ganigan. I'll lead him there. I hope it's empty. Empty when I checked the roll. I can't look, I'll tip my hand. Keep a poker face. Come on, Miller, follow me. Follow me so I can crack your ugly skull in two. Come on, you louse. One of us goes, Miller. And it's not going to be me.

"Nossir, Mr. Daddy-oh, we ain't gonna bother with you no more. No more tests, and no more of your noise. Just your face, Mr. Daddy-oh. Just gonna fix your face so nobody'll wanna look at you no more."

One more row, Richard calculated. Back up one more row. Reach. Swing. One. More. Row.

The class followed the two figures with fascination. Miller stalked Richard down the long aisle, stepping forward on the balls of his feet, pace by pace, waiting for Richard to back into the blackboard. Vota rolled over on the floor and groaned again.

And Richard counted the steps. A few more. A . . . few . . . more . . .

"Shouldn't have hit me, Mr. Daddy-oh," Miller mocked. "Ain't nice for teachers to hit students like that, Mr. Daddy-oh. Nossir, it ain't nice at . . ."

The chair crashed into Miller's chest, knocking the breath out of him. It came quickly and forcefully, with the impact of a striking snake. Richard had turned, as if to run, and then the chair was gripped in his hands tightly. It sliced the air in a clean, powerful arc, and Miller covered his face instinctively. The chair crashed into his chest, knocking him backwards. He screamed in surprise and pain as Richard leaped over the chair to land heavily on his chest. Richard pinned Miller's shoulders to the floor with his knees and slapped him ruthlessly across the face.

"Here, Miller, here, here, here," he squeezed through clenched teeth. Miller twisted his head from side to side, trying to escape the cascade of blows that fell in rapid onslaught on his cheeks.

The knife, Richard suddenly remembered! Where's the knife? What did he do with the . . .

Sunlight caught the cold glint of metal, and Richard glanced up instantly. Vota stood over him, the knife clenched tightly in his fist. He grinned boyishly, his rotten teeth flashing across his blotchy, thin face. He spat vehemently at Richard, and then there was a blur of color: blue steel, and the yellow of Vota's hair, and the blood on Miller's lip, and the brown wooden floor, and the gray tweed of Richard's suit. A shout came up from the class, and a hiss seemed to escape Miller's lips.

Richard kicked at Vota, feeling the heavy leather of his shoes crack against the boy's shins. Miller was up and fumbling for Richard's arms. A sudden slice of pain started at Richard's shoulder, careened down the length of his arm. Cloth gave way with a rasping scratch, and blood flashed bright against the gray tweed.

From the floor, Richard saw the knife flash back again, poised in Vota's hand ready to strike. He saw Miller's fists doubled and hard, saw the animal look on Vota's face and again the knife threatening and sharp, drenched now with blood, dripping on the brown, cold, wooden floor.

The noise grew louder and Richard grasped in his mind for a picture of the Roman arena, tried to rise, felt pain sear through his right arm as he put pressure on it. He's cut me, he thought with panic. Vota has cut me. And the screaming reached a wild crescendo, hands moved with terrible swiftness, eyes gleamed with molten fury, bodies squirmed, and hate smothered everything in a sweaty, confused, embarrassed embrace.

This is it, Richard thought, this is it.

"Leave him alone, you crazy jerk," Serubi was shouting.

Leave who alone, Richard wondered. Who? I wasn't . . .

"Lousy sneak," Levy shouted. "Lousy, dirty sneak."

Please, Richard thought. Please.

Levy seized Miller firmly and pushed him backward against a desk. Richard watched him dazedly, his right arm burning with pain. He saw Busco through a maze of moving, struggling bodies, Busco who was caught cheating, saw Busco smash a book against Vota's knife hand. The knife clattered to the floor with a curious sound. Vota's hand reached out and Di Pasco stepped on it with the heel of his foot. The knife disappeared in a shuffle of hands, but Vota no longer had it. Richard stared at the bare, brown spot on the floor where the knife had been.

Whose chance is it now, he wondered? Whose turn to slice the teacher?

Miller tried to struggle off the desk where Levy had him pinned. Brown, a Negro boy, brought his fist down heavily on

Miller's nose. He wrenched the larger boy's head back with one hand, and again brought his fist down fiercely.

A slow recognition trickled into Richard's confused thoughts. Through dazzled eyes, he watched.

Vota scrambled to his feet and lunged at him. A solid wall seemed to rise before him as Serubi and Gomez flung themselves against the onrushing form and threw it back. They tumbled onto Vota, holding his arms, lashing out with excited fists.

They're fighting for me! No, Richard reasoned, no. But yes, *they're fighting for me!* Against Miller. Against Vota. For me. For me, oh my God, for me.

His eyes blinked nervously as he struggled to his feet.

"Let's . . . let's take them down to the principal," he said, his voice low.

Antoro moved closer to him, his eyes widening as they took in the livid slash that ran the length of Richard's arm.

"Man, that's some cut," he said.

Richard touched his arm lightly with his left hand. It was soggy and wet, the shirt and jacket stained a dull brownish-red.

"My brother got cut like that once," Ganigan offered.

The boys were still holding Miller and Vota, but they no longer seemed terribly interested in the troublemakers.

For an instant, Richard felt a twinge of panic. For that brief, terrible instant he imagined that the boys hadn't really come to his aid at all, that they had simply seen an opportunity for a good fight and had seized upon it. He shoved the thought aside, began fumbling for words.

"I . . . I think I'd better take them down to Mr. Stemplar," he said. He stared at the boys, trying to read their faces, searching for something in their eyes that would tell him he had at last reached them, had at last broken through the wall. He could tell nothing. Their faces were blank, their eyes emotionless.

He wondered if he should thank them. If only he knew. If he could only hit upon the right thing to say, the thing to cement it all.

"I'll . . . I'll take them down. Suppose . . . you . . . you all go to lunch now."

"That sure is a mean cut," Julian said.

"Yeah," Ganigan agreed.

"You can all go to lunch," Richard said. "I want to take Miller and Vota . . ."

The boys didn't move. They stood there with serious faces, solemnly watching Richard.

". . . to . . . the . . . principal," Richard finished.

"A hell of a mean cut," Gomez said.

Busco chose his words carefully, and he spoke slowly. "Maybe we better just forget about the principal, huh? Maybe we oughta just go to lunch?"

Richard saw the smile appear on Miller's face, and a new weary sadness lumped into his throat.

He did not pretend to understand. He knew only that they had fought for him and that now, through some unfathomable code of their own, had turned on him again. But he knew what had to be and he could only hope that eventually they would understand why he had to do it.

"All right," he said firmly, "let's break it up. I'm taking these two downstairs."

He shoved Miller and Vota ahead of him, fully expecting to meet the resistance of another wall, a wall of unyielding bodies. Instead, the boys parted to let him through, and Richard walked past them with his head high. A few minutes ago, he would have taken this as a sign that the wall had broken. That was a few minutes ago.

Now, he was not at all surprised to hear a high falsetto pipe up behind him, "Oh, Daddy-oh! You're a *hee*-ro!"

Short Short Story

In March of last year, I wrote a letter to your magazine which you subsequently published in May. You will recall that I described myself as a bald-headed though virile man of seventy-six with a walrus mustache and a preference for well-built redheaded midgets (female). In that letter, I related the story of my first and only sexual experience with a redheaded midget, and told of the ecstasy I had derived from that brief encounter. I explained that whereas I was now married to a very tall blond woman (five feet five inches), I nonetheless had never forgotten that fleeting affair so many years ago, and was still unable to quell my longings and urgings for female midgets with scarlet tresses. While praising abundantly the various women of height and undeniable girth who have graced the pages of your fine magazine, I asked at that time if your plans for the future included running a centerfold photograph of a nude minikin with an auburn thatch. I also asked if any of your readers shared my feelings about midgets with ruddy locks.

I certainly did not anticipate the overwhelming tide of letters that were published in your July issue, most of them complaining that my comments about female midgets, especially redheaded ones, reflected nothing but the basest sort of male chauvinism. I had not felt, nor do I now feel, that my admitted lust for miniature redheaded women is in any way sexist, and I was quite frankly surprised and annoyed by these accusations, and by the suggestion from one of your readers (Dr. J. M., Seattle, Washington) that my "aberration" (as he called it) was nothing but a role-reversal acting-out of "the

Snow White syndrome." His diagnosis continues to baffle me. Full-blown sex in a king-sized bed with a perfectly formed little woman is hardly the same thing as cavorting with a gang of gnomic old men. I would like to call the good doctor's attention to the definition of "midget" in the *American Heritage Dictionary of the English Language*: "An extremely small person who is otherwise normally proportioned."

Needless to say, the storm of protest quite unsettled me. Until then, I had enormously enjoyed your "Letters" column, which I found to be spirited, uninhibited, and literary besides. Such elevated dialogue, it seemed to me, was necessary in a free society, where sexual acts considered strange, bizarre, perverse, or merely monstrous might be revealed as natural and normal through a sincere exchange of ideas among consenting adults. I was surprised to learn, for example, how many men are sexually attracted to women with back problems, especially those wearing braces. Or, as a further example, I would never have dreamt that certain types of women are irresistibly drawn to men who have undergone surgery for the removal of knee cartilage. (For my tardy enlightenment, I thank the young lady who signed her letter *M. S., Dallas, Texas*, in your giant holiday issue.) And I was thoroughly amazed to learn how many couples use flavored yogurt to enliven their sexual encounters in or out of bed. My own aversion to yogurt remains undiminished, but an understanding of the needs and gratifications of others surely goes a long way toward an understanding of oneself. Returning to the point, the angry and hysterical letters you published concerning the apparently taboo subject of sexual intercourse between a female midget and a male of normal size (I myself am five feet eight and one-half inches tall, and built accordingly) shocked me, dismayed me, and caused me to reassess with regret what are surely preponderantly puritanical attitudes in this nation. It was not until your August issue, however, that the *real* problem started.

You'll remember that you published my letter in May of last year, and that you headlined it (somewhat cutely, I felt) SMALL WONDER, and signed it *Name and address withheld.* Your "Letters" column (as I'm sure you know) warns that *"Letters for publication should carry name and address—in capitals, please—though these will be withheld by the Editor on request."* I requested that you withhold *my* name and address only because it seemed *de rigueur.* For example, most of the gourmands who wrote in to describe the flavorsome uses to which they had put yogurt asked that *their* names and addresses be withheld, though God only knows why. To be perfectly honest, I once believed your editors were inventing all those unsigned letters. This was before you published *my* letter in May, of course, which I knew was genuine since I myself had written it. I assumed, too, that the July issue's firestorm was equally genuine, and I thought I had seen the last of the correspondence in that issue—but instead, another letter appeared in your August issue. I reproduce that letter now, verbatim, including the precious headline which I'm sure was created by the same editor who headlined *my* letter.

TINY TURN ON

 As a twenty-two year old redheaded (and red-blooded) female midget, I must say I was really turned on by that bald, mustached macho male who wrote to say he preferred abbreviated beauties to overblown broads. If ever you decide to pick up on his suggestion and run a midget in your centerfold, I hereby volunteer my face and form. My proportions, if you're seriously interested, are a spectacular 24, 20, 25, and since your centerfold measures almost twenty-four inches opened wide, and since I measure only thirty-eight inches similarly, a nude centerfold photograph of me would be something very close to life-size. Think about it, and if you decide to go ahead with it, why not send the guy with the walrus mustache to take the picture? I'd be happy to oblige him in every way possible. L. E., Oaken Bow, North Carolina.

My first response to L.E.'s letter was, I am not ashamed to admit, anatomical. The very thought of photographing all three-feet two-inches of her in the nude was enough to trigger the wildest memories of what had happened with my first (and last) redheaded midget almost five decades before. Was it possible that your magazine would actually *consider* running a centerfold of a nude midget? Was it equally possible (vain desire!) that you would assign *me* to the pleasurable task of photographing L.E. in Oaken Bow, North Carolina?

And then I began to doubt.

Was the letter bona fide, or had it been concocted to spur another avalanche of angry responses from your readers? Immediately, I resurrected my earlier theory that all unsigned or otherwise anonymous letters were written by your staff editors, and concluded that the letter from L.E. had been written by one Louis Edwards, whose name appeared on your masthead—and who apparently had been sloppy enough to have used his own initials when signing his imaginary epistle. I even doubted the existence of Oaken Bow, North Carolina, until I looked it up in the Atlas that night after dinner—and then my entire perspective changed.

Oaken Bow *did* exist. It was a town in McDowell County, and it had a population of 787, and it could be found on the North Carolina map on page 109 at location D4, which I discovered was in the Blue Ridge Mountains, some twenty miles southeast of Asheville. I cannot begin to describe the enormous pleasure I derived from the simple act of locating Oaken Bow on the North Carolina map. If Oaken Bow existed, then it was entirely possible that L.E. *also* existed, that L.E. was in fact one of the 787 people living there, a twenty-two-year old redheaded (*and* red-blooded) midget who had invited me in print (was that legally binding?) to come take her picture in the nude for the centerfold of your magazine! I slammed the Atlas shut and turned to find my wife staring at me. I mumbled something about never having known Tasmania was so close to New Zealand, and then I spent the rest of the night longing for morning to come.

At the crack of dawn, I rose, showered, shaved, dressed, and was out of the apartment by seven-thirty. Instead of going directly to my office on East 40th Street, I went instead to Grand Central Station, where I searched through the out-of-town telephone directories until I found one for McDowell County, with combined listings for Garden City, Glenwood, Providence, Oaken Bow, Marion, Old Fort, and Sevier. My heart was pounding furiously as I scanned the "E" listings, and then my forefinger and my heart stopped almost simultaneously—I had found a listing for a woman named *Lillian Eaton!* It was the only L.E. listing in Oaken Bow, and I was certain even before I dialed the number that I had found my fiery-haired minikin.

The woman who answered the phone sounded senile.

I asked if I might talk to Lillian Eaton, and she said she was Lillian Eaton.

I asked if there were a *younger* Lillian Eaton there, her daughter perhaps, or her granddaughter, and she said she was a ninety-four year old spinster, and the only Lillian Eaton in that house, or for that matter in all of McDowell County.

She was also a little hard of hearing. When I asked her if she was by any chance a midget, she said there was nobody named Bridget in that house. I decided she was not the lady who had written the letter to your magazine. (It was interesting to learn, by the way, just how many men are sexually attracted to novagenarians, as reported in your article on *Geriatric Sex* in the February issue.)

Limp and dejected, I walked the two blocks to my office, knowing full well I would be unable to rest until I had taken a train or a plane to Oaken Bow and searched that town from house to house for my enigmatic, monogrammatic love. (Yes—*love!* I had already begun to think of her as such, even though I had never laid eyes on the creature.) I agonized for the better part of August. I am a bookkeeper with a large accounting firm, and am rarely if ever required to go out of town on business. But so driven was I by the thought of locating the L.E. who had promised to "oblige me in every possible way," so determined was I to experience after almost five decades an encore of that first blissful interlude, so *obsessed* was I that I created an opportunity to absent myself from New York. I told my wife a furniture company we represented had burned to the ground in Old Fort, North Carolina, and that I would have to go there in an attempt to reconstruct their destroyed books. The lie was based on an actual furniture company fire in Schenectady four years earlier, at which time one of our accountants had gone upstate to do exactly what I was pretending to be doing now. On the fifth of September, then, a Friday night—I flew from the airport in Newark, New Jersey, to the Asheville-Hendersonville airport in North Carolina, and then I rented a car and drove to Oaken Bow. On Saturday morning, September the sixth, I began looking for L.E. in earnest.

I could not find her.

I searched through Oaken Bow all day Saturday and part of Sunday. On Sunday afternoon, I canvassed the nearby communities, but none of the people to whom I spoke had the faintest knowledge of a redheaded midget with the initials L.E. On Sunday evening, I went back to the only hotel in town and learned to my dismay that McDowell County was dry, and that the package stores in the nearby wet county were closed on Sunday. Deprived of even the solace of alcohol (I am not normally a drinking man, but my inability to locate L.E. was both frustrating and distressing), I sat in the lobby of the hotel and eventually struck up a conversation with a one-armed former blackjack dealer who mentioned in passing that he had read in a man's magazine (I don't believe it was yours) an article stating that certain types of women found one-armed men sexually attractive.

We then began discussing my penchant for midgets, and he said I should have been down there in June when the circus had pitched its tents on the fairgrounds. He said there must've been six or seven good-looking midgets in town, wouldn't have minded getting hold of one of them himself, he said, though his tastes usually ran to larger women.

I asked him if he had happened to notice a redheaded midget, a girl of about twenty-two, and he said there *might* have been a redheaded midget but he couldn't say for sure because in addition to his one arm being missing, he was also color blind. (Though he had read in a magazine that many women found it sexually stimulating to go to bed with men who were color blind.) I told him that this particular midget would have had the initials L.E., and he asked me if I mightn't be thinking about Ellie Carpenter, who was a midget who'd been there with the circus in June, and who used to come over to the hotel every now and then to turn tricks, since what she doubled as in her spare time away from the sideshow was a hooker. She'd been around for two weeks, while the circus was there, and then she'd left when the circus had.

On the plane back to New York, I pondered what he had told me. Was it possible that Ellie Carpenter, a redheaded midget passing through Oaken Bow with the circus in June, had read my letter in your June issue, and had answered it while in Oaken Bow (hence the address) and had asked that it be signed with the homophonic initials L.E.—for Ellie? In November, telling my wife that a furniture store in Sarasota had gone up in smoke, I flew down to the winter quarters of the circus in a further attempt to locate Ellie Carpenter. The man I spoke to had been with the circus for the better part of his life, and he told me that the only redheaded midget they'd employed in recent years was a woman named Else Kopchek, who was twenty-two years old, and Polish, and from Philadelphia, Pennsylvania. But she had left the circus immediately after the season, mentioning in parting that there was bigger money to be made elsewhere. She had not even remotely hinted where "elsewhere" might be.

It now seemed entirely possible to me that Else Kopchek might indeed have called herself Ellie Carpenter while turning tricks at the Oaken Bow Hotel, and it seemed further likely that she had not gone back to Philadelphia, Pennsylvania, it being common knowledge that *nobody* goes back to Philadelphia, Pennsylvania. (I certainly hope this casual remark does not unleash another cageful of beastly letters, if you'll pardon the metaphor. My *first* letter has caused me problems enough.) The very thought of reliving that thrilling youthful experience with a new and different partner—but oh so similar in size and coloration—was enough to send me to Philadelphia the very next weekend, hoping against hope that soon I might disrobe an elfin Ellie, discard her dainty delicate underthings, pat her seemingly pubescent peaks, probe her pithy pussy, manipulate her miniature mons veneris and Lilliputian labiae, caress her compact clitoris and crisp pauciloquent pubic—please, an elderly man should not carry on so in a public forum.

Suffice it to say, I went to Philadelphia.

I found a man there named Karl Kopchek who told me his daughter was indeed a redheaded, twenty-two year old midget named Else Kopchek. Karl was six-feet three-inches tall and had black hair. He told me he had last seen his daughter when she'd come home for Christmas. At the time, she said she was doing social work in San Juan, Puerto Rico, but he had not heard from her since, and did not know where she was or what she was doing now.

And neither do I.

And that's why I'm writing to you once again.

Is Ellie Carpenter (née Else Kopchek) indeed the L.E. who extended her kind invitation to me in the pages of your magazine? If she is, I will of course continue the search for her as long as I have breath, and I will *find* her one day, I *know* I will, and then, beware you lovers of yore! We shall scale Parnassian heights, we two, and shatter legends and myths! But, sirs, *is* she my L.E.? Only you can say, for only you have her original letter, written from Oaken Bow last June but presumably carrying a name and address (in capitals, please) as asked for at the very top of your "Letters" column. I implore you now for your educated advice. Should I now curtail my quest for this carmine-curled, concise, and curvaceous munchkin whom I believe to be the L.E. who first wrote to you? In short, is my minor marvel a myth, or a midget worth pursuing? Tell me, sirs. *Is* Else Kopchek the L.E. who wrote to you last June? Consult your files, I beg of you, and send me your response in the enclosed stamped, self-addressed envelope. I shall be eternally grateful for your speedy reply.

Name and address withheld.

The Beheading

The paid previews had begun on the day before Easter.

I spent Easter Sunday with my family in the country, and then packed a bag on Monday afternoon and left for an apartment on West Tenth Street in the Village, graciously loaned to me by two friends who were spending Easter week in Chicago. The apartment was small and comfortable, with one bedroom, a tiny kitchen overlooking an enclosed back yard, and a living room with a real wood-burning fireplace. In the bedroom fronting on Tenth, there was a large double bed with brass headboard and footboard, covered with an opulent red brocade bedspread. A reading lamp hung over the bed on the wall, a radio-alarm clock was on the bedstand beside it, and a note from Dotty was pinned to one of the pillows:

Dear Gene:

The sheets were changed yesterday, there is fresh linen if you need it in the closet near the kitchen. Help yourself to anything in the fridge or the bar, use Mike's spare razor if you want to, and also my typewriter which is on the desk in the bedroom near the windows. Paper is in second drawer left, erasers, etc. The cleaning woman name of Eudice out of South Carolina comes on Thursday, I've already explained you'll be using the apartment. Have yourself lots and lots of lovely previews, we will be back in time for the opening.

Love,
Dotty

I read the note and settled in. Actually, there wasn't very much settling to do since I'd packed only one bag with a half-dozen clean shirts, a sweater, socks, a pair of pajamas, a toothbrush and my own electric razor. I felt strange in an apartment in New York City. Natalie and I had moved to the country shortly before our first child was born. Peter was ten when the play went into rehearsal, which meant that we had been living in the old gray-shingled Cape Cod for close to eleven years. The house had a widow's walk, and once— while we were still negotiating for rights to the play, and I stayed late in the city over too many martinis—Natalie stood waiting for me on the narrow platform running around the second story of the house, her hands clasped in the classic pose of the seafarer's wife, back straight, head erect, silhouetted against the dying sun.

I missed her that first night alone in the city. The automobile sounds below seemed incessant. At three a.m., I heard a girl laughing and thought for an insane moment that Natalie was with me in the bedroom. I got out of bed and walked to the window. The girl was wearing a green dress. She was blond, and she was leaning against her escort, helpless with laughter, one hand draped languidly on his shoulder. I went back to bed, and at last I fell asleep. The radio-alarm went off at nine the next morning. Rehearsal was scheduled to start at ten.

By noon, I knew what had to be done.

I suppose I should explain that a strange sort of self-hypnosis gradually overcomes the people working on a play. The writing of a play is a solitary task, but once it has been optioned for production it becomes of necessity a group effort. I used to think that the only *pure* production of a play was the one the author saw on the stage of his mind while he was writing it. There was no human error then, no actor who might nullify a character through inadequacy or misinterpretation, no director who might call for an emotion never intended, no designer who might visualize a setting contrary to the one the author imagined. There was, instead, a marvelously unique creation, a newborn child who miraculously was not the result of any collaboration, who (as ugly as he may have been) seemed radiantly beautiful to his only parent. I used to think that a play was not only being *written* while it was in the typewriter, it was being staged and performed and cheered by capacity audiences as well.

I now know that a play is nothing but a manuscript until it is put on the boards. It is only then that it comes to life, and the life it realizes is sometimes quite different, and very often immeasurably better than the one it aspired to on paper.

We had been rehearsing my play for five weeks, and we had nine days of previews still ahead of us, with two performances on Wednesday and another two on Saturday. I had, of course, rewritten many scenes in the play even before we went into production, and I had since rewritten almost half of the second act. I had watched our cast of six explore their respective roles, come to grips with the characters they were portraying, settle into performances they were now polishing and refining before opening night. I had seen our director wrestling with difficult scenes, badgering and cajoling his actors, desperately seeking the play's inner secret, the single factor that would transform it into a semblance of reality, an illusion of vibrant flesh and blood. I had eaten breakfast, lunch, and dinner with each of the people involved in the show, either separately or together, I had listened to complaints and petty quarrels, I had even resisted a blatant seduction attempt by the ingenue who was determined to "get close to the well-spring," as she put it. I had been at every rehearsal but one (when I had to rush crosstown to talk with a man from the *Times* who was doing a piece on me) and I had been convinced completely and utterly that we were on the right track, that we were all working together toward the successful realization of my play.

And then suddenly, that Tuesday morning, the spell broke as sharply as though a hypnotist had snapped his fingers and commanded me to open my eyes. I saw the play, *really* saw it, for the first time since rehearsals had begun. I saw it from beginning to end, and I wanted to weep. I left the theater as soon as Danny, our director, began giving his notes to the actors. I walked up Broadway and wondered what I should do, and then I decided to call Natalie. I caught her in the middle of leaving for nursery school to pick up Sharon, our four-year old daughter.

"Nat," I said, "we've got trouble."

"What is it?"

"The play stinks."

"The play does not stink," Natalie said.

"Honey, I just sat through it, and it's terrible. I don't know what to do."

"What do you want to do?"

"I don't know."

"Gene, you *do* know."

"Yes, I do. I think I want to get rid of Danny."

"Yes."

"I think I've wanted it all along."

"I know you have."

"But, honey, I *like* him."

"Is he harming your play?" Natalie asked.

"Yes."

"Then replace him before it's too late."

"Honey . . ."

"Honey," she said, "you spent a year writing this play. Do you want to see it die?"

"No, but . . ."

"Then do it. Replace him."

We were both silent. Outside the corner phone booth, a traffic jam was starting, horns honking, a patrolman approaching a stalled Cadillac, his arms in frantic motion.

"All right," I said at last.

"I have to get Sharon."

"All right."

"Gene?"

"Yes?"

"I love you. Call me later, will you?"

"Yes, sure."

"How's the apartment?"

"It's nice."

"All right, I'll talk to you later."

"Right, right," I said, and hung up.

I had lunch at the Automat, and then went back to the afternoon rehearsal. I took a seat in the balcony and tried to see the play objectively, telling myself that this morning's shock may have been due to pre-opening jitters, willing everything on that stage to come to unexpected life. But nothing happened. The actors went through scene after scene, the play unfolded listlessly; it was make-believe, it was fake, it was rotten. Unobserved, I listened to the actors when Danny called a break. Scenes that once were clear to them now seemed troublesome; they were asking far too many questions for a company that would be opening in a week. And worse, Danny had no answers to give them. If he had ever understood the play, he did not seem to grasp it now. I listened as he fumblingly tried to explain the relationship of the father to his young son in a scene I had sweated over for months, and I fairly screamed aloud from the balcony when I realized he was only confusing it beyond all comprehension. If I had had any doubts, they evaporated in that moment.

I went upstairs to the executive offices of the theater and asked Phillip, our general manager, where I could find Beth. He said he thought she was across the street in Ho Tang's. Beth was my producer, a woman of forty-eight, twice divorced and childless. Thirty-nine years ago, she had first set foot on a New York stage as a child actress, and some of her friends still called her Baby Beth despite her flinty blue eyes and imperious mouth. She was sitting with Edward, our stage manager, at a table in the bar section of the restaurant. Ho Tang's specialized in a Chinese-Korean cuisine and though we had never once tasted the food there, it was rumored to be excellent. We used the place as a command post, meeting there to drink and discuss the play, as Beth and Edward were presumably doing when I approached the table. Edward was my age, forty-three, but he looked a good deal older; perhaps the horn-rimmed spectacles accounted for that. He always wore a trench-coat, day or night, fair weather or foul, indoors or out. He gave the impression of someone expecting a phone call that would force him to leave immediately for another appointment.

"Here's Gene," he said.

Beth pulled out the chair beside her. Her eyes studied my face, and she said immediately, "Is something wrong?"

"Yes," I said. "I think Danny's lost control of the play and the actors, and I think he should be replaced."

The table was silent for an instant. Beth looked across at Edward. I thought he nodded almost imperceptibly but that may have been in understanding of what I'd said, rather than in agreement with it.

"We were just talking about the same thing," Beth said.

"Do you agree with me?"

"I'm not sure. I want to watch tonight's performance."

"Will you know then?"

"Yes," she said.

I did not get a chance to talk to her after the evening performance because Danny was with us when we went over to Ho Tang's for our customary drinks and critique. He was exhausted after a full day of rehearsal and a grueling performance during which he could not have failed to sense the enormous apathy of the audience. His weariness showed in his face. He was a tall man, fifty years old, with graying hair and a small bald patch at the back of his head. His eyes were a deep brown, darting and alert, as searching as an inquisitor's. He had a habit of pointing with his entire head, jutting it forward sharply to ask a question. His nose was a trifle too keen for his otherwise soft features, emphasizing the head thrust each time it came. His mouth was gently rounded, curving upward at either end to give him an expression of perpetual amusement. I was waiting for him to go to the jukebox to play his favorite song, a tune called "One More Time" which had, through over-exposure during the last five weeks, practically become the show's theme. As soon as he left the table, I said, "Well?" and Beth sharply whispered, "Later."

"One More Time" erupted into the bamboo bar, its tempo insinuatingly tropical, its lyric hypnotically repetitious. Danny came back to the table and we began the usual post mortem, discussing the play in minute detail, lines, movement, nuance, everything but what was essentially wrong with it: Danny.

At twelve-thirty in the morning, we left Ho Tang's and put Beth into a taxi. I still had not spoken to her. I hailed a cab for myself and arrived at the Tenth Street apartment at a quarter to one. Beth's line was busy when I called. I tried again in five minutes and she answered the phone on the second ring.

"Gene?" she said.

"Yes."

"I was just talking to Edward."

"And?"

"We think you're right," she said. "We've got to replace Danny."

"How shall we do it?"

"I don't know yet," she said.

"Who'll we get?"

"I don't know."

"Beth, we've got to move . . ."

"Tomorrow's a matinee day," she said calmly. "I'll make some excuse not to be there. Meet me outside the Plaza at two-thirty. We'll figure it out then."

"You do agree . . ."

"Yes, I think he's lost control of it," Beth said, and sighed. "Darling, I'm exhausted, we'll talk about it tomorrow."

"Yes," I said, "good night."

"Good night, Gene."

I hung up, and then called Natalie to tell her what we'd decided. She listened intently and then said she thought we were doing the right thing. I turned out the light and tried to sleep. I kept listening for the blond girl in the green dress, but there was no laughter that night.

The streets of New York were thronged with college kids home on vacation. I walked up Fifth Avenue, envying each and every one of them. They all seemed to be smiling or laughing, sporting their new Easter outfits, enjoying the mild spring day, window shopping, chattering gaily.

Beth sat alone on the lip of the fountain outside the Plaza, bathed in sunlight. She was wearing a blue suit, and her hands were clasped over her bag, which she held in her lap, her head bent, the sunshine touching her short blond hair. Six months ago, when my agent had finished his negotiations with her, he had called me immediately and said, "Baby Beth, my ass, she almost chewed the rug off the floor." She had then gone out to raise eighty thousand dollars in less than a month, assembled cast and director and crew in half again that time, booked a theater, and hired her press agents and advertising representatives—all of this accomplished effectively and tirelessly in a business that boasted its only good producers were men. She was a tough beautiful broad. I had never seen her looking as forlorn or as vulnerable as she did that day outside the Plaza, sitting in sunshine on the lip of the fountain.

I hesitated before approaching her. She seemed to be caught in one of those intensely private reveries it is almost sinful to interrupt. But I walked to her at last, and my shadow fell over her crossed hands on the bag in her lap, and I said, "It's not the end of the world, dear."

She looked up, gave me a fleeting smile and a brief nod, and then patted the fountain rim beside her. I sat with my hands clasped between my knees, my head turned toward Beth. I felt suddenly old, like a tired vagrant watching pigeons.

"So," I said, "what do we do now?"

"We get another director, of course," Beth said.

"Isn't it too late?"

"No, I don't think so. We've got a full week, we don't open until next Wednesday night. I've seen shows saved in less time than that."

"What if we *don't* fire him, Beth?"

"I think we'll be killed." She shook her head. "The actors smell it. They've lost faith in him." She shook her head again.

94

"It's a goddamn shame, but that's what's happened, and we've got to fire him or die for him." Her eyes met mine, bright and blue and cold and hard in the warm sunshine. "I don't think you want to die for Danny, do you?"

I hesitated. Then I said, "No, I don't want to die for Danny."

"I didn't think so," Beth said. She took my hand in hers. We might have been lovers sitting in the sunshine, except that we were discussing an execution. "You've written a good play, Gene," she said. "I've done everything I can for it so far, and now I've got to do the rest. I've got to fire Danny, and I've got to do it fast because time is the one luxury we haven't got."

"Couldn't we postpone?"

"Yes, but that costs money. We're stretched very thin as it is." She sighed heavily. "You don't know how I hate doing this," she said. "I've known Danny a long time. This isn't our first show together, you know."

"Yes, I know."

"He's had a rough time these last five years. I don't want to hurt him."

"Neither do I." I hesitated and then said, "Look, maybe we ought to forget it, just take our chances and see what happens."

"No," she said.

"It's only a play, Beth."

"*Is* it only a play, Gene?" I did not answer her. She nodded wearily. "We'll do what has to be done," she said. "The only thing . . ."

"Yes?"

"I want it to come from him. I want him to realize for himself that it's no good anymore. I want *him* to suggest that we bring in another director."

"Who have you got in mind?"

"I've already spoken to Terry Brown. He says he's interested."

"When did you do that?"

"This morning. Would you agree to Terry?"

"Of *course* I would."

"Fine then," she said, and nodded.

We sat in silence for several moments. And then, because we had completed the difficult part of our discussion, deciding unanimously that we were ready and willing to sacrifice Danny for the sake of the play, we now rushed into the easy part—how to commit our homicide. We spoke in whispers; there was the hard beat of urgency to our words.

"When will we do it?"

"Tonight," Beth said. "After the performance."

"Where?"

"Ho Tang's. We'll gradually lead up to what's wrong, try to make Danny see he's hurting the show."

"Then what?"

"When he suggests getting another director, I'll pretend Terry is a spur-of-the-moment idea."

"Why all the duplicity?" I said. "Why can't we just tell him straight out?"

"I told you. I don't want to hurt him."

"Suppose he doesn't suggest . . ."

"I've thought of that," Beth said.

"I mean, it may never even *occur* to him that we should get another director."

"In that case, I'll just have to tell him," Beth said. "Straight out," she said, and sighed.

I sighed, too.

We shook hands then, and glanced over our shoulders like the conspirators we surely were. Beth walked off up Central

Park South. I went down Fifth to Forty-Sixth and then cut crosstown to the theater.

The matinee had not yet broken.

I stood on the sidewalk and looked up at the marquee.

The new title of the play had been suggested by Danny a week before we went into rehearsal. Every time I looked at it, or heard it spoken, or even *thought* about it, I felt a pang of guilt, as though I had honestly named my baby Max, only to have agreed later that his name should be changed to Percy. The stars' names were above the title—their credits rigidly predetermined by contract and scrupulously respected by those professionals who design window cards, three-sheets, and newspaper ads—in the same size, style, weight, color, and color background as the title. Listed below their names was the title itself (I felt the pang of guilt) and then my name as author (25% of the title) and then the names of the supporting players (50% of the title) and then Danny's name as director (100% of the title, on the strength of the hit show he had directed for Beth five years back). I stood studying the marquee in despair, not because my name was the smallest one on it, but only because I suspected I might wish it were even *smaller* come opening night, illegible perhaps, known to only a few loved ones like my mother and my wife, otherwise hidden from the rest of the scornful world.

I stared at the marquee only a moment longer.

Then I walked up to Sixth Avenue and found a bar.

I did not call Natalie until just before dinner, when I told her the plan and announced that I might very well shoot myself before the night was over.

"Don't shoot yourself," she said matter-of-factly.

"Give me one good reason why."

"I'll give you *four* good reasons why," she said. "Me,

Sharon, Peter, and the dog."

"Hell with the goddamn dog," I said.

"Have you been drinking a little, dear?" she asked sweetly.

"I have been drinking a *lot*," I said. "Natalie," I said, "I have the feeling that before this day is through I will have consumed more alcohol than I have previously in my entire life included."

"Darling," she said, "go back to the apartment and take a shower."

"All right, honey, I'll take a shower."

"Good." She paused. "Make it a cold one."

"Very good," I said, "a cold one. Goodbye, darling, I'll call you later."

"Whatever time it is," she said. "Good luck."

I didn't take a shower. I walked from Forty-sixth to Thirty-fourth instead, and then I took a cab back to Forty-fourth and Sixth and ate four hot dogs with sauerkraut at the hot dog stand on the corner there, and then walked up to Columbus Circle and sat near the statue and wondered where the pigeons went when it got dark. I was waiting in Ho Tang's when Danny and Beth came in. Edward was a step behind them. Danny walked jauntily to the juke box, and "One More Time" pierced the Korean dusk.

"Gene," he shouted, "where the hell were you? You missed the best performance we've ever had!"

"I had to meet . . ."

"It was *tremendous*," he said, coming over to the table, "absolutely tremendous!"

". . . my agent," I mumbled. "Had to meet him." My eyes sought Beth's as she took off her Persian lamb and draped it over the back of the chair beside me. I could read nothing on her face.

"The audience *loved* it!" Danny said. He slid into the

booth behind the table, so that Beth and I were facing him. Edward sat on his right and a jutting mirrored wall was on his left. It occurred to me that we had him surrounded, escape was impossible. "They laughed in all the right places," he said, "they were quiet when they were supposed to be, they cried when . . . Beth, did you hear how still it got during the marbles scene?"

"Yes," she said, "they were very attentive." Her voice was noncommittal. I still knew nothing.

We ordered a round of drinks while Danny went on to relate to me all I had missed, going over each and every line the audience had howled at, explaining how the father-son scene had torn out their hearts, telling me he had seen an old lady openly weeping in the lobby after the second act curtain. I listened apprehensively, waiting for a cue from Beth. Were we to go through with this or not? Had she changed her mind after tonight's performance?

"There's still a lot wrong with it," she said at last, and I glanced at her quickly. We were going ahead as planned. I sighed and lifted my glass.

"Oh, sure," Danny said, "lots of little things wrong with it, but nothing we can't fix in the next week. I tell you, I've never felt more confident about a show in my life. I wouldn't have said this a few days ago, but everything suddenly seemed to come together tonight."

He grinned charmingly, boyishly, his eyes glowing with enthusiasm. He was raising his drink to his mouth when Beth said, "Well, I'm glad you know it still needs work, Danny."

"Oh, sure," Danny said, and drank. "You should have been there tonight, though, Gene. You'd have been amazed."

"Well, I saw it last night," I said. "And I was at yesterday's rehearsal."

"No comparison," Danny said, and lifted his glass again.

"Am I right, Beth? Two different shows."

"Miracles don't happen overnight," I said.

"Are you telling *me? Nothing* happens overnight," Danny said. "A lot of hard work went into making this show what it is."

"About yesterday's rehearsal . . ." I said.

"Forget yesterday's rehearsal. Wait'll you see it tomorrow. Listen, what kind of an author are you, anyway? How can you possibly stay away from your own show a week before it opens? He's jaded, that's what," Danny said, and laughed, and nudged Edward. Edward, sitting with his back to the wall, the collar of his trench coat raised, looked like a Mafia henchman in horn-rimmed glasses. He had not yet said a word.

"I thought you gave them the wrong slant on the father-son scene," I said. I knew I was pressing. A warning flashed in Beth's eyes.

"What do you mean?" Danny said.

"Yesterday. At rehearsal. I think the actors came away . . ." I hesitated. "Confused," I said.

"Yeah?" Danny shrugged. He lifted his glass and drained it. "You wouldn't have known it tonight. If anybody on that stage was confused . . ."

"Well, I think Gene may be right," Beth said cautiously. "I'm still not sure that scene is coming off."

"Oh?" Danny said. He signaled to the waiter and then leaned forward. "Where do you think it's wrong, Beth?" he asked. His voice was interested, concerned, respectful. He kept watching Beth's face. The waiter arrived just then, sparing her an immediate answer. We asked for another round. "One More Time" started again on the jukebox.

"Beth?" Danny said.

"I wouldn't know where to begin," she answered.

"Oh, come on," Danny said, and laughed. "The scene can't be *that* wrong."

"It is," Edward said suddenly. The flatness of his voice startled all of us. Danny turned toward him as if he'd been struck with a closed fist.

"The scene with the father and son?" he asked incredulously.

"Yes," Edward said, and nodded.

"Well, gee, I'm . . ." Danny paused. "Tell me what's wrong with it, will you?"

"Great *many* things wrong with it," I mumbled.

"What?"

"I said . . ."

"He said there are a great *many* things wrong with it," Beth said.

"Like what?" Danny said, and reached into his pocket for a notebook. He produced a pencil, opened the notebook on the table before him, and poised the pencil over a clean page. "Okay, let's have it," he said, and thrust his head forward. "Come on, come on, that's what we're here for."

"The actors don't understand it," I said.

"I've explained it to them often enough," Danny said.

"Yes, but they *still* don't understand it."

"Then I'll just have to explain it to them again," he said, and nodded. He looked up at me suddenly, his head darting forward again. "*I* understand it, don't I? I mean, *I* haven't misinterpreted it, have I? If there's one thing I think I know, Gene, it's your play," he said, and gave a short laugh.

"Well, the *actors* don't seem to know what they're doing," I said, hedging.

"We'll take care of that scene, don't worry," he said. "I'll look at it first thing tomorrow."

"It's not just *that* scene," Beth said. "The actors don't

seem to know what they're doing at *all*."

"In the *play*, do you mean?" Danny said.

"Yes."

"In the whole *play?*"

"Yes."

The waiter arrived with our drinks. Danny was staring at Beth across the table. Her eyes did not waver from his face.

"I'm not sure I get your meaning," he said.

"I mean," Beth said, "the actors need more direction."

"Direction?"

"Yes."

"You mean motivation?"

"I mean *direction*," Beth said.

"Look, I've discussed motivation with them till I'm blue in the . . ."

"I said *direction*." She paused. Her eyes were blue and hard and cold and bright. Danny was pinned against the wall, surrounded, and she would not let him escape those penetrating eyes. "Direction," she repeated. "From a director."

The first sign of fear flickered on Danny's face. Hypnotically, he kept staring into Beth's eyes, and then forcibly turned his head away, glancing first at Edward, and then fixing his gaze on me across the table.

"You think I should get tougher with them, is that it?" he asked.

"Danny," I said, "we feel . . ."

"Danny," Edward said, "it just isn't working, really it isn't. Maybe you're too close to it, maybe . . ."

"No closer than any of us," Danny answered. "I thought it went fine tonight. Give me a performance like that on opening night, and . . ."

"It was no different tonight," Beth said flatly.

"I thought . . ."

"It doesn't matter what you thought," Beth said. "The actors don't know what they're doing, and you haven't yet told them what's wrong."

"Well, look, honey, if you *know* what's wrong, I wish you'd let me in on the secret," Danny said, his voice rising. "Just tell me what the hell it is, and I'll fix it."

"We don't think you can," Beth said.

She delivered the words softly, the way she might have if she were underplaying a particularly powerful scene on stage, except that she was not acting. She turned her head toward me as she spoke, avoiding Danny's eyes, ducking her chin toward her right shoulder.

"I don't understand," Danny said, but I knew he had understood at last, I knew that the meaning was now absolutely clear, he had been told, and he had understood, and there was nothing left to do now but administer the *coup de grâce*.

I do not know where I found the courage. I think it was spawned only by Beth's sudden weakness, the way her chin was still turned into her shoulder. "We want to replace you," I said, and felt suddenly sick to my stomach.

"Then why the hell didn't you say so?" Danny snapped at once.

"It's just not working," I said.

"Sure, sure."

"We've still got a week," Edward said, "we may be able to save it."

"Sure."

"Danny, please understand," Beth said.

"Don't ever say that again!" Danny shouted, and the table fell silent. He looked down into his drink. He seemed suddenly embarrassed, as though his inability to have understood graciously and immediately was somehow shameful, as though his having failed to make it easier for us was something that now brought him very close to tears. I found it painful to watch him, and yet I could not take my eyes from his crumbling face. "You didn't have to give me a song and dance, you know," he said, "I'm not a beginner. If you want another director, then get one, that's all. I'm not a beginner."

"Danny," Beth started, and she reached across the table for his hand.

"Yes, we want another director," I said sharply, terrified that she would blow it all in the final moment, touch his hand and lose all her resolve, allow sympathy and loyalty to stand in the way of what had to be done, what had almost already been done.

"Do *we* want another director," Danny asked, "or is it just *you*, Gene?"

His eyes clashed with mine, and then he turned slowly to Beth. Her hand had stopped midway across the table, still reaching. Something passed between them, something I could not define, as delicate as air, caught in their locked glances. It hovered silently, painfully, endlessly. And then Beth pulled back her hand, clenched it in her lap and said, "*I* want it, too, Danny. We *all* want it."

"All right," he said, and nodded briefly, and glanced at the jukebox, as though fearful even his song would run out too soon. He nodded again. "Who?" he said.

"We thought Terry Brown."

"Have you spoken to him?"

"No, not yet," Beth said quickly.

"Is he in town?"

"I think so."

"Well, go on, call him then."

"Danny, I wish . . ." Beth started.

"Call him," I said.

She sighed, and nodded, and said to Edward, "Have you

got a dime?" and then she went to call the man who would save my play.

We stood together, Beth and I, at the rear of the theater on opening night. I could see Natalie sitting in the sixth row center, flanked by my parents on her left and her parents on her right. She was wearing a long green velvet gown, pearls at her throat. She looked as beautiful as she had almost twenty years ago when she'd walked over to me in the small park outside N.Y.U., wearing sweater and skirt, put her hands on her hips and said, "My friend Nancy said you wanted to know my name. Why?" As radiant as that.

We knew, of course, five minutes after the curtain went up. The first laugh line rushed past without a titter from the audience, and I felt Beth stiffen beside me, and actually crossed my fingers, something I had not done since I was a boy of seven. And then another laugh line followed, with no response from the audience, and the actors felt the apathy and began pushing, playing it more broadly, forgetting what the play was about, concentrating only on getting those laughs when they were supposed to come, estranging the audience completely. By the time they got to the serious stretch in the middle of the first act, they had alienated everyone in the house. The audience was coughing and sniffling and stirring restlessly when the first act curtain fell.

I took Natalie's hand as she came running up the aisle. Her eyes were wide with questions. I nodded and said, "Natalie, I think we're dead," and she squeezed my hand and said, simply, "Yes, Gene."

We went backstage to talk to the actors between acts, encouraging them, telling them everything was going fine, just don't press, the audience is loving it, we've got a sure hit on our hands. And the actors, flushed with the excitement of the night, involved in performances they had been preparing for six long weeks, believed every word we said and went out prepared to clinch their victory in the next two acts.

I met Beth at the rear of the theater.

"Do you need a drink?" she asked.

"I think so," I said.

She took my arm, and we went across the street to Ho Tang's welcome dusk. The jukebox was silent. Neither of us put any money into it. We sat at the bar and ordered our drinks. Beth was in a black gown with a diamond pin just below the yoke. I was wearing a dinner jacket and a frilled shirt, and the studs and links Beth had given me as an opening night gift. We raised our glasses and touched them together, and Beth said, "Here's to the next one, Gene."

"To the next one," I said.

We drank.

"It's a goddamn rotten shame," she said.

The reviews would come in much later that night, we would hear them read to us over the telephone from the *Times* and the *News* and later the *Post*, and then we would actually see the morning papers and read what we had earlier heard on the telephone, and we would commiserate into the night while the celebration party at Sardi's dissolved and eventually disappeared around us. But we would be numb by that time, and so we sat in Ho Tang's now and shared the death of the play together, and for the first time in a long time, we talked about other things, my children and the fact that Sharon had to have her tonsils out, the difficulty Beth was having getting a maid, the chances of the Mets this year, how lovely the weather had been this past week.

We both drank more than we should have, not going back to the theater for the second-act curtain, trying to obliterate what was happening across the street, and finally succeeding.

Awash at last in boozy self-pity, I put four quarters into the juke, and we listened solemnly to the music, and nodded a lot, and stared mournfully into our glasses, and sighed, and ordered more whiskey, and began talking in an endless drunken round I will remember quite forever, despite my own drunkenness.

"Did we do the right thing?" Beth asked, and put her hand on my arm, and leaned into me.

"I hope so," I said, and tried to light a cigarette.

"No, tell me," she said. "Did we do the right thing, Gene?"

"I don't know."

"It was difficult."

"It was very difficult, Beth."

"Do you know how difficult it was for me that night?"

"What night?"

"The night we told him."

"Very difficult," I said.

"Yes, but do you know *how* difficult?"

"How difficult?"

"We were lovers," she said.

I was looking full into her face, she was leaning very close to me, clinging to the bar and my arm, her eyes misting over. "Danny and I," she said, and I nodded, and she said, "Long time ago."

"Listen," I said, "maybe we ought to get back."

"Back where?" she said.

"Across the street."

"What for? Nothing's changed across the street."

"Even so . . ."

"Nothing's changed." She lifted her glass, drained it, and put it down on the bartop. "I've never been lucky with men," she said. "Never. Do you want another drink? Two more," she said to the bartender. "Lasted longer with Danny than I thought it would," she said. "I met another man, an instructor at Yale, I was up there trying out a new show. In New Haven, I mean."

"Yes," I said.

"And we fell in love." She shrugged, looked to see if the bartender was fixing our drinks, and then said, "We were living on Fifty-eighth Street at the time, Danny and I. Little apartment on Fifty-eighth. I drove down from New Haven at three in the morning. On the Merritt. You know the Merritt?"

"Sure, I know the Merritt."

"It was empty. This was three o'clock in the morning. Danny was in bed when I got back to the apartment. Everything was very quiet. I had to tell him. I figured that was best. Not to lie about it, not to pretend everything was . . . the same. So I sat on the edge of the bed, it was very quiet, I don't know, it was almost, I don't know, the building was so *still*. I said, 'Danny, it's finished.' "

"Martini straight up, and a scotch on the rocks," the bartender said.

Beth picked up her glass. She sipped a little of the whiskey, and then said, without looking at me, "Danny wouldn't believe it. He said, 'No, Beth, it isn't true.' It was so goddamn *quiet* in that building. I told him there was another man, and he just kept saying, 'No, no,' and you could hear this awful silence everywhere around us, as if the world had already come to an end. 'No, no,' he kept saying, and I said, 'Please understand, Danny.' "

"Let's get back," I said. "Beth, I want to see what's happening."

"So last week, I did the same thing to him all over again. And I asked him to understand again." She lifted her glass and drained it. "I did it for your play," she said.

"I know you did."

"I don't mean hiring him. That was for *me*. To square it, to make amends for having kicked him out. Give him something back, you know? A chance. But firing him was for you and your play." She shook her head. She was very close to tears. I kept watching her. It all seemed suddenly senseless. The play across the street was a failure.

"It *had* to be done," she said, fiercely, her eyes snapping up at me, blue and hard and cold. "Sure, now that we've got a flop, it's easy to say we should have stuck by him, seen it through with him, sure. But tell me something, Gene. Suppose the play had been a *hit?* Would it have been worth it then?"

And because I was drunk, I had no answer.

The Birthday Party

He was still very intoxicated when the pilot or the purser, or whoever it was, made the announcement. His head rolled over to one side, and he gazed through the window just level with his right shoulder and down to the ground below where he could see beginning pinpoints of light in the distance. He was wondering what it was the loudspeaker had announced, when a blond stewardess came up the aisle and paused and smiled. "Would you please fasten your seat belt, sir?" she asked.

"I would be happy to," he answered. He smiled back at her, and then began looking for the seat belt, lifting his behind and reaching under him to pull it free, and then fumbling very hard to fasten it, while the blond stewardess stood patiently smiling in the aisle.

"May I help you, sir?" she asked.

"Please," he said.

She ducked her head a little as she moved toward him past the empty aisle seat. Smiling, standing balanced just a bit to his left, she caught up both ends of the seat belt and was clasping them together when he lightly and impishly ran his right hand up the inside of her leg. She did not jump or scream or anything. She just continued fastening the seat belt, with the smile still on her face, and then she backed away into the aisle again, saying, "There you are, sir."

He was enormously surprised. He thought Now that is poise, that is what I really call poise, and then he wondered whether there possibly hadn't been a short-circuit from his brain to his hand, causing the brain command to be issued but not executed. In which case, nothing at all had happened and the girl's tremendously impressive icy poise and aloofness, her ability to remain a staid and comforting mother-image in the face of danger was really nothing to marvel at, boy am I drunk, he thought.

He could not imagine how he had got so drunk since he absolutely knew for a concrete fact that it was an ironbound rule of airplane companies the world over never to serve any of its passengers more than two drinks of whiskey. He suspected, however, that he had been drinking a stupefying amount of booze long before he'd boarded the plane, though he couldn't quite remember all of it too clearly at the moment, especially since everything seemed to begin spinning all at once, the lights below springing up to his window in startling red and green and white proximity, oh mother, we are going to crash, he thought.

He recognized at once, and to his enormous relief, that the plane was only banking for a turn on its approach to an airport, probably New York though he could not remember ever seeing lights like those on the approach to New York, scattered for miles, spilled brokenly across the landscape, oh that was a beautiful sight down there, he wished he knew where the hell he was.

The poised young blond stewardess opened the folding door between sections, and then walked briskly forward again, preparatory to taking her own seat and fastening her own belt. She was carrying a blanket or something, they always seemed to be tidying up an airplane just before it landed. He said, "Miss?" and when she stopped he noticed that she kept her distance. "Miss, where are we? We're coming down someplace, aren't we?"

"Yes?"

"Well, *where* are we coming down?" he asked.

"Los Angeles," she said.

"Oh good," he answered. "I've never been to Los Angeles before." He paused, and then smiled. "Miss?"

"Yes, what it is? I've got to take a seat."

"I know. I just wanted to ask you something. Did I put my hand under your skirt?"

"Yes, you did."

"Just a little while ago?"

"Yes."

"Thank you," he said.

"Is that all?"

"Yes, thank you."

The stewardess smiled. "All right," she said. She started up the aisle again, stopped, turned back, leaned over, and whispered, "Your hands are cold."

"Thank you," he said.

"All right," she answered, and smiled, and left.

He pressed his forehead to the glass and watched the lights drawing closer and closer. He could see moving automobiles below now, and neon signs, and traffic signals blinking on and off, the Lionel train set his father had bought him for Christmas long ago, toy houses puffing smoke, reach down like God and lift the little automobiles, the movie with Roland Young where the huge pointing finger of God came down over his head. There was speed suddenly, a sense of blinding speed as the ground moved up and the airport buildings flashed by in a dizzying blur. He felt the vibration of the wheels when they touched.

He thought, It's all over.

"We have just landed at Los Angeles International Airport," a voice said. He knew for sure it wasn't the pilot this time, unless they allowed women to fly jet aircrafts. "The local time is six forty-five p.m., and the temperature is seventy-eight degrees. May we ask you to please remain seated until we have taxied to the terminal building and our engines have stopped? It has been our pleasure to serve you, and we hope you will be flying with us again in the near future. Thank you, and Merry Christmas."

"Thank *you*," he said aloud, "and a Merry Christmas to you, too." He immediately unfastened his seat belt and rose to take his coat from the rack overhead. The stewardess' voice came over the loudspeaker in gentle warning. "Ladies and gentlemen, *please* remain seated until the aircraft has taxied to a stop. Thank you."

"Thank you," he said again, "you forgot to say Merry Christmas." He did not bother to sit because he figured the aircraft must surely have taxied to a stop by now, although he could still hear engines. He was putting on his coat when the blond stewardess came up the aisle to him. "Sir," she said, "would you please remain seated until we have taxied and stopped?"

"Certainly," he said, but he did not sit.

"Sir, we'd appreciate it . . ."

"You are the most poised young lady I ever met in my life," he said.

"Thank you, but . . ."

"Are you Swedish?"

"No, sir, I . . ."

"We have a girl in our office from Sweden, she's very poised, too. At the Christmas party today, she jumped off the window."

"She *what?*" the stewardess said. "She jumped out of the window?"

"No. Of course not! She jumped *off* the window. *Off* it. The sill."

"Oh," the stewardess said.

"What's your name?" he asked her.

"Miss Radley."

"That doesn't sound Swedish at all," he said. "*My* name is Arthur. Everyone calls me Doc."

"Are you a doctor?"

"No, I'm an art director, but everyone calls me Doc. *What* did you say your name was?"

"Miss Radley. Iris Radley."

"Boy, that is some funny name for a Swedish girl," he said.

"Why do they call you Doc?" she asked.

"Because I wear eyeglasses."

"Well, Doc," she said, "you've successfully remained standing all the while we taxied."

"Thank you," he said.

"Have a nice time in Los Angeles."

"I will. I've never been here before."

"It's a nice city."

"I'm sure it's a beautiful city. It has beautiful lights."

"Do you know where the baggage area is?" she asked, concerned. They were walking forward now, toward the exit. His overcoat felt very bulky all at once.

"No," he said, "where *is* the baggage area?"

"Have you got your claim tickets?"

"No," he said.

"Oh, dear, did you lose them?"

"No. As a matter of fact, I don't *have* any baggage. I'm traveling light. Well," he said, turning to the exit and peering through it down the steps and beyond to the terminal building, "Los Angeles." He extended his hand. "Goodbye, Miss Radley, and Merry Christmas."

"Merry Christmas," she said.

He went down the steps.

He knew at once that he had done the right thing. The air

was balmy, it touched his cheeks, it kissed his face, it riffled his hair. He took off his coat, oh, he had done the right thing, he had most certainly done the right thing, though it was unimaginable to even imagine having done the wrong thing after so many drinks and kissing Trudy in MacLeish's darkened office. It was impossible to imagine having made the wrong decision, not after feting old Mr. Benjamin of Benjamin Luggage, and racing out of the building with whoever the hell those girls were from Accounting, her hand so warm and moist in his pocket, the air crisp, church bells bonging, bonging someplace, Salvation Army virgins playing horns and drums. Oh what a city at Christmas, what a New York, how could anything be wrong, everything *had* to be right, right, right. They talked an off-duty cab driver into taking them out to Kennedy Airport. The cabbie was anxious to get home, "too much goddamn traffic in this goddamn city," but he slipped him a fin even before they opened the door, and suddenly there was no more traffic in the city, suddenly everything was Christmas Eve again and church bells were bonging joy to the world.

Long Island was where Kennedy International Airport was, you had to remember not to call it Idlewild anymore because that would automatically date you as being forty-one years old, that was very bad, going on forty-two imminently. Trudy was nineteen, she wore candy-striped stockings and a short suede skirt, and he had kissed her in MacLeish's office. She had said, "Why, Mr. Pitt, how nasty," but he had kept right on kissing her, and she, too, back. The girls from Accounting, and Arthur, and Benjamin had made the plane in plenty of time, the cabbie was that anxious to show his Christmas spirit after the five-spot tip, had to get old Benjamin Baggage, excuse *me*, Benjamin Luggage, onto that Chicago plane or else Lake Michigan would drift out to sea or something. They stole a plaque from one of the airline counters, it said, "Mr. Schultz," and they gave it to Benjamin as a keepsake. The Chicago plane took off in a roar of screaming jets. Arthur and the two girls from Accounting stood on the observation deck and watched as it soared almost vertically into the sky and then vanished into the clouds. He had an arm around each girl. They were all very drunk, and the girls sighed when the plane disappeared.

"Tomorrow is my birthday," he said to the redhead.

"Happy birthday," she said.

"I only get one present," Arthur said, "because they fall on the same day. My birthday and Christmas. I mean, I get a *lot* of presents, but only *once*. We only celebrate *once*, do you know what I mean?"

"No, I don't," the redhead said, "but you're very cute. Do you know what he means, Alexis?"

Alexis said, "No, I don't know what he means, gee I miss Mr. Benjamin."

"Listen, I have an idea," Arthur said. "Let's go to Chicago."

"Why not?" the redhead said.

"Listen, what's your name?" he asked.

"Rose."

"Rose, let's you and me and Alexis here go to Chicago and surprise Mr. Benjamin, what do you say?"

"Okay, why not?" Rose said. "But first let's have another drink."

"Boy, will he be surprised," Alexis said, and giggled.

"Okay, so let's go," Arthur said, but he knew even then they would not go to Chicago. He knew at once that they would all have another drink, and then the girls would start reconsidering and remembering that it was Christmas Eve and they should be getting home to family and dear ones, and after all Benjamin wasn't expecting them, and did anyone even know where he lived, and how long would it take them to get to Chicago, and all the rationalizing crap that people always came up with when something exciting or adventurous was proposed. He knew they would back out, and he wasn't at all surprised when they asked him to get a taxi for them.

Well, tomorrow is my birthday, he thought, standing just outside the terminal building and watching their taxi move into the distance. Well, happy birthday old Doc, time to go home to the family and dear ones, the loved ones, time to go home. Nobody ever wants to go anywhere anymore, boy, what a bunch of party poops. He looked at his watch, but couldn't read the gold numerals on the dial because it was late afternoon, with that curiously flat winter light that causes whites to become whiter and gold to blend indefinably into them, and besides he was drunk. He went back into the terminal to look at the big clock over the counter, and he saw that it was twenty minutes to four, well what the hell, he thought, home James, home to Merry Christmas and such, boy, nobody ever wants to *go* anywhere anymore, boy, what a drag. He heard them calling a flight, and he walked over to the counter and said, "Excuse me, Captain, but what flight was that you just called?"

"The four o'clock flight to Los Angeles," the captain answered, though Arthur knew he wasn't a captain at all, he was just making him feel good.

"I've never been to Los Angeles," he said.

"No?" the captain answered politely.

"No. How much does it cost?"

"How much does what cost?"

"A ticket to Los Angeles, that's the city of Angels, did you know that?"

117

"That's right, so it is. First-class, sir?"

"First-class, of course."

"First-class round trip to Los Angeles is three twenty-one eighty. Plus tax."

"How much is the tax?"

"Sixteen-oh-nine, sir."

"That sounds very reasonable. Will you take a check?"

"Sir?"

"For the flight you just called. I have identification, if that's what's troubling you."

"No, sir, it's just . . . I don't even know if there's room on that flight, sir. Christmas is our busiest . . ."

"I don't need a room, just a seat." Heh-heh, he thought, how'd you like *that* one, Sonny?

"Well, I'd have to . . ."

"Yes, well go ahead and do it. You said it leaves at four, didn't you?"

"Are you *serious*, sir? Do you really want me to . . . ?"

"Certainly, I'm serious. Of *course* I'm serious. Nobody the hell *goes* anyplace anymore!"

He knew he would not go through with it, he was just having a little fun with the captain, what the hell tomorrow was his birthday. He knew he would not do it because old Arthur Doc Pitt simply didn't do things like that, flying away from home and hearth on Christmas Eve, what would Fran say? Fran would take a fit, that's what Fran would say. And besides, this really had nothing whatever to do with Fran or anyone else. It had only to do with old Doc Pitt, who knew he could never never never do something like this, the same way he could not that time in Buffalo when the man sitting in the lobby had asked him if he would like to spend the night with a burlesque queen, or was it even a burlesque queen, *that* part may have been just imagination. In any case, he could not do it then, and he would not do it now, but there was no harm in having a little fun with the good captain here, hanging up the phone now, and putting on a bright smiling cheerful airlines face.

"Well you certainly are lucky, sir," he said. "There've been some cancellations in the first-class section."

Yeah, well I was only kidding, Arthur thought.

Something started inside him. He knew it was the alcohol, he knew he had had absolutely too much to drink. He knew it was kissing Trudy in MacLeish's office and putting his hand under the short suede skirt, the candy-striped stockings, he knew it was that, nineteen years old, Trudy. He knew it was the wild ride to the airport with the two girls from Accounting, and the soaring disappearance of Benjamin's plane into the clouds, the sudden desperate knowledge that the party was going to end without ever having begun. He knew it was all that, but he suspected it was something more as well, and so he allowed the excitement to grow inside him, teasing himself, saying to himself Go ahead, do it, go ahead, why don't you? And then soberly regarding himself through his eyeglasses, Don't be ridiculous, and then looking at the captain's expectant face and thinking the thing to do was reach into his pocket and slap his checkbook on the counter and write that goddamn check, he had always wanted to do things like that. The captain was waiting, and the excitement was rising inside Arthur, something that started down in his groin for which he blamed Trudy in MacLeish's office, and climbing up into his chest and his throat and then suddenly leaping into his fingertips which positively twitched with the need to reach into his pocket and slap his checkbook onto the countertop, You like that Rolls-Royce, kid? It's yours.

The captain was waiting.

"Okay," Arthur said, and reached into his pocket and

slapped his checkbook onto the counter.

"Where to, Mac?"

"A good hotel," he said.

"Lots of good hotels in Los Angeles."

"Like what?"

"You want the city, or Beverly Hills, or what?"

"Beverly Hills," he said. "Why not?"

"Which one in Beverly Hills?"

"The best one."

"They're all good."

"There is only one best one."

The cab driver set the car in motion. "You want the Beverly Hills?"

"I already told you I wanted the Beverly Hills."

"I meant the Beverly Hills *Hotel*."

"Okay, why not?"

"You in the movie racket?"

"No, I am in the advertising game," he said.

"What do you advertise?"

"Benjamin Luggage," he said. "Among other fine products."

"Never heard of it."

"Well, I never heard of the Beverly Hills Hotel," he said.

"They're crying," the cab driver answered, and stepped on the gas.

"This looks like Long Island," Arthur said.

"It ain't," the cabbie replied.

"It sure looks like it. What are all these hot dog stands for? What do you do out here, eat hot dogs all the time?"

"That's right, we eat hot dogs all the time," the cabbie said.

"That's what I thought," Arthur answered. "Boy, what a

city. It looks like Long Island. I've never been to Los Angeles."

"That's a shame," the cabbie answered.

"All you do out here is frolic, huh?" he said.

"Yeah, that's all we do out here," the cabbie said.

"What's this we're on now?"

"The San Diego Freeway, heading north."

"Is that where Beverly Hills is?"

"North, right. You been drinking a little bit?" the cabbie asked, which Arthur thought was very clever.

"Yes, a little bit. I have been drinking since twelve o'clock noon New York time."

"That means you've been drinking since nine o'clock this morning, California time."

"That's very clever," Arthur said. "What time is it in London?"

"Who the hell knows?"

"It's seven A.M. Christmas morning," Arthur said, not having the faintest idea what time it was in London or even Bangkok.

"Well, Merry Christmas," the cabbie said, and again lapsed into silence.

"What is this Beverly Hills Hotel?" Arthur asked. "Some kind of fancy hotel, is that what it is?"

"That's what it is."

"In that case, you'd better take me back to the airport," he said.

"What?"

"The airport, the Los Angeles International Airport where it is now six forty-five California time and the temperature is seventy-eight degrees."

"What?"

"You must think I'm crazy or something," he said,

"coming all the way out to Los Angeles on Christmas Eve when my wife and family are waiting at home for me."

"Mister, you're not crazy," the cabbie said, "you're drunk."

"You *bet* I am," Arthur said. "I was only kidding, so what the hell am I doing here in Los Angeles?"

"Mister, I don't know. Sometimes I wonder what the hell *I'm* doing here in Los Angeles."

"Well, I don't want to go to the Beverly Hills Hotel," he said.

"Okay, so where *do* you want to go?"

"I don't know."

"You know what my mother told me? My mother told me never pick up no drunks, son, because they will give you gray hairs and a hernia. I'm a working man, mister, I've got a wife and kids waiting home for me, too, this is Christmas Eve. I'd like to get a few calls in and then go home to trim the tree, okay? So where shall it be? The Beverly Hills, the airport, downtown Los Angeles, name it."

"Where's the Beverly Hills?"

"On Sunset Boulevard."

"No, sir," Arthur said. "Absolutely not a hotel on Sunset Boulevard, I saw that movie." He shook his head. "Why don't you take me to the airport where I *want* to go?"

"Okay, I'll get out at the next exit and swing around."

"Are you going to take me to the airport?"

"That's where you want to go, that's where I'll take you."

"Chicken!" Arthur said.

"What?"

"I said you are chicken."

"Now, look, mister, drunk or not . . ."

"Running home to trim your goddam tree!"

"Mister . . ."

"Aren't there any hotels except on Sunset Boulevard? You think I came out here to drown face down in a swimming pool?"

"You want the Hilton, mister?" the cabbie said, sighing.

"*What* Hilton?"

"The Beverly Hilton."

"That's very clever," Arthur said. "The Beverly Hilton. I'll bet my bottom dollar it's in Beverly Hills, am I right?"

"You're absolutely right."

"Boy, that's clever," Arthur said. "You people out here are certainly clever."

"That's because we eat so many hot dogs," the cabbie said.

"Yes, and witty, too. Well, do you know what I want to do? I want you to turn off this highway, thruway, freeway, *whatever* you call it out here, and stop at the *first* hotel you see. The very first hotel you see, *that's* where I want to go. Impromptu," Arthur said. "Im*promp*tu."

"Boy, pick up drunks," the cabbie said.

He felt refreshed and sober when he came out of the shower. There were at least eight mirrors in the bathroom, but he couldn't see himself in any of them because he had taken off his glasses before climbing into the tub. Besides, the bathroom was all steamed up from the hot water he had used, this was certainly a fine hotel with lots of mirrors and good hot water to sober up a wandering soul on Christmas Eve.

I'd better call Fran, he thought.

He put on his glasses, and picked up his watch. It was still set with New York time, he hadn't bothered to reset it when he got off the plane. In New York, in White Plains to be exact—which is where he and Fran and Michael and Pam lived, the four little Pitts in a white clapboard house on Robin

Hood Lane—it was now eleven p.m., one hour to Christmas, and Fran was probably frantic. Naked, he put on his watch, and walked out of the bathroom. He found a white ivory telephone on the night table near his bed, wondered whether he should call her or not, and then decided of *course* he had to call her.

He felt chilly all at once. He went to the closet where the bellhop had hung his cashmere overcoat and, lacking a bathrobe or any other boudoir attire, put on the overcoat. The lining was silk. The coat felt luxurious and comforting. He sat on the edge of the bed and crossed his legs and looked at the phone and then became absorbed in reading the dial which listed all the various places you could call in the hotel. There was a little red light on the telephone, too, and he supposed you used that if you wanted a direct line to a red light district, which he might very well want before this night was through. In the meantime, he had to call Fran so that she wouldn't alert the police or call the hospitals or, God forbid, his mother. That's all he needed was for Fran to call his mother. What do you mean he's not home? his mother would shout; his mother always shouted. On Christmas *Eve,* he's not home? Yes, Virginia, for that was his mother's name, your son is not home on Christmas Eve.

That's right, Mom, he thought, I'm here in Los Angeles.

I'd better call Fran.

He hesitated again, not because he was afraid of Fran—he did in fact feel invulnerable, invincible, courageous, adventurous, a naked wild man in a luxurious cashmere overcoat—but only because he did not want to spoil his party. He had never had a birthday party in his life because dear Virginia his mother had been inconsiderate enough to become pregnant nine months to the day before Christmas. Who wants to attend anyone's birthday party when the biggest birthday in history is in the midst of celebration? *Next* Year, Virginia would always say, *Next* Year, we'll have some of your friends in later in the day, the afternoon perhaps, or the evening, there's no reason we can't celebrate your birthday just because it happens to fall on Christmas. She had said *Next* Year every year but eventually they ran out of years. By that time he had married Fran, and not having a birthday party had become habit. Besides, you have to have your birthday parties when you're still a kid wearing eyeglasses. When you're thirty-five and wearing eyeglasses, and then forty and wearing eyeglasses, it doesn't matter a hell of a lot anymore. Until you're about to be forty-two, and still wearing eyeglasses, and a party is about to start and you feel it slipping out of your hands, trickling through your fingers like all the sands of next year, next year, next year—and you want it to be *this* year, *now.*

He was not afraid of Fran, but he was afraid she would spoil his party.

He picked up the phone receiver.

Instead of calling Fran, he dialed 7 for the valet and was told the valet had gone home, this is Christmas Eve, sir. He asked if the housekeeper had gone home, too, and was informed that a housekeeper was *always* on duty and she could be reached by dialing 4. He dialed 4 and a woman with a foreign accent answered the phone. He could not place the accent.

"Do you have an iron?" he asked.

"An iron? To press?"

"That's right."

"Yes, I have an iron. Why you don't call the valet? He presses."

"He's gone. It's Christmas Eve."

"Oh. You want to press?"

"Yes. I'd like to press my pants because I'm having a party, you see, and they're all wrinkled from the plane ride. I don't like to have a party in wrinkled pants."

"What room you in? I send."

"One-oh-eight," he said.

"You return?"

"Yes, I return," he said.

"Good. I send."

"Good, you send. Thank you."

He hung up. He called the bell captain then and asked if there was a liquor store in the hotel. The captain told him he could order liquor in the pharmacy, which sounded like a peculiar place to be ordering liquor, but he hung up and then dialed the operator and asked for the pharmacy. When he was connected, he told whoever answered the phone that he wanted two bottles of scotch sent to room 108 and charged to his bill.

He did not begin pressing his suit with the borrowed steam iron until after the whiskey was delivered. He poured a stiff double hooker into one of the glasses that were ranged on the counter top facing the entrance door, and then discovered there was an ice-making machine under the counter, this was *some* hotel all right. From the bathroom, he took a clean towel and spread it out on the counter and then put his trousers on top of the towel and began pressing them while he sipped at the scotch.

The idea was to keep the party going. He did not know what his next move would be after he pressed his pants and his jacket, but he did know that he had two bottles of whiskey and he would not be forty-two for almost an hour, so the idea was to keep the party going. Maybe he would just dial the operator and ask her to ring several rooms in the hotel and when he got them he would say, "Hi, this is Doc Pitt in room 108.

I'm having a little birthday party, and I wonder if you'd like to come down and join me. It's right off the pool, room 108." Maybe he'd do that, though he doubted it. What he *would* do was press his pants and his jacket, and maybe his tie as well, and then have a few drinks and then leave this nice hotel room and see what Beverly Hills was all about.

The telephone rang.

He propped up the steam iron, started for the phone, decided he'd better be more careful, went back to unplug the iron, and then ran to the phone to answer it.

"Hello," he said, wondering who would be calling him in Los Angeles since he didn't know a soul out here but the movie stars.

"Sir," a very nice cultured Choate voice said, "I'm awfully sorry to be calling you, but would you mind lowering your radio?"

"My *what?*" he said.

"Your radio, sir. I'm terribly sorry, but the guest in the room next door is trying to nap, and it seems your radio is on very loud."

"My radio isn't on at *all*," he said. *"Not* at *all."*

"Just a moment, sir."

He waited.

"Sir?"

"Yes?"

"Is this Mr. Pitt in room 108?"

"Yes, this is Arthur Pitt in room 108, that's right. *That* part of it is absolutely right."

"Mr. Pitt, would you mind lowering your radio, sir?"

"Listen, are you a cretin?" Arthur asked. "I just told you that my radio is not on. *Not* on. *Off.* I am pressing my pants and drinking some scotch, and my radio is not on. It is off. O-double-F. Off."

"Sir, the guest who made the complaint is in the last room on the floor, and your room is the only room next door, so it *must* be your radio, sir."

"Is this a gag?" Arthur asked suspiciously.

"No, sir."

"Then perhaps you would like to take a walk down here and see for yourself, *listen* for yourself, I mean. My radio is off. Do you hear a radio?"

"No, sir, but the guest in 109 . . ."

"Yes, well you tell the guest in 109 that my radio is off."

"Yes, sir, if you say so."

"Thank you. This is *some* hotel," he said, and hung up. Boy, he thought, how do you like that? How the hell do you like that? I'm standing here in my undershorts, minding my own business, and some fat old bastard with a cigar begins having auditory hallucinations and calls the desk to tell me to turn off my radio which isn't even on, boy this is some hotel all right, I'm telling you.

Angrily, he walked back to the counter, plugged in the steam iron, picked up the half-filled glass of scotch, and drained it. Boy, he thought. Next door, he heard the phone ringing. That would be the desk clerk from Choate who would be calling 109 to report that 108 said his radio was not on. The phone stopped ringing. 109 had answered it. Arthur stood silently with the steam iron in one hand and tried to hear the conversation next door. He could not hear a word, some hotel. Well, I'd better press my pants, he thought, and get the hell out of here before they call again to say the wild party in my room has simply got to stop. He ran the iron over his trousers several more times, held them up to examine them, and then pulled them on. They were nice and warm, they made him feel very cozy. He went to the closet for his jacket, studied it when he took it off the hanger, and decided it did not need pressing. He poured himself a very tiny shot of scotch, drank it down, figured he'd have just one more tiny one before leaving the room, and was pouring it over the cubes in his glass when his telephone rang again.

Choate again, he thought. He decided to turn up the radio full blast before answering the telephone, and then did not do it. "Hello," he said into the receiver.

"Mr. Pitt? This is the desk clerk again."

"Well, this is a surprise," Arthur said.

"Mr. Pitt, I wanted to apologize. I spoke to the young lady in 109, sir, and apparently there was some mistake. Apparently what she heard were the loudspeakers around the pool, sir, and she thought it was the radio in the room next door. I'm terribly sorry if I inconvenienced you, sir."

"That's quite all right," Arthur said, "no inconvenience at all. Where'd you go to school?"

"Sir?"

"What prep school?"

"I didn't go to any prep school, sir. I went to a high school in downtown Los Angeles."

"Oh. Did you ever hear of Choate?"

"No, sir."

"Did you ever hear of the Beverly Hills Hotel?"

"Yes, sir."

"That just goes to show," Arthur said, and hung up. He was smiling. He was having a very good time. So the guest next door in 109 was a young lady, huh? Well, good. Maybe he'd just give her a ring on the telephone and they'd have a little laugh together over the misunderstanding. Why not? This was going to be one hell of a birthday party, and he was going to enjoy every goddamn minute of it until it was over. He did not like to think of it as ever being over, especially now when it had just really started, so instead of thinking about it he went back to the counter and poured himself the drink he had promised himself, though not as tiny as he had promised. He drank it down, said, "Ahhhhh," and was putting on his jacket when the telephone rang again.

"Hello," he said into the receiver. "Just a minute, I forgot to unplug the iron."

He went back to the counter, unplugged the iron, poured himself another drink while he was there, and then carried the glass back to the phone with him.

"Yes?" he said.

"This is the bell captain, sir."

"Yes, hello, what can I do for you?"

"I've got a bottle of champagne for you, sir."

"You have?" Arthur said, astonished. "Who's it from?"

"I don't know, sir. It was delivered just a few moments ago."

"Well, that's very nice," Arthur said. "Put it in an ice bucket and send it on over, why don't you?"

"Yes, sir," the bell captain said, and hung up.

Still astonished, Arthur sat on the edge of his bed, certain that the champagne had been ordered by the hotel management who, in their haste to set things right after the recent misunderstanding, were now outdoing themselves lavishly. Well, never look a gift horse, he thought. A party is in progress, and we need all the champagne we can get, not to mention several satin slippers from which to drink it.

The telephone rang again.

He stared at it unbelievingly, thinking the hotel management was really going a bit *too* far, really, and wondering what they had up their sleeves this time. Gardenias? A basket of California oranges? He would flatly refuse. He would say Thank you, your apologies are accepted, but if you send any further gifts, I will have to consider us engaged.

Giggling, he lifted the receiver. "Hello?" he said.

"Is this Mr. Pitt in room 108?"

"Yes, this is he," he said.

"I'm sorry, Mr. Pitt."

"That's quite all right, no need to apologize."

"This is the bell captain again, sir. I'm sorry about that bottle of champagne, sir, but it isn't for you, after all."

"Oh?"

"It's for the young lady in 109, sir. I rang the wrong room, sir, I'm terribly sorry."

"That's all right."

"I'm sorry, sir. Merry Christmas."

"Merry Christmas to you," Arthur said, and hung up.

He felt suddenly demolished. The idea that the champagne was not for him at all but rather for the young lady in 109, the idea that a gift had been extended to him and then just as abruptly withdrawn filled him with a despair that was unbearable. I'd better call Fran, he thought, what the hell.

He picked up the phone receiver.

He was studying the holes in the dial, trying to decide which one would connect him with the long-distance operator, when he heard the splash outside his window. He thought at once that someone had fallen into the pool; it was still winter in his mind, and people did not voluntarily jump into a swimming pool on Christmas Eve. He immediately replaced the receiver and ran to the sliding glass door, peering through at the pool and the lanai area. At first, he couldn't see anyone either in the pool or around it. Soft recorded violin music was being piped over the loudspeakers. He could see the muted lights illuminating the palms surrounding the pool, and the single immense white Christmas tree in the pocket formed by the U of the hotel's wings—but no one in the pool or around it. And then a head burst through the water and a blond girl surfaced and swam to the side of the pool, swinging herself up over its tiled lip, and gracefully walking toward the diving board. She was wearing a black, two-piece bathing suit, not a bikini, but cut very low on her waist, the halter top scarcely containing her breasts. She flicked her head to one side, the long mop of blond hair flapping soddenly away from her face, and then continued walking with that peculiar graceful flatfooted stamp of athletes and dancers, one hand cupping thumb and forefinger over her nose to clear it, the other tugging the seat of her trunks down over the partially-exposed white swell of her buttocks. She mounted the ladder to the diving board and walked to its end where she stood with her hands on her hips and stared down at the water.

She stood that way for the longest time, absorbed, her head bent, one hip jutting. He had no idea who she was, could not in fact see her face too clearly in the muted light surrounding the pool. But she was tall and blond and poised, and he could think of only one person in all of Los Angeles who was tall and blond and very poised. It seemed entirely possible to him that she, who else could it be, had come directly to this fine hotel where after her long and tedious flight she had attempted to take a nap only to be awakened by the poolside music—whereupon she had instantly ordered herself a bottle of champagne, of course, and decided on a midnight swim instead. The girl standing still and serene on the end of the board could not conceivably be anyone but Miss Iris Radley, a strange name for a Swedish girl, and what a pleasant surprise, even though he could not yet see her face, who else could she *possibly* be?

More and more convinced, he watched her captured in reverie, her head and body motionless, her blond hair glittering with reflected light. At last, she heaved a long heavy sigh, her shoulders moving—he could almost hear that long mysterious sigh through the closed plate glass door—and walked back to the ladder. Her body was tight and slim and tanned, she glided through the soft California night and then turned a short pirouette and moved forward suddenly, not running, drifting, moving magically to the very end of the board. Her knee came up, she made a precise figure four with one taut straight leg, one bent, sprang and hung suspended, the board vibrating beneath her. Head back, body arched, arms wide, she hung against the night for an eternity, and then plummeted to the water below, her arms and hands coming together an instant before she disappeared. He watched. She surfaced some ten feet beyond and then swam in an easy crawl to the shallow end of the pool, executed a clean racer's turn, swam to the deep end, turned again, and continued swimming back and forth tirelessly, effortlessly.

He watched her world.

There was in that world all the things he had never known, the burlesque queen he had not had in Buffalo that time, the birthday gifts that blended with Christmas gifts and left a strange aching void, the bottle of champagne offered and then withdrawn.

He wanted to call out to her, wanted to shout, "Hey, are you *really* Miss Radley who said my hands were cold? Are you really the girl in 109? Hey, how would you like to come to my party? How's the water?"

Trembling, he looked at his watch. It was seven minutes to midnight in White Plains. He would be forty-two years old in seven minutes.

Go ahead, he thought. Call Fran.

He reached for the stem of his watch and pulled it out. Slowly and carefully, he set the watch back to ten fifty-three, and then nine fifty-three, and then eight fifty-three. He snapped the stem back into the case with a small final click, walked swiftly to the sliding door, and pulled it open.

The girl was just coming out of the water.

He knew goddamn well she was not Miss Iris Radley, and possibly not even the girl in 109. But his step was curiously light, and his heart was beating wildly as he hurried toward the pool to invite her to his party.

The Movie Star

She had just come out of Mr. Mergenthaler's office, and was heading for Cost when Jerry Schneider stopped her and said, "Nora, would you mind very much if I told you something?"

"What is it you want to tell me?" she asked. She was really in a hurry because Mr. Mergenthaler had said to get those invoices to Cost immediately, but Jerry was a nice high school kid of about sixteen who was only working for Mergenthaler and Harris during the summer, and she didn't want to seem abrupt with him.

"I guess people have told you this a hundred times," Jerry said.

"Told me what?"

"That you look like Kim Novak."

"Oh, sure, Kim Novak."

"I mean it."

"Kim Novak is a blond."

"That don't make any difference," Jerry said. "I know your hair is brown, Nora, but that don't make any difference. You look just like her, I mean it. It's the look right in here . . ." He raised his hand before her face and made a vague defining gesture. "Right in here, the eyes and nose and mouth."

"My eyes are blue," she said. "Hers are . . ."

"I know, but . . ."

"Hers are supposed to be lavender or something."

"I didn't mean the color," Jerry said, "though the color is pretty close, too. I meant the *look* in her eyes, you've got the same kind of distant look she gets in her eyes. And your nose

135

is hers exactly, Nora, I mean it. Exactly." He paused. "Your mouth, too."

"Oh, come on, Jerry," she said. "Kim Novak is a beautiful girl."

"Well, so are you, Nora. You could be her twin sister, I mean it."

"Sure."

"I mean it."

"You'd better have your eyes examined," she said and shrugged. "I have to hurry. Thank you, anyway."

She smiled, and then walked quickly down the corridor to Cost. She was still smiling when she entered the office. Marvin Krantz, who was the company's cost accountant, looked up and said, "What's the big grin for?"

"Oh, Jerry Schneider," she said. "Here are some invoices Mr. Mergenthaler said I should get to you in a hurry."

"What'd he do?"

"Who? Oh, Jerry, you mean?" She smiled again. "He's a silly kid."

"Yeah, but what'd he do?" Marvin asked.

"He said I look like Kim Novak."

"Well, you do," Marvin said immediately.

"What?"

"Sure. Didn't you know it?"

"Oh, come on, Marvin. Stop kidding me."

"Everyone in the office says so."

"How come *you* never told me before?"

"Maybe I didn't think it was very important," Marvin said.

"Well, I mean, if a girl looks like Kim Novak . . ." She shrugged. "Oh, come on, you're kidding me."

"Nora, you're a very pretty girl," Marvin said solemnly.

"But Kim Novak is a movie star."

"So? Does that make her not a person?"

"You know what I mean."

"No. What do you mean?"

"She's a movie star. She's Kim Novak."

"So? You're Nora Feldman. I'll tell you something, Nora. I think Kim Novak would be delighted to learn that *she* looks like *you*."

"Oh, sure, I'll just bet she would. Besides, we don't look alike at all," she said, and walked out of the office.

On her way to the subway that night, she bought three movie magazines. One of them had Kim Novak's picture on the cover. She didn't get a seat until the train reached 149th Street and the Grand Concourse, and then she studied the picture on the cover as well as several pictures inside all three magazines. Nora supposed she was as tall as Kim Novak, or at least as tall as she *imagined* her to be, since none of the magazines gave a height. Nora was five feet seven in her stockinged feet, and Kim Novak seemed to be at least that tall, if not taller. But that was exactly where the resemblance ended, she thought. Even so, she continued to look at the pictures all the way uptown to Mosholu Parkway.

The benches outside the park were crowded with the usual collection of fellows who would whistle and call every time Nora walked past. They always made her feel clumsy and exposed, she didn't know why, as though they could somehow see through her clothes. She always wished she could walk past with her head high and her nose tilted, just ignoring them. That night, she suddenly wondered why she never wore high-heeled shoes to work. Because I'm too tall, she thought, and then immediately remembered that Kim Novak was at least as tall as she was. Yes, but she's a movie star, Nora reminded herself, and walked quickly past the benches, looking down at the sidewalk.

Her grandmother was cooking borscht in the kitchen of their Knox Place apartment. Nora put the magazine on the enamel-topped kitchen table and said, "Grandma, do you think I look like this girl?"

Her grandmother turned from the pot, looked at the picture of Kim Novak on the cover of the magazine, and said, "Who's this?"

"Kim Novak."

"Who?"

"Kim Novak. She's a movie star."

"A what?"

"A movie star."

"She looks to me like a shiksa," her grandmother said.

"She is."

"So this is what you want to look like? A shiksa?"

"Grandma, I didn't say I *wanted* to look like her. I only asked if you *thought* I looked like her."

"By me, that's the same thing."

"Oh, boy, you're impossible," Nora said. "Never mind, I'll ask Daddy when he gets home."

"Sure," her grandmother said. "Go ask him if you look like a Hollywood shiksa. That's a nice thing you should ask a man when he gets home from work, to give him a heart attack."

When she asked her father that night, he kissed her on both cheeks and hugged her and said, "Sweetheart, you look like Kim Novak and Elizabeth Taylor and Ava Gardner all rolled into one." His voice lowered. "You also look very much like your dear mother," he said, "may she rest in peace."

The next day was Friday which was always a very busy day at Mergenthaler and Harris, not because Mr. Harris always left very early on Friday to go to his beach club in New Rochelle, but only because Friday was the day new lots of dresses always were shipped out, though God knew why on a Friday, the last day of the week. This Friday was just like every other Friday at Mergenthaler and Harris, except that it rained which meant Mr. Harris didn't go to his beach club in New Rochelle, but instead was underfoot and in everybody's way, especially with a lot of sixteen hundred dresses coming off the factory floor at three o'clock in the afternoon, and everyone anxious to get them sorted and packed and out before quitting time. Mr. Harris was a great help with his foul-smelling cigar, snapping orders at floor boys and packers and even some cutters who had nothing at all to do with the packing and shipping operation. Also on this Friday which was raining and hectic, Marvin Krantz asked Nora if she would like to go to dinner and a movie with him after work. She accepted and then called her grandmother to tell her she wouldn't be home for dinner.

"Do you know this is the Sabbath?" her grandmother asked.

"Yes, grandma."

"So where are you going on the Sabbath?"

"To dinner and a movie."

"To see a Hollywood shiksa?"

"Grandma, there are a lot of Jewish people in Hollywood," Nora said.

"Yes, I see them," her grandmother answered, "on all the covers of the magazines."

"Grandma, as a matter of fact, one of the biggest stars in Hollywood is Jewish."

"Yes, who?"

"Elizabeth Taylor."

"Sure," her grandmother said, and hung up.

All during dinner, Marvin kept saying that he was taking Nora to "a very special movie" tonight, being very mysterious about the whole thing, but not mystifying her at all. She knew pretty well what he had planned, and wasn't at all surprised when they approached a marquee with the name KIM NOVAK across it in big black letters.

"Here we are," Marvin said. "Now I prove my point."

"What point, Marvin?"

"That you're beautiful."

"But I'm not."

"You admit that Kim Novak is beautiful, don't you?"

"Oh, of *course.*"

"Okay. If I can prove you look like her, then maybe you'll realize just how beautiful you really are."

"You make me feel silly," Nora said.

"Why?"

"Well, first because I *don't* look like Kim Novak. And also . . . well, because you keep telling me I'm beautiful."

"You are."

"I wish you'd stop, Marvin."

"Why?"

"Well, you sound so serious."

"Suppose I am?"

"I'm only twenty-one years old," Nora said.

"Old enough to have dozens of babies," Marvin said.

"Well, thank you, but I don't want dozens of babies."

"What do you want, Nora?"

"I don't know." She shrugged. "Everything. I want *everything,* Marvin."

"Well," Marvin said, very seriously, "I can't give you *everything,* Nora."

"Then why don't we just go see the movie?" she said, and they went inside.

A strange thing began happening to her as she watched the picture. She knew what Kim Novak looked like, of course, but she had never really watched her before, or at least never studied her the way she was studying her now. What she was trying to do was to sort of superimpose a picture of herself up there on the screen beside the picture of Kim Novak, to see if they really did look at all alike. She finally decided that both Jerry Schneider and Marvin Krantz were out of their minds. Side by side, the images of Nora Feldman and Kim Novak bore no resemblance to each other whatever. To begin with, Nora was much shorter than Kim Novak. Nora's hair was brown whereas hers was a pale blonde. Nora's bust was nowhere as full. Nora's legs were certainly not as good. Nor did her eyes, nose, or mouth look at all like the eyes, nose or mouth of Kim Novak. She didn't even *sound* like her. She was about to tell Marvin how crazy she thought he was when the strange thing began happening.

As the picture got close to the end, Kim Novak was running along the cliff chasing an old lady in a wheelchair. It was pretty exciting and pretty funny at the same time, and Nora was laughing along with everyone else in the theater and of course was excited, but suddenly her heart began to pound so hard she thought it would push itself right out of her chest.

"Hey, easy," Marvin said, and she realized she was squeezing his hand very tightly, so she dropped it and instead clasped both her hands together and discovered they were covered with sweat. It was then that Nora began to believe it. It was then that she felt it was *she* who was chasing that old lady in the wheelchair, and not Kim Novak. Why, it's *true,* she thought. We *do* look alike.

She was suddenly very scared and also sort of pleased. She kept looking at the screen with a strange smile on her face. She'd always thought of herself as only herself, but now, well . . . now she realized that she *did* look very much like Kim Novak, who was a movie star. Little Nora Feldman from Knox Place looked like a movie star.

She shrugged.

Boy, she thought.

"Well, what do you think now?" Marvin asked as the house lights went up.

"I don't know," Nora said.

That night, when Marvin took her home, she bleached her hair a pale blond.

If there was any remaining doubt in her own mind concerning her resemblance to Kim Novak, the bleaching of her hair settled it at once. On Saturday morning, when she went down to the candy store on Gun Hill Road to buy the *Daily News*, the owner of the store—whose name was Gregory but whom everyone called Gus—said to her, "You know something, Nora?"

"What, Gus?"

"With your hair this way, you look just like Kim Novak."

"Thank you," Nora said.

"It's amazing," Gus said. "You could be her twin sister."

"Well, thank you," she said, and walked home with her newspaper. At eleven o'clock, she went down for a walk in the park and was stopped five times by people she knew who told her that with her hair this way she looked just like Kim Novak. By Sunday, everyone in her neighborhood, which was bounded by Mosholu Parkway and Gun Hill Road, had grown used to the blond hair and the idea that she looked like Kim Novak, so no one else mentioned it to her. But on Monday morning, the man in the change booth of the Mosholu Parkway elevated station said to her, "Miss, you're a dead ringer for Kim Novak," and Nora thanked him and accepted her token, smiling. When she reached the office, Mr. Mergenthaler buzzed her and told her to come in at once with her pad, and she ran into his office and listened while he reeled off a list of things he wanted done in a hurry and then he looked up abruptly and said, "What the hell did you do to your hair?"

"I tinted it, Mr. Mergenthaler."

"Yeah?"

"Yes, sir."

"My daughter tints her hair," Mr. Mergenthaler said. "Why do you women do that, anyway?"

"I don't know. Does it look awful, Mr. Mergenthaler?"

"Awful? No, it's very nice. In fact . . ." He pursed his lips and frowned at her, looking extremely puzzled. "Well, never mind," he said. "We've got a lot to do this morning."

It wasn't until after lunch that he buzzed her again and said, "Now I know what it is."

"What what is, Mr. Mergenthaler?"

"Who you look like with your hair this way."

"Who, Mr. Mergenthaler?"

"That movie star," he said. "Kim Novak. Did you ever hear of her?"

"Yes, sir."

"Well, there's a very strong resemblance between you two girls."

"Thank you, Mr. Mergenthaler."

"Don't mention it. Did you give my message to the cutting room foreman?"

"Yes, sir, I did."

"Good," Mr. Mergenthaler said, and clicked off.

When Jerry Schneider saw her later that afternoon, he immediately slapped his forehead and said, "Wow! Now you've done it, Nora, I mean it. Now you look *just* like her!"

"Do you think so, Jerry?"

"Boy, *do* I!" Jerry said. "Listen, Nora, if I bring a camera to work tomorrow, will you take a picture with me in front of the building? On our lunch hour?"

"Why?"

"So when I get back to school, I can show it to the guys and they'll think I know Kim Novak."

Nora smiled and said, "All right," and then shrugged.

She put off going into Marvin's office until late in the afternoon. Marvin, busily adding a column of figures, barely glanced up at her as she put a batch of invoices on his desk.

"Hello, Nora," he said. "Did you have a nice weekend?"

"Very nice, Marvin."

She waited by his desk, hoping he would look up, but he kept working with his head bent.

"Marvin?" she said at last.

"Mmm?" he said, without looking up.

"Look at me."

He raised his eyes.

"Do you like my hair this way?"

Marvin studied her for a moment and then said, "It's blond. When did you do that?"

"Friday night. After you dropped me off."

"Why?"

"I thought it would be fun."

"You look very pretty, Nora," Marvin said. "But then, you've always looked pretty."

"Do you like it better?"

"I like it the same."

"But don't you think I . . . ?" She hesitated and then shrugged.

"Don't I think you what?"

"Nothing," she said, and left his office. She began practicing her new voice when she got home that night. She'd been thinking about it all the way uptown on the subway, so that by the time she got home she could almost hear it inside her head. When her father went into the spare room after dinner, to watch television, Nora and her grandmother began doing the dishes, and that was when she tried the new voice for the first time.

"Speak up," her grandmother said. "I can't hear you."

"Grandma, I'm purposely trying *not* to shout like a fishwife."

"Yes, so instead you're whispering like somebody in a hospital, God forbid."

"I'm trying to cultivate my voice," Nora said.

"For what?"

"Just to sound better."

"Then speak up," her grandmother said, "and you'll sound better."

She practiced the new voice all through the next morning, answering the telephone in a breathy whisper that was a little startling to some of the customers of Mergenthaler and Harris. Just before lunch, in fact, one of the customers said, "Excuse me, this *is* Mergenthaler and Harris?"

"Yes, sir," Nora said in the same voice. "Whom did you wish to speak with?"

"I'll tell you the truth, young lady, you almost make me forget," the man said, and Nora laughed a funny sort of laugh that seemed to originate somewhere way back in her throat.

On her lunch hour, she posed for a whole roll of pictures with Jerry Schneider outside the building. After lunch, she surprised Mr. Schwartz, who ran an outlet store in a Pennsylvania farmer's market, by using her new phone voice on him. And later, she caused poor Mr. Harris to puff very anxiously on his cigar when she gave him the funny laugh from the back of her throat. For the remainder of that week, she practiced the voice and the laugh almost constantly. She also went all

145

the way down to Fourteenth Street to see Kim Novak in a revival *of The Man With The Golden Arm*, and she bought as many movie magazines as she could find, searching for photos of Kim Novak and remembering what Jerry had said about that distant look in her eyes. Nora studied the look, and tried imitating it in her bathroom mirror, but she only looked either stupid or sleepy until one night she just stumbled upon it accidentally and almost scared herself half to death.

Oh my God, Nora thought, look at that.

Fascinated, she stared at this person in the mirror. Then she shivered and went to bed.

On Tuesday of the second week after she'd bleached her hair, Nora wore high heels to work.

"Where are you going?" her grandmother asked as she was leaving the apartment. "To a party?"

"I'm going to work."

"With shoes like that?"

"What's the matter with these shoes?" Nora asked.

"Speak up, I can't hear you," her grandmother said.

"This is my normal speaking voice," Nora whispered.

"It sounds to me like laryngitis."

"I'm terribly sorry," Nora said.

"Such shoes to work," her grandmother said, and shook her head.

The shoes *were* a bit high perhaps, and Nora felt a little self-conscious throughout part of the morning, but only until she got used to the extra two inches they added to her height. Some of the girls in the office told her they'd never realized how tall she was, and one of the salesmen said, "Nora, you are positively statuesque. Did anyone ever tell you you look like Kim Novak?"

"Yes, a few people," she said.

"You even sound like her."

"Do you think so?" Nora whispered, and then laughed her throaty laugh and gave him her look.

"I'll be damned," the salesman said.

That night, on her way home from the elevated station, she walked past the boys on the park bench with her head very high, her heels clicking on the pavement, the distant smoldering look on her face. The boys on the bench were dead silent. There were no whistles and no catcalls. They stared at her as she walked past, and didn't even begin whispering about her until she was well past the bench. Her eyes heavy-lidded, her face inscrutable, she allowed a tiny half-smile of triumph to play about her lips.

The next day, it really began happening.

It began happening on her lunch hour. She had walked cross-town to Fifth Avenue and then decided to have lunch in Schrafft's. She was wearing her favorite color, which was lavender, and her blond hair was combed loosely about her face. She walked with a confident sway in the high-heeled shoes, coming into the restaurant and pausing to look for the hostess, a distant expression on her face.

She was unaware of anything around her because she was frankly very hungry and was thinking of what she would order. The hostess led her to a table, and Nora smiled at her and then picked up the menu and looked at it. A waitress came over and stood grinning a little foolishly, her pencil poised over her order pad. Nora looked up and said, in her breathy quiet voice, "I'd like a grilled cheese sandwich and a cup of coffee."

"Yes, Miss Novak," the waitress said, and grinned again, and immediately left the table before Nora could correct her.

Almost as soon as the waitress was gone, a young girl in a dark blue skirt and white blouse came to the table carrying a pen and a sheet of paper.

"Excuse me," she said. "Could I have your autograph, Miss Novak?"

Nora looked at her and smiled. "I'm sorry," she said. "I'm not Kim Novak."

The little girl seemed puzzled. "You're not?" she asked.

"No. I'm not."

"Gee, you sure look like her," the girl said.

"Yes, but I'm not." Nora said. The girl continued to stare at her, and Nora realized all at once that the girl didn't believe her. "Really," she said, "I'd be happy to give you my autograph if I *were* Kim Novak. But I'm not."

"Well," the girl said, "thank you," and she smiled weakly and went back to her table. At the table, Nora heard the girl say to her mother, "She wouldn't give it to me."

Nora frowned. When her grilled cheese sandwich came, she began eating it in silence.

"Will that be all, Miss Novak?" the waitress said.

"I'm *not* Kim Novak," Nora said.

"You aren't?" the waitress asked. Her voice managed to convey disbelief, disappointment, and scorn—all at the same time.

"I'm sorry," Nora said. "I'm not."

That afternoon, on the way to the subway, a boy pushing an empty dress rack stopped her and asked for her autograph. Nora told him she was sorry, she was not Kim Novak. On Thursday, in Penn Station, a girl with a valise chased her all the way to the street and then breathlessly told her she loved all of her pictures and could she please write *To Louisa, With Warmest Wishes,* and then sign it? Nora told the girl that she was sorry, she was not Kim Novak. On Friday, she ate lunch in a little Italian restaurant near Eighth Avenue, sitting alone at a table in the rear of the place. She was asked for her autograph five times during lunch. Each time she said she was sorry, she was not Kim Novak.

That night, when Marvin asked her where she wanted to go for dinner, she immediately said, "Sardi's."

"Why Sardi's?"

"Why not? The food is very good there," Nora answered.

"What?" he asked. "I'm sorry, Nora, I can't hear you. You're almost whispering."

"I said the food is good there, isn't it?"

"Well, yes."

"Then let's go."

She was very much aware of the stir she caused as she entered the restaurant. She saw the heads turning at all the tables, and she put her hand lightly on Marvin's arm and whispered something about the pictures of the celebrities on the walls, and then smiled and stared smolderingly into the distance. At the bar on her right, she heard a man saying, "Look, honey, there's Kim Novak."

"We don't have a reservation," Marvin said to the head waiter.

The head waiter smiled genially. "That's all right, sir," he said. "We'll see what we can do."

He snapped his fingers, and they found a table for Marvin and Nora at the front of the restaurant, not too far from the entrance door.

"It's very hard to get seated downstairs without a reservation," Marvin said.

"Is it?" Nora asked.

"Yeah. This is a very good table."

"We didn't seem to have any trouble getting it."

"No, we didn't. That's unusual."

"Yes," Nora said.

"Would you like to have a drink?" Marvin asked.

"No, thank you. Not now."

"Would you mind if I had one?"

"Not at all."

"Because, to tell you the truth, Nora, by the time Friday's over, I really *need* a drink, believe me."

"Go right ahead."

Marvin ordered a double scotch on the rocks. The waiter took the order and then turned to Nora and smiled. "Nothing for you, Miss Novak?" he asked.

"Not right now, thank you," Nora said, and the waiter smiled and left the table.

"*What* did he call you?" Marvin asked.

"Who?"

"The waiter. Did he call you 'Miss Novak'?"

"I didn't hear him," Nora said.

"Boy, I'm sure he . . ."

"I didn't hear him."

When the waiter came back with Marvin's scotch, he put the glass down and turned again to Nora. "Miss Novak," he said, "are you sure you won't have something? A little dry sherry perhaps?"

"Thank you, no," Nora said in her quiet, breathy voice. The waiter smiled and left the table.

"He called you 'Miss Novak'," Marvin said.

"Did he?"

"Didn't you hear him? He said it plain as day."

"No, I didn't hear him."

"Well, how could you miss hearing him? He said, 'Miss Novak, are you sure you won't have something?' Didn't you hear him say that?"

"No, I . . ."

"Excuse me, Miss Novak."

They both turned at the same time. The man standing beside the table was holding a Sardi's menu in one hand and an open fountain pen in the other. He was a rather stout man, sweating a bit, beaming happily out of his round face.

"I hate to intrude this way," he said. "My name is Roger Forbes, I'm from Oregon." He paused self-consciously. "Eugene, Oregon."

Marvin looked at the man in puzzlement and then turned to Nora, who was smiling patiently and sympathetically.

"I wonder . . ." the man said. "My daughter is a big fan of yours, Miss Novak. I wonder if . . ."

"You're making a mis . . ." Marvin started.

". . . you'd sign this menu for her?" the man said.

"I'd be happy to," Nora answered.

Marvin's eyes opened wide. Nora smiled at him, and then took the menu from the man.

"What's your daughter's name?" she asked.

"Marie."

On the menu, Nora wrote *To Marie, With Warmest Wishes,* and then signed it *Kim Novak.*

"Thank you, Miss Novak," the man said.

"Not at all," she said, and smiled at him graciously as he left the table.

"Why did you do that?" Marvin whispered.

"It's easier than denying it all the time," she said.

"That's against the law," Marvin said, leaning over the table, whispering.

"Don't be ridiculous."

"You are impersonating Kim Novak," he whispered.

"I am not impersonating anyone. The man asked me for my autograph, and I gave it to him."

"He asked for Kim Novak's autograph, not yours."

"It's not my fault he made a mistake. I'm not going to go through the rest of my life saying I'm sorry I'm not Kim Novak."

"But you're *not* Kim Novak."

"*He* thought I was."

"How the hell does that change anything?"

"Oh, I don't know," she said. "Let's get out of here."

"We haven't had our dinner yet."

"I don't care." She rose suddenly and began walking toward the door. At the entrance, the head waiter asked, "Is everything all right, Miss Novak?" and she said, "Yes, everything is fine," and walked out onto the sidewalk. Two teenage boys walking past turned and smiled at her.

"Hi, Kim!" one of them shouted.

"Hey, Kim," the other one called, "you want to go out with my friend?" and then they both burst out laughing and ran toward Broadway.

The doorman was grinning. "Taxi, Miss Novak?" he asked.

"Yes. Please."

"We'll walk," Marvin said, coming up behind her.

"I want to go home, Marvin," she said.

"We'll walk to the subway."

"The subway?"

"Yes," Marvin said, and he took her elbow and began walking her toward Times Square. They shuttled across to Grand Central and then boarded the Woodlawn Road Express. Marvin seemed not to notice the turning heads, the craning necks, the pleased smiles and excited whispers of the riders everywhere around them on the subway. When they got off at Mosholu Parkway, he walked Nora into the park, and they sat together on a bench some distance from the nearest light.

"Nora," he said, "there's something I've got to tell you."

"What?" she said.

"Nora, do . . . do you know how I feel about you?"

"I think so."

"I love you," he said.

"Mmmm."

"I love you," he repeated.

"Mmmm."

"Is that all you can say? I just told you I loved you. Twice."

"What do you want me to say, Marvin?"

"I don't know. Say you love me, too, or say you hate me, but don't just say 'Mmmm' as if I told you it's a nice day or something."

"Marvin, you don't love *me*," Nora said.

"I don't, huh?"

"No." Her voice lowered. "You only love Kim Novak."

"Who?"

"You heard me."

"Kim Novak? I don't even *know* Kim Novak. How could I . . . ?"

"Marvin, it's because I look like her, and that's all."

"Nora, I don't care if you look like Kim Novak or Phyllis Diller, believe me."

"Then why did you take me to that movie with her in it?"

"Because I wanted to tell you I thought you were beautiful, that's all. Nora, what do I care *who* you look like? To me, you look like Nora Feldman, that's who."

"No, Marvin . . ."

"Nora, I love you. I've loved you from the first day Mr. Mergenthaler brought you into my office and said he wanted me to meet his new secretary. I was pricing that shantung, do you remember?"

"I remember."

"So how could I be in love with Kim Novak? Did Mr. Mergenthaler ever bring Kim Novak into my office?"

"No, but . . ."

"Nora, I'm in love with you. *You.*"

"Who am I?" Nora asked. "Tell me that, Marvin."

"What?"

"Who is Kim Novak, for that matter? If we look the same, and walk the same, and talk the same, maybe we *are* the same."

"No, Nora, because . . ."

"A man in a restaurant thinks I'm Kim Novak, and I sign Kim Novak's name on his menu, so he goes home and tells his daughter he got Kim Novak's signature for her, and who knows the difference? Does *he* know the difference? Does his daughter? Does even Kim Novak *herself* know the difference?"

"Nora," Marvin said very gently, "do *you* know the difference?"

"Yes," she said. "The difference is being somebody when I walk into a restaurant."

"Nora, when you walk into a restaurant you *are* somebody. Nora, to me you are everybody in the room."

"Oh, Marvin, don't you see? It means somebody caring whether or not I would like a little dry sherry before my meal."

"Nora, *I* care. Nora, if you would like a little dry sherry before your meal, I would swim to Spain for it."

"Or yelling out 'Hi, Kim!' on the street."

"Nora, I'll yell 'Hi, Nora' from the rooftops. I'll yell it twenty-four hours a day, if that's what you want."

"Marvin, don't you see? Everybody *loves* Kim Novak."

"Not me," Marvin said. "*I* love Nora Feldman."

They were silent for a long time. Outside the park, on the street comer, the boys were telling jokes, and Nora could hear their laughter. At last, Marvin cleared his throat.

"There . . . there's something I want to ask you, Nora," he said.

"Don't," she told him.

"Nora, will you be my . . ."

"No, *don't,*" she said, and stood up. "I want to go home, Marvin. I want to go home now."

Marvin stood up and looked at her, and then he sighed and

said, "All right, Nora. I'll take you home."

They walked past the boys on the corner and then up the block and into Nora's building. Outside her door, Marvin said goodnight and tried to kiss her, but she turned her face away and began looking for her key. She opened the door and heard his footfalls on the steps going down the street. The minute she turned on the lights, her grandmother said, "Who is it?"

"Me," Nora answered.

Her father must have heard their voices because from his room he called, "Who is it?"

"It's Kim Novak, who do you think?" her grandmother said, and Nora smiled and turned out the lights and found the way to her room. She undressed and then washed out her underwear and set her hair and sat up for a while reading some of the fan magazines. One of them said that Kim Novak was left-handed. She hadn't known that. After a while, she felt drowsy, so she put out the light and got into bed and instead of falling asleep, she stared up at the ceiling and wondered why she'd stopped Marvin just when he was about to propose, wondered why she'd turned away when he tried to kiss her. He was really a very nice fellow, and he'd said he loved her. She lay there thinking about Marvin and about being married to him, and finally she got out of bed. She walked to the window and looked out. She could see the lights of the elevated platform on Jerome Avenue. She went to her desk and turned on the lamp, and then she opened the top drawer and took out a sheet of stationery. She picked up her pen. She was about to begin writing when she remembered what she'd read in the fan magazine. She shifted the pen to her left hand.

Then, over and over again, she wrote Kim Novak, Kim Novak, Kim Novak . . .

Barking at Butterflies

Damn dog barked at everything.

Sounds nobody else could hear, in the middle of the night the damn dog barked at them.

"He's protecting us," Carrie would say.

Protecting us. Damn dog weighs eight pounds soaking wet, he's what's called a Maltese poodle, he's protecting us. His name is Valletta, which is the capital of Malta. That's where the breed originated, I suppose. Some sissy Maltese nobleman must've decided he needed a yappy little lapdog that looked like a white feather duster. Little black nose. Black lips. Black button eyes. Shaggy little pipsqueak named Valletta. Who barked at everything from a fart to a butterfly. Is that someone ringing the bell? The damn dog would hurl himself at the door like a grizzly bear, yelping and growling and raising a fuss that could wake the dead in the entire county.

"He's just protecting us," Carrie would say.

Protecting us.

I hated that damn dog.

I still do.

He was Carrie's dog, you see. She rescued him from a husband-and-wife team who used to beat him when he was just a puppy—gee, I wonder why. This was two years before we got married. I used to think he was cute while she was training him. She'd say, "Sit, Valletta," and he'd walk away. She'd say, "Stay, Valletta," and he'd bark. She'd say, "Come, Valletta," and he'd take a nap. This went on for six months. He still isn't trained.

Carrie loved him to death.

As for El Mutto, the only thing on earth *he* loved was Carrie. Well, you save a person's life, he naturally feels indebted. But this went beyond mere gratitude. Whenever Carrie left the house, Valletta would lie down just inside the door, waiting for her to come home. Serve him a hot pastrami on rye, tell him, "Come, Valletta, time to eat," he'd look at me as if he'd been abandoned by the love of his life and never cared to breathe again. When he heard her car in the driveway, he'd start squealing and peeing on the rug. The minute she put her key in the lock, he jumped up in the air like a Chinese acrobat, danced and pranced on his hind legs when she opened the door, began squealing and leaping all around her until she knelt beside him and scooped him into her embrace and made comforting little sounds to him: "Yes, Valletta, yes, Mommy, what a good boy, oh, yes, what a beautiful little puppyboy."

I used to joke about cooking him.

"Maltese meatloaf is delicious," I used to tell Carrie. "We'll pluck him first, and then wash him real good, and stuff him and put him in the oven for what, an hour? Maybe forty-five minutes, the size of him. Serve him with roast potatoes and—"

"He understands every word you say," she'd tell me.

Damn dog would just cock his head and look up at me. Pretended to be bewildered, the canny little son of a bitch.

"Would you like to be a meatloaf?" I'd ask him.

He'd yawn.

"You'd better be a good dog or I'll sell you to a Filipino man."

"He understands you."

"You want to go home with a Filipino man?"

"Why do you talk to him that way?"

"In the Philippines they *eat* dogs, did you know that, Valletta? Dogs are a delicacy in the Philippines. You want to go home with a Filipino man?"

"You're hurting him."

"He'll turn you into a rack of Maltese chops, would you like that, Valletta?"

"You're hurting *me*, too."

"Or some breaded Maltese cutlets, what do you say, Valletta? You want to go to Manila?"

"Please don't, John. You know I love him."

Damn dog would rush into the bathroom after her, sit by the tub while she took her shower, lick the water from her toes while she dried herself. Damn dog would sit at her feet while she was peeing on the toilet. Damn dog would even sit beside the bed whenever we made love. I asked her once to please put him out in the hall.

"I feel as if there's a *pervert* here in the bedroom watching us," I said.

"He's not watching us."

"He's sitting there *staring* at us."

"No, he's not."

"Yes, he is. It embarrasses me, him staring at my privates that way."

"Your privates? When did you start using *that* expression?"

"Ever since he started staring at it."

"He's not staring at it."

"He is. In fact, he's *glaring* at it. He doesn't like me making love to you."

"Don't be silly, John. He's just a cute little puppydog."

One day, cute little puppydog began barking at *me*.

I came in the front door, and the stupid little animal was sitting smack in the middle of the entry, snarling and barking at me as if I were a person come to read the gas meter.

"What?" I said.

He kept barking.

"You're barking at *me?*" I said. "This is my house, I *live* here, you little shit, how *dare* you bark at me?"

"What is it, what is it?" Carrie yelled, rushing into the hallway.

"He's barking at me," I said.

"Shhh, Valletta," she said. "Don't bark at John."

He kept barking, the little well-trained bastard.

"How would you like to become a Maltese hamburger?" I asked him.

He kept barking.

I don't know when I decided to kill him.

Perhaps it was the night Carrie seated him at the dinner table with us. Until then, she'd been content to have him sitting at our feet like the despicable little beggar he was, studying every bite we took, waiting for scraps from the table.

"Go ahead," I'd say, "watch every morsel we put in our mouths. You're *not* getting fed from the table."

"Oh, John," Carrie would say.

"I can't enjoy my meal with him staring at me that way."

"He's not staring at you."

"What do you call what he's doing right this minute? Look at him! If that isn't staring, what is it?"

"I think you're obsessed with this idea of the dog staring at you."

"Maybe because he *is* staring at me."

"If he is, it's because he loves you."

"He doesn't love me, Carrie."

"Yes, he does."

"He loves *you.*"

"He loves you, too, John."

"No, just you. In fact, if you want to talk about obsession, *that's* obsession. What that damn mutt feels for you is *obsession*."

"He's not a mutt, and he's not obsessed. He just wants to be part of the family. He sees us eating, he wants to join us. Come, Valletta, come sweet puppyboy, come little Mommy, come sit with your family," she said, and hoisted him off the floor and plunked him down on a chair between us.

"I'll get your dish, sweet babypup," she said.

"Carrie," I said, "I will not have that mutt sitting at the table with us."

"He's not a mutt," she said. "He's purebred."

"Valletta," I said, "get the hell off that chair or I'll—"
He began barking.

"You mustn't raise your hand to him," Carrie said. "He was abused. He thinks you're about to hit him."

"*Hit* him?" I said. "I'm about to *kill* him!"
The dog kept barking.
And barking.
And barking.
I guess that's when I decided to do it.

October is a good time for dying.
"Come, Valletta," I said, "let's go for a walk."
He heard me say "Come," so naturally he decided to go watch television.

"Is Daddy taking you for a walk?" Carrie asked.
Daddy.
Daddy had Mr. Smith and Mr. Wesson in the pocket of his bush jacket. Daddy was going to walk little pisspot here into the woods far from the house and put a few bullets in his head and then sell his carcass to a passing Filipino man or toss it to

a wayward coyote or drop it in the river. Daddy was going to tell Carrie that her prized purebred mutt had run away, naturally, when I commanded him to come. I called and called, I would tell her, but he ran and ran, and God knows where he is now.

"Don't forget his leash," Carrie called from the kitchen.

"I won't, darling."

"Be careful," she said. "Don't step on any snakes."

"Valletta will protect me," I said, and off we went.

The leaves were in full voice, brassy overhead, rasping underfoot. Valletta kept backing off on the red leather leash, stubbornly planting himself every ten feet or so into the woods, trying to turn back to the house where his beloved mistress awaited his return. I kept assuring him that we were safe here under the trees, leaves dropping gently everywhere around us. "Come, little babypup," I cooed, "come little woofikins, there's nothing can hurt you here in the woods."

The air was as crisp as a cleric's collar.

When we had come a far-enough distance from the house, I reached into my pocket and took out the gun. "See this, Valletta?" I said. "I am going to shoot you with this. You are never going to bark again, Valletta. You are going to be the most silent dog on earth. Do you understand, Valletta?"

He began barking.

"Quiet," I said.

He would not stop barking.

"Damn you!" I shouted. "Shut up!"

And suddenly he yanked the leash from my hands and darted away like the sneaky little sissydog he was, all white and furry against the orange and yellow and brown of the forest floor, racing like a ragged whisper through the carpet of leaves, trailing the red leash behind him like a narrow trickle of blood. I came thrashing after him. I was no more than six feet behind him when he ran into a clearing saturated with golden light. I followed him with the gun hand, aiming at him. Just as my finger tightened on the trigger, Carrie burst into the clearing from the opposite end.

"No!" she shouted, and dropped to her knees to scoop him protectively into her arms, the explosion shattering the incessant whisper of the leaves, the dog leaping into her embrace, blood flowering on her chest, oh dear God, no, I thought, oh dear sweet Jesus, no, and dropped the gun and ran to her and pressed her bleeding and still against me while the damn dumb dog barked and barked.

He has not barked since.

For him, it must seem as if she's gone someplace very far away, somewhere never even remotely perceived in his tiny Maltese mentality. In a sense this is true. In fact, I have repeated the story so often to so many people that I've come to believe it myself. I told her family and mine, I told all our friends, I even told the police, whom her brother was suspicious and vile enough to call, that I came home from work one day and she was simply gone. Not a hint that she was leaving. Not even a note. All she'd left behind was the dog. And she hadn't even bothered to feed him before her departure.

Valletta often wanders into the woods looking for her.

He circles the spot where two autumns ago her blood seeped into the earth. The area is bursting with fresh spring growth now, but he circles and sniffs the bright green shoots, searching, searching. He will never find her, of course. She is wrapped in a tarpaulin and buried deep in the woods some fifty miles north of where the three of us once lived together, Carrie and I and the dog.

There are only the two of us now.

He is all I have left to remind me of her.

He never barks and I never speak to him.

He eats when I feed him, but then he walks away from his bowl without once looking at me and falls to the floor just inside the entrance door, waiting for her return.

I can't honestly say I like him any better now that he's stopped barking. But sometimes . . .

Sometimes when he cocks his head in bewilderment to observe a floating butterfly, he looks so cute I could eat him alive.

Motel

The January wind was blowing fiercely as he put the key into the unfamiliar door lock and then twisted it to the right with no results. He turned it to the left, and the door opened, and he pushed it wide into the motel room, and then stepped aside for her to enter before him. She was wearing a short beige car coat, the collar of which she held closed about her throat with one gloved hand. Her skirt, showing below the hem of the coat, was a deeper tan. She was wearing dark brown leather boots, almost the color of her shoulder-length hair. Her eyes were browner than the boots, and she lowered them as she stepped past him into the room. There was an air of shy nervousness about her.

Fumbling to extricate the key from the lock, Frank almost lost his homburg to a fresh gust of wind. He clasped it to his head with his free hand, struggled with the damn key again, and finally pulled it free of the lock. Putting the key into the pocket of his overcoat, he went into the room, closed the door behind him, and said immediately, "I hope you won't misinterpret this."

"Why should I?" she asked.

"Well, a motel has connotations. But I couldn't think of any other way."

"We're both adults, Frank," she said. "I don't see why it shouldn't be possible for two adults to take a room and . . ."

"That was precisely my reasoning," he said.

"So please don't apologize."

They stood just inside the entrance doorway, as though each were reluctant to take the steps that would propel them deeper into the room. There were two easy chairs on their right, in front of the windows facing the courtyard outside. A table with a lamp on it rested between the two chairs. On the wall immediately to their left, there was a dresser with a mirror over it, another lamp on one end of it. An air-conditioning unit was recessed into a window on the wall opposite the door. The bed was covered with a floral-patterned spread that matched the drapes. Its headboard was against the wall opposite the dresser. A framed print of a landscape hung over it.

"Millie," he said, "I honestly *do* want you to see this film."

"Oh, I honestly *want* to see it," she said.

"We talked about it so often on the train that it just seemed ridiculous not to show it to you."

"Of course," she said.

"Which is why I mentioned it at lunch today, and suggested that maybe we could take a room someplace, for just a few minutes, a half-hour maybe, so I could show you the film. Still, I don't want you to think the only reason I asked you to lunch was to show you the film." He grinned suddenly. "Though I am very proud of it."

"I'm dying to see it," she said.

"I'll just be a minute, okay?" he said, and went to the door, and opened it, and stepped outside into the windblown courtyard, leaving the door open. She debated closing the door behind him, and decided against it. She also debated taking off her gloves, and decided against that as well. Outside, she heard the sound of the automobile trunk being slammed shut. A moment later, he came into the room carrying a motion picture projector.

"I was wondering how you were going to show it," Millie said.

"I had this in the trunk," he said, and put it down on the floor.

"Do you always carry a movie projector in the trunk?"

Smiling, he said, "Well, I can't pretend I didn't *plan* on showing you the film." He took a small reel of film from his coat pocket, held it up for her to see, and then put it on the dresser top. Taking off his coat, he went to the rack in one corner of the room, and hung it on a wire hanger. He took off the homburg and placed that on the shelf over the rack. He was wearing a dark, almost black, shadow-striped business suit.

"Did your wife say anything?" she asked.

"About the projector? Why would she say anything?"

"I guess she wouldn't," Millie said. "I guess lots of men take movie projectors to work in the morning."

"Actually, she didn't see it," Frank said. "I put it in the car last night." He looked around the room. "I was hoping the walls would be white," he said. "Well, maybe the towels are white."

"Did you plan to take a bath first?" she asked.

"No, no," he said, walking toward the bathroom door. "I just want to make a screen." From the bathroom, he said, "Ah, good," and was back an instant later carrying a large white towel. "Let's see now," he said, "I guess I can hang this over the mirror, huh? Move the table there, and set my projector on it. Um-huh." As she watched, he went to the dresser, reached up over it, and tucked the towel over the top edge of the mirror, covering it. She had not moved from where she was standing just inside the door. Turning to her, he said, "Wouldn't you like to take off your coat?"

"Well . . . is it a very long film?" she asked.

"Sixty seconds, to be exact."

"Oh, well, all right then."

She took off her gloves and her coat. She was wearing a smart, simple suit and a pale green blouse. As she carried the coat to the rack, Frank took the lamp off the table, moved the table, set the projector down and plugged it into a wall socket.

"Isn't sixty seconds very short?" she asked.

"No, that's the usual length. Some are even shorter. Thirty seconds, some of them." He looked up from where he was threading the film. "You don't have to hurry back or anything, do you?"

"No, no," she said. "As long as I'm back before dinner."

"What time is that, usually?"

"Seven-thirty, usually. But I have to be back before then. My husband gets home at seven, you see. And he likes to have a drink first. So I should be home around six-thirty, seven. Not that I have to account for my time or anything, you understand."

"Well, even if you did," Frank said, "there's nothing wrong with two adults having lunch together."

"If I thought there was anything wrong with it, I wouldn't have accepted."

"In fact, it seems entirely prejudicial that a man and a woman can't enjoy each other's company simply because they happen to be married to other people—you didn't tell your husband, did you?" he asked.

"No. Did you tell your wife?"

"No," he said. "I never even told her I'd met you on the train."

"It's really silly, isn't it?"

"It certainly is," he said. "But you know, the truth of it is that most people just wouldn't understand. If I told my wife . . . or *anyone*, for that matter . . . that I'd taken you to lunch . . ."

"And to a motel later . . ."

"To show you a film . . ."

"Who'd believe it?"

"There," he said. "Let me just close these drapes." He pulled them across the rod, darkening the room, and then snapped on the projector. As the leader came on, he adjusted the throw and the focus, and framed the film on the center of the towel. "Here goes," he said, just as a heraldic blast of trumpets sounded from the projector's speaker. The film appeared on the towel. There were two ten-year old children in the film. The children were singing.

"Hot buttered popcorn," they sang,

"We like it, you like it.

"Hot buttered popcorn

"From Pike, it's

"Great!"

The children were digging into a box of popcorn now. One of the children asked, "Do you like popcorn?"

"I love popcorn," the other child said.

"Me, too."

The children fell silent. On the screen, there were close shots of their hands digging into the box of popcorn, other close shots of the popcorn being transferred to their mouths. The camera pulled back to show their beaming faces.

"Good, huh?" the first child asked.

"Delicious," the second child said.

"What is it?"

"Popcorn. What do you think it is?"

"Yeah, but what *kind* of popcorn?"

"Hot buttered popcorn."

"I mean, the name."

"Oh. I dunno."

"Is this it here on the box?"

"Yeah, maybe."

The camera panned down to the front of the popcorn box, and the words PIKE'S POPCORN printed on it.

"Pike's!" one of the children shouted. "*That's* the name!"

Together, they began singing again.

"Hot buttered popcorn,

"We like it, you like it.

"Hot buttered popcorn

"From Pike, it's

"Great!"

The screen went blank. Frank snapped off the projector, and then turned on the room light. Millie was silent for what seemed an inordinately long time. Then she said, "I didn't realize it would be in color."

"Yes, we shoot everything in color nowadays," he said. "What'd you think of it?"

"I don't know what to say," she said. "Did you write the song, too?"

"No, just the dialogue. Between the kids."

"Oh," Millie said.

"It was very easy and natural for me," he said. "I have three kids of my own, you know."

"Yes, you told me that. On the train. Two boys and a girl."

"No, two girls and a boy," he said.

"Yes. How old are they?"

"The boy's nineteen. The girls are fifteen and thirteen."

"That's older than my girls," Millie said. "Mine are eight and six."

They looked at each other silently. The silence lengthened. And then, into the silence, the telephone suddenly shrilled, startling them both. He moved toward the phone, and then stopped dead in his tracks. The phone kept ringing. Finally he went to it, and warily lifted the receiver.

"Hello?" he said. "Who? No, there's no Mr. . . . . oh, yes!

Yes, *this* is Mr. McIntyre. The *what?* Yes, the Mercury is mine. In *what?* In the parking space for seventeen? Oh, yes, certainly, I'll move it. Thank you." He hung up, and looked at Millie. "I parked the car in the wrong space," he said.

"Is that the name you used? McIntyre?"

"Yes, well, I figured . . ."

"Oh, certainly, what's the sense of . . . ?"

"That's what I figured. I'd better move the car. It's supposed to be in sixteen."

As he started for the door, she said, "Maybe we just ought to leave."

"What?" he said.

"Well . . . you've shown me the film already. And since you have to move the car, anyway . . ."

"Yes, but we haven't discussed it yet," he said. "The film. In depth, I mean."

"That's true. But we could discuss it in depth in the car on the way back to the city."

"Yes, I guess we could do that," he said. "Is that what you'd like to do?"

"What would you like to do?"

"Well, I thought I'd move the car to number sixteen, and then maybe we could discuss the film afterwards. In depth. If that's what you'd like to do."

"Well, whatever you want to do."

"Well, fine then."

"Fine."

"I'll move the car," he said quickly, and went out, and closed the door behind him., She debated sitting on the bed, and decided against it. She debated sitting in one of the chairs near the windows, and decided against that as well. She settled for leaning on the dresser. She was leaning on it when he came back into the room, blowing on his hands.

"Whoo, it's cold out there," he said. "I can't remember a January this cold, can you?"

"You should have put on your coat."

"Well, I figured just to move the car . . ."

"Did you move it?"

"Yep," he said, "all taken care of. Room sixteen in space sixteen."

"What kind of car was it?"

"Mine? Oh, you mean room seventeen. A big black Caddy. With a fat old man behind the wheel."

"Alone?"

"No, he had a girl with him. A frumpy blonde."

"Probably has a film he wants to show her," Millie said, and smiled.

"Probably," he said, and returned the smile. "So . . . what'd you think of it?" Without waiting for her answer, he said, "I got quite a bit of praise for it. In fact, the Head of Creation called me personally to . . ."

"God?"

"No, Hope. Hope Cromwell. She's the agency's creative head. That's her official title."

"What's *your* official title?"

"Me? I'm just a copywriter, that's all."

"Well, I wouldn't say *just* a copywriter."

"Well, Hope's a vice president, you see. I'm just . . ." He shrugged. "Just a copywriter."

"Michael's a vice president, too," she said. "My husband. He's a stockbroker, did I tell you that?" She paused, and then said, "Is Hope attractive?"

"No, no. Well, yes, I suppose so. I suppose you could call her attractive. I suppose you could call her a beautiful red-head."

"Oh," Millie said. "Is she a nice person, though?"

"Actually, she's a pain sometimes."

"So's Michael," Millie said. "Especially when he starts discussing futures. Are you, for example, interested in soy beans?"

"No, but men like to discuss their work, you know. I guess he . . ."

"Oh, I understand that. But I've never even *seen* a soy bean, have you?"

"I've seen soy bean sauce," Frank said.

"But have you ever seen a soy bean itself?"

"Never."

"So why should I be interested in something I've never seen in my entire life?"

"You shouldn't."

"*Or* its future," Millie said. "Of course, Michael's interesting in other ways. He has a mathematical turn of mind, you see. I'm a scatterbrain, but Michael . . ."

"I wouldn't say that."

"I am, believe me. If it weren't for Michael, I wouldn't know how to set the alarm clock. Well, I'm exaggerating, but you know what I mean. He has this very logical firm grasp on everything, whereas I just flit in and out and hardly know what I'm doing half the time. I'm very impulsive. I do things impulsively."

"Like coming to lunch today," Frank said.

"Yes. And like coming here to the motel."

"That was impulsive for me, too," he said.

"Well, it wasn't as impulsive for you as it was for me. Because, after all, you *did* put the projector in your car last night."

"That's right," Frank said. "Yes, in that respect, it wasn't as impulsive, you're right."

"What would you have said if your wife saw you putting the projector in the car?"

"I guess I'd have said I was bringing it in for repair or something."

"Would she have believed that? Does she trust you?"

"Oh, sure. I've never given her reason not to trust me. Why shouldn't she trust me?"

"Well, if you go around sneaking movie projectors into your car . . ."

"I didn't *sneak* it in. I just carried it out. She wasn't even home, in fact."

"Where was she?"

"At the shop. Mae owns a little antiques shop in Mamaroneck."

"Oh? What's it called?"

"Something Old."

"Really?" Millie said. "That's a darling shop! Does your wife really own it? I've been in there several times. Which one is your wife?"

"Well, there are only two of them in the shop, and one of them's sixty years old. My wife's the other one."

"The little brunette? She's very attractive. I bought an ironstone pitcher from her last month. What'd you say her name was?"

"Mae."

"That's a pretty name. Very springlike."

"Yes. Well, it's M-A-E, you understand."

"Oh, not M-A-Y?"

"No, M-A-E," he said, and they both fell silent.

"Well," she said.

"Well," he said.

"Did you register as Mr. and Mrs. McIntyre?" she asked.

"Yes. Well, I couldn't very well register as Mr. and Mrs. Di Santangelo, could I?"

"Why not?"

"I'd still be up there signing the card," he said, and laughed. "Di Santangelo's an unusually long name, you see."

"My maiden name was longer. Are you ashamed of being Italian?" she asked abruptly.

"Ashamed? No, no, why should I be ashamed?"

"It just seems strange to me that you'd choose a Wasp name like McIntyre . . ."

"It's not a Wasp name."

"Did you choose it last night? When you were putting the projector in the car?"

"No, I chose it when I was registering."

"My mother would die on the spot if she knew I was in a motel room with a Wasp named McIntyre."

"It's not Wasp, it's Roman Catholic."

"Worse yet," Millie said. "Is your wife Italian, too?"

"She's Scotch."

"Do you think we can get something to drink?" Millie asked.

"As a matter of fact, I have a bottle in the car," Frank said.

"My, you're very well appointed, aren't you?" she said, and smiled. "A projector in the trunk . . ."

"Well, I figured . . ."

"But maybe we just ought to leave," she said. "Find a bar on the way back."

"Oh, sure, we can do that, if you want to."

"Is that what you want to do?"

"Well, this is a nice comfortable room, we might just as well . . . *would* you like a drink, Millie?"

"I would love a drink," she said, and he rose instantly and started for the door. "But not if it's any trouble."

"No trouble at all," he said, and went outside again.

She debated taking off her boots, and decided against it.

She sat on the edge of the bed instead. There was a Magic Fingers box on the side of the bed. She read the instructions silently, took off the boots after all, inserted a quarter into the box, and lay back on the bed. The bed was still vibrating when Frank came back into the room. He was carrying a brown paper bag.

"Are you having a massage?" he asked.

"It said 'soothing and relaxing.' "

"Is it?"

"It's soothing," she said. "I don't know how relaxing it is." The machine suddenly stopped, the bed stopped vibrating. "Ooo," she said. "Now I miss it."

"Shall I put another quarter in?"

"No, I think a drink might be more relaxing," she said, and sat up. "I don't ordinarily drink, you know. Michael's the big drinker. Do you have a drink when you get home at night?"

"Oh, yes."

"How many drinks do you have?"

"One or two. Usually two."

"Michael also has one or two, but usually three. For a fellow who's on such a strict diet, he sure knows how to put away his whiskey. Jewish men aren't supposed to be big drinkers, you know. There are statistics on that sort of thing." She smiled and said, "I probably married the only Jew in Larchmont who has three glasses of whiskey before dinner. *Big* glasses, too."

"Are you from Larchmont originally?" Frank asked.

"No, the Bronx. Michael was born in Larchmont, though. We met at a dance. He used to play alto saxophone in a band. Would you like to hear something strange? The first time he took me out, he told me he was going to marry me. Don't you think that's strange?"

"No, that's what I told Mae the first time I dated her."

"Really?"

"Mm-huh. Let me get some glasses and ice," he said, and went into the bathroom.

"Is there a little instruction booklet or something?" Millie asked.

"No, just the ice machine," he said. "Under the sink here."

"I mean, that you fellows consult before dating a girl for the first time. I think it's extraordinary that you and Michael would have used the same line on two separate girls. Don't you think that's extraordinary?"

"No," he said, coming out of the bathroom. "In fact, it wasn't a line with me. I really meant it." He walked to the dresser, and poured Scotch into both glasses. "I knew immediately that I wanted to marry her. Did you want water in this?"

"No, thanks," she said.

Frank handed her one of the glasses. "Well . . . cheers," he said, and clinked his glass against hers.

"Cheers," Millie said, and drank. "Wow!" she said.

"Too strong? I can . . ."

"No, no, it's fine," she said, gasping. "Before you got married . . . ?"

"Yes?"

"Did you go to bed with your wife? I don't mean to be personal."

"No, no, that's a perfectly legitimate question. We're both adults, after all, and if we're going to be honest with each other, we should be entirely honest."

"Precisely," Millie said. "*Did* you go to bed with her?"

"Yes."

"A lot?"

"Every now and then," Frank said. "We were at school together, you see. The University of Pennsylvania. It was very convenient."

"It was very convenient for Michael and me, too."

"It's even more convenient for the kids nowadays. My son, for example . . ."

"How old did you say he was?"

"Nineteen. He's a sophomore at Yale."

"Does he have a beard?"

"A mustache."

"Michael has a mustache, too."

"I was saying that the kids don't give a second thought to it nowadays. It's all very natural and casual with them."

"Natural maybe," Millie said, "but I don't think casual."

"Well, it *should* be a very natural thing, you know. Sex, I mean."

"Yes, but not casual. I don't think it should be casual, do you? Sex, I mean."

"No. But I *do* think it should be natural. Would you like to take off your jacket or something?"

"It *is* warm in here, isn't it?" She took off the suit jacket, and tossed it to the foot of the bed. "You were saying about your wife . . ."

"My wife?"

"About sleeping with her all the time."

"Well, not *all* the time. But we were on the same campus for four years."

"That's a long time to be sleeping with somebody."

"Especially if her father is a Methodist minister," Frank said.

"*My* father runs a Buick agency in the Bronx," Millie said. "Did you deliberately set out to marry a Wasp? I mean, because you're ashamed of being Italian and all?"

"Hey, come on," Frank said, laughing, "I'm *not* ashamed of being Italian. And besides, I don't think of Mae as a Wasp."

"What do you think of her as?"

"A woman," he said, and shrugged. "My wife. Whom I happen to love very much."

"I happen to love Michael very much, too," she said, "though he is a pain sometimes. This is very good, this Scotch. No wonder Michael belts it down every night. Could I have just a teeny little bit more?"

He took the bottle of Scotch from the dresser and went to her, and poured more of it into her glass, and then sat on the edge of the bed beside her.

"Thank you," she said.

"You're welcome," he said.

"That must have been very nice," she said, "going to an out-of-town college, I mean. I went to N.Y.U. I used to commute from the Bronx every day."

"When did you graduate?"

"Ten years ago. In fact, Michael and I went to a reunion just before Christmas. It was ghastly. Everyone looked so old."

"How old *are* you, Millie?"

"Thirty-two," she said.

"Do you realize that when I started at the University of Pennsylvania you were still being pushed around in a baby carriage?"

"You're how old? Forty-six?"

"Four."

"That's only twelve years older than I am," she said, and shrugged.

"Exactly my point. When I was twenty-two . . . ."

"Why'd you start college so late?"

"I was in the Army. My point is that when I was starting college . . . did you want some more of this?"

"Just a drop, please," she said, and held out her glass again. He poured liberally into it, and she raised her eyebrows and said, "That's like one of *Michael's* drops."

"Anyway, when I was starting college, you were only ten years old."

"Yes, but that's not in a baby carriage."

"No, but it's very young."

Sipping at her drink, she said, "Is that why you want to make love to me?"

"What?" he said.

"Make love," she said. "To me," she said. "Because I'm twelve years younger than you are?"

"Well, who . . . well, who said anything about . . . ?"

"Well, you *do* want to make love to me, don't you?"

"Well, yes, but . . ."

"Well, is that the reason?"

"Well, that's part of it, yes."

"What's the other part? That I'm Jewish?"

"No. What's that got to do with . . . ?"

"If that's part of it, I really don't mind," she said. "A lot of Gentiles find Jewish girls terribly attractive. And vice versa. Jewish girls, I mean. Finding Italian men attractive."

She looked at him steadily over the rim of her glass. She rose then, and walked to the dresser, and put her glass down, and began unbuttoning her blouse.

2

The motel courtyard was washed with sunshine, the trees were in full leaf. It was April, and Millie was wearing a bright cotton dress that echoed the blues, greens, and yellows of the season. Frank was wearing a business suit, but the tie he wore seemed geared to spring as well—a riot of daisies rampant on a pale green field. He unlocked the door knowledgeably, and removed the key with familiar dexterity. Millie entered the room first. She went swiftly to the dresser and put down her bag. As Frank locked the door from the inside, she went quickly to the drapes and pulled them closed across the windows. Frank threw the slip bolt and was turning away from the door, when Millie rushed into his arms. She kissed him passionately, and then moved out of his arms and disappeared into the bathroom.

Frank went to one of the easy chairs. He turned on the lamp between the chairs, and then began taking off his shoes and socks. Millie came out of the bathroom, carrying a facial tissue. She went to the mirror and began wiping off her lipstick. Frank took off his jacket. Millie slipped out of her pumps. Frank carried his jacket to the clothes rack, and hung it neatly on a wire hanger. Millie padded over to him barefooted, turned her back to him, lifted her hair from the nape of her neck and waited for him to lower the zipper on her dress.

"What's the use?" he said.

"Huh?" she said, and turned to look at him, puzzled.

"What's the use, what's the use?" he said despairingly, and went to one of the chairs, and sat in it, and began wringing his hands. "How am I supposed to put my heart in this when my mind's a hundred miles away? She's driving me crazy, Millie. If she doesn't stop, I'll just have to leave, that's all."

"Leave?" Millie asked, surprised.

"Leave, leave, right," he said, and rose and began pacing in front of the dresser. "I've warned her. I've told her a hundred times. She can't treat me this way, damn it. I'm not some adolescent kid fresh out of college."

"You've *told* her?" Millie said, and her eyes opened wide.

"A hundred times. More often than that. Repeatedly. Over and over again. A *thousand* times. Then today . . ."

Alarmed, Millie said, "What happened today?"

"What's today?"

"Tuesday. You know it's Tuesday. We meet every Tuesday."

"I mean the date. What's the date?"

"April sixth."

"Right. So that means *she* was five days late to begin with. So what's she jumping all over me for?"

"Five days late?"

"Right. And she yells at me about it. When *she's* really the one to blame."

"Frank, I thought we agreed a long time ago that we wouldn't discuss anything like this."

"Like what?"

"Like Mae or Michael."

"Who's discussing Mae or Michael? I'm talking about Hope. Hope Cromwell. She came in first thing this morning and said, 'Where is it?' So I reminded her that she'd only told me about the damn thing Friday, five days *after* it was due, and she said it seemed to her it shouldn't take that long to do a thirty-second spot when I knew the client was waiting for a presentation, and maybe I'd get the material in on time if I didn't take such long lunch hours every Tuesday. So I told her to take a look at her *own* lunch hour, which starts at eleven in the morning and ends at three, so don't talk to *me* about long lunch hours, baby."

"Did you really say that?"

"I certainly did."

"You called her 'baby'?"

"No, no, I wouldn't call her 'baby'. The point is I don't like being bawled out for something that's not my fault. And anyway, if I want to take a long lunch hour every Tuesday, so what? I've got half a mind to tell her what she can do with the job."

"Why don't you?"

"Huh?"

"Why don't you call her and tell her what she can do with the job?"

"Tell *Hope,* you mean?"

"Sure."

"Well, she's probably out to lunch right now."

"Let's try her," Millie said, and went to the phone.

"Well, perhaps it's best not to act too impulsively," he said. "There are millions of copywriters in New York, all of them just as good as I am."

"I doubt that very much," Millie said. She lifted the receiver and handed it to him. "Call her."

"Just a second, Mil," he said. "Let me *think* about this a minute, okay?"

"What's there to think about? Just tell her, that's all."

"I'll tell her when I get back to the office."

"Do you promise?"

"I promise."

Millie put the receiver back onto the cradle, and turned her back to him again. Lifting the hair from the nape of her neck, she lowered her head and waited for him to unzip her dress. "You don't have to take that kind of abuse, Frank," she said. "You're a very *good* copywriter."

"Yeah," he said, and lowered the zipper.

"So tell her."

"I will," he said, "don't worry." He unknotted his tie and threw it onto the seat of the closest chair. Unbuttoning his shirt, he said, "I'll tell her I don't have to take that kind of abuse."

"Right."

"I'll tell her I don't like to be blamed for something that's not my fault. She should have told me about the presentation earlier."

"That's right, she should have."

"Damn *right,* she should have," Frank said. "I'll tell her there are millions of copywriters in this city, but not many of them are as good as I am. And if she continues to hand out the kind of abuse she did this morning, I'll just head over to one of the other agencies where they won't treat me like an adolescent."

"Good," Millie said, "tell her." In bra, half-slip and panties, she padded to the clothes rack and hung up her dress.

"As for the lunch hour," he said, gathering steam, "I'll tell her to stop behaving as if it's a *banquet!* It isn't a banquet, it's just an ordinary long lunch hour, and that's that." He nodded, took off his shirt, and draped it over the back of one of the chairs. Millie was silent for what seemed like a long time.

"Frank, have you ever done anything like this before?" she asked suddenly.

"With another woman, do you mean?"

"Yes, with another woman."

"Besides Mae, do you mean?"

"Yes, besides Mae."

"Never," he said. "Why? Have you?"

Millie walked to the air conditioner. "Do you think this thing works?" she asked, and stabbed at a button on its face. "There," she said, and went to the bed, and neatly folded back the spread, and then carried it to one of the chairs.

"Millie?" he said. "You haven't answered my question. Have *you* ever?"

"Have I ever what?"

"Done this?"

"With another man, do you mean?"

"Yes, with another man."

"Besides Michael, do you mean?"

"Yes, besides Michael."

"Do you want an honest answer?"

"Of *course* I want an honest answer."

"Yes," she said.

"Jesus!" he said.

"You wanted to know."

"Who was it?"

"Another man."

"I *know* that! Who?"

"You don't know him. His name is Paul."

"Where'd you meet him?"

"In the Chock Full O'Nuts on Sheridan Square."

"Having a nice long lunch, was he?"

"No, he was eating a cream cheese sandwich on toasted raisin bread."

"I don't want to know anything else about him," Frank said. "In fact, I think we'd better get dressed."

"Why?"

"Because I want to leave." He went to the chair and picked up his shirt. He started to put it on, but one of the sleeves was pulled inside out. Angrily, he shoved at the sleeve, and finally managed to get his arm through it.

"He's a sculptor," Millie said.

"I don't care what he is."

"I posed for him once. Just my belly button."

"Your *what?*" Frank said.

"He does belly buttons. Not always, you understand. That was his project at the time. When I met him. He was doing these enormous sculptures of belly buttons. It was really quite fascinating. I mean, things take on a completely different perspective when you see them larger than . . ."

"I don't want to hear about your goddamn sculptor and his belly buttons!" Frank shouted. Calming himself, he said, "Get dressed, please," and began buttoning his shirt.

"He filled a very important need in my life," Millie said softly.

"I'm sure he did."

"And I could hardly have known at the time that I was going to meet you on the eight forty-six from Larchmont. Besides, I stopped seeing him right after I met you. In February."

"That's *not* right after you met me," Frank said. "That's a full *month* after you met me."

"Well, it takes time to end things," she said.

"More time than it takes to begin them, I'm sure."

"Now you sound like Michael."

"Oh, did you tell *him* about your sculptor, too?"

"Of course not."

"How come I'm so privileged?"

"I thought you'd understand."

"I don't. Put on your clothes, and let's get out of here."

"I wasn't looking for anything, Frank, I hope you realize that. It just happened."

"How? What'd you do, show him your navel in the middle

of Chock Full O'Nuts?"

"I didn't do anything of the sort."

"Then how'd he know he wanted to sculpt *your* navel? There are six million women in the city of New York, how'd he happen to pick *your* navel?"

"He picked a lot of navels," Millie said. "Not only mine."

"How many?"

"At least fifty of them."

"Now that's sordid, that's positively sordid," Frank said.

"It wasn't sordid at all."

"Where'd you pose for him?"

"He has a big loft in Greenwich Village. There. But not the same day."

"Oh, that makes an enormous difference. When *did* he sculpt you, if you'll pardon the expression?"

"A month later. On October sixth."

"You remember the exact date, huh?" Frank said. "That really *is* sordid, Millie, remembering the exact date."

"Only because it was his birthday," she said.

"What'd you do? Drop in on the loft, strip down and yell 'Happy Birthday, Paul!' "

"Not Paul's birthday. Michael's."

"Oh, Jesus!" Frank said.

"And I didn't just go there. Paul called and asked me to come."

"Oh, you gave him your number, did you?"

"He looked it up, the same as you."

"He seems to have done a *lot* of things the same as me," Frank said. "Will you for God's sake get *dressed?*"

"It was just like open heart surgery," Millie said.

"What was?" Frank asked.

"Doing my navel. I didn't have to expose any other part of me. He had me all covered up with a sheet, except for my

Motel

navel. It was very professional."

"When did it start getting *un*professional?" Frank said, and whipped his tie from the seat of the chair, and walked angrily to the mirror.

"After he cast it in bronze."

"Did he put it on the living room table?" Frank asked, and lifted his collar and slid the tie under it, and then began knotting the tie, and had to start all over again because somehow he'd forgotten how to knot a tie. "I think that would've been touching," he said. "A bronze belly button instead of a pair of baby shoes."

"It would've been too big to put on a table, anyway," Millie said. "I told you, the whole idea of the project was . . ."

"The whole idea of the project," Frank said, "was to get fifty stupid housewives into *bed* with him!"

"We weren't all housewives," Millie said.

Calming himself again, carefully knotting his tie, Frank said, "In any case, Millie, I think we should leave. I don't know how to sculpt, you see. I wouldn't know how to sculpt a goddamn navel. Or how to pick up a goddamn lady in the Chock Full O'Nuts on Sheridan Square."

"You did fine on the eight forty-six from Larchmont," she said.

"Oh, *I* did. I see. *I'm* the one who seduced the innocent little housewife, led her down the garden . . ."

"Well, *I* certainly didn't have the movie projector in *my* trunk!"

The telephone rang, shocking them into silence. They both turned to look at it, but neither made a move for it. The phone kept ringing.

"Why don't you get it?" Frank said. "Maybe it's Paul. Maybe he's doing buttocks this week."

Millie did not answer him. With great dignity, she padded

187

to the phone, and lifted the receiver. "Hello?" she said. "Who? Yes, just a moment, please." She held out the receiver to Frank. "It's the manager. He wants to talk to Mr. McIntyre."

Frank took the receiver from her. "Hello?" he said. "Yes? The *what's* too loud?" He looked across the room at the television set. "It isn't even *on*," he said, "so how can it be on too loud? Well, you just tell the man in seventeen that perhaps the television on the *other* side of him is on. In eighteen, that's right. Tell him it is *not* on in sixteen. Goodbye," he said, and banged down the receiver. "Stupid ass," he said. "Good thing we won't be coming back *here* anymore."

In a very tiny voice, Millie said, "Won't we?"

They looked at each other silently.

"I didn't know you'd get so angry," she said. "I'm sorry."

"Then why'd you tell me, Millie?"

"I had to."

"Why?"

"Because of what you said."

"When?"

"Just a little while ago."

"What did I say?"

"You said this wasn't a banquet."

"Huh?"

"You said it was just an ordinary long lunch hour. Well, to me it's a banquet. And if it's just an ordinary long lunch hour to you, then you can go to hell. If you're in the habit of taking lots of women to a motel in New Jersey . . ."

"I have never . . ."

"Putting a projector in your trunk . . ."

"I have never . . ."

"And showing them your lousy sixty-second commercial . . ."

"I thought you *liked* my commercial," he said.

"Not if it's been seen by every stupid housewife in the city of New York!"

"It's been seen by stupid housewives all over *America*," Frank said. "It's been aired approximately two hundred and twenty times. Listen, Millie, how did *you* suddenly become the injured party. *I'm* the injured party here. *I'm* the one who's been betrayed."

"Betrayed?" she said. "Oh my God, you sound *just* like Michael."

"Leave Michael out of this, if you don't mind. Let's get back to Paul."

"Why? Paul was nothing but an ordinary long lunch hour."

"A little while ago, you said he filled a very important need in your life."

"That's right, he did."

"You can't have it both ways, Millie. Either he was meaningful or he was a cream cheese sandwich on whole wheat."

"Toasted raisin."

"Whatever."

"He was both."

"Perhaps you'd like to explain that."

"Perhaps I wouldn't."

"Fine. Let's get dressed."

"Fine," she said.

She walked angrily to the rack, took her dress off its wire hanger, and slipped it over her head. "I thought you'd understand, but apparently you've never been neglected in your own home." He did not answer. "Apparently Mae adores you completely," she said, walking to him. She turned her back to him, and he zipped up her dress. "Thank you," she said. "Apparently Mae never treated you in a way that might force you to consider addressing a stranger in Chock Full O'Nuts. But when someone is concerned solely with Puts and Takes and selling short, then perhaps a woman may feel the need for conversation . . ."

"Conversation!" Frank said. "Jesus!"

"Yes, with someone whose interests extend beyond commodities. With someone who doesn't think of a *woman* as just another commodity. Paul thought of me . . ."

"As just another navel," Frank said.

She stared at him icily, and then said, "Paul thought of me as a very exciting individual. *That's* how he filled a need in my life. And that's why I'll always be grateful to him."

"Fine," Frank said, and put on his jacket. "Are you ready?"

"Not quite," Millie said. "Which isn't to say that I didn't enjoy the other aspect as well."

"Millie," he said, "you have said it all, you have really said it all. Now let's just get out of here, okay?"

"I'm not dressed yet," she said, and sat and put on her pumps, and then walked to the dresser and rummaged in her bag for her lipstick. "Haven't *you* ever felt like going to bed with somebody?"

"I have," he said.

"Not Mae, I mean."

"Not Mae."

"Who?"

"Hope."

"Hope? The Head of Creation?"

"Yes."

"Hope!"

"That's right."

"That's disgusting," Millie said. "She's your *boss!*"

"She's also a beautiful redhead."

"And a Wasp besides," Millie said.

"She happens to be an atheist."

"Has Mae ever met her?"

"She has."

"Does she like her?"

"Not particularly."

"Good," Millie said, and capped the lipstick and dropped it into her bag. "I'm ready," she said.

"Let's go then."

"Let's go," she said, and started for the door, and then suddenly stopped, and turned back to look into the room.

"Got everything?" he asked.

She hesitated.

"What'd you leave?"

"Nothing, I guess," she said, and shook her head. At the door, she hesitated again, and then said, "Frank, there's just one thing I'd like to know. Why do you find Paul so threatening?"

"I do not find him in the least threatening," he said.

"Then why are you so angry?"

"I am not in the slightest bit angry," he said.

"I was stupid to tell you," she said, and shook her head again. "Michael's right. Stupid is stupid, that's all." She sighed, and then said, "Let's go."

"What do you mean, Michael's right?"

"He's right, that's all. He thinks I'm stupid, and I am."

"You are definitely not stupid," Frank said.

"Michael thinks so. Maybe that's because he's so smart."

"Has he ever actually *said* he thinks you're stupid?"

"Not in so many words. But what he does is I'll make a suggestion about something, you know, and he'll say, '*Thank you, Millicent,*' with just the proper inflection and tone, you know, to make me feel like an absolute moron. As far as he's concerned, if I keep my mouth shut and dress the girls properly and help him watch his damn calories, that's enough. Do you want to know something, Frank? I've known you for only four months, and I feel closer to you than I do to my own husband. What do you think of that?"

He did not answer.

"Well, it's true," she said. "Which is why I can't understand why you feel threatened about something that happened . . ."

"I don't feel threatened."

"You *all* feel threatened," she said. "If I'd ever told Michael about even *posing* for Paul, he'd probably have hit me or something."

"What do you mean? Are you trying to tell me he beats you?"

"Don't be silly, he's Jewish."

"So was Louis Lepke," Frank said.

"Yes, but he got mixed up with a lot of Italians. Now don't get offended."

"I'm *not* offended."

"You *do* find it threatening, don't you?"

"No, I don't find it threatening," he said. "In fact, I find it lovely. In fact I find it delightful that you picked up a belly-button sculptor, and posed for him, and went to bed with him, and can still remember the exact date, October eighth . . ."

"Sixth," she corrected.

"Yes, I find that all perfectly damn *won*derful," he said, his voice rising. "I thought we were, for Christ's sake, supposed to be in *love* with each other! I thought we were supposed to be able to trust each other and . . ."

There was a sudden hammering on the wall opposite the bed. Frank stopped mid-sentence, and turned to look at the wall.

"The black Cadillac," Millie whispered.

There was more hammering now, louder this time.

"Stop that banging!" Frank shouted, and it stopped immediately. "Fat bastard," he said, and Millie giggled. "Thinks he owns the place. Move the car, lower the television, bang, bang, bang with his goddamn fist!" He glared at the wall. Millie was still giggling. "Go ahead!" he shouted. "I dare you to hit that wall one more goddamn time!"

There was no further hammering. Frank turned from the wall. Millie had stopped giggling. She was watching him steadily.

"*Are* we supposed to be in love with each other?" she asked.

"That was my understanding," he said quietly.

"That was my understanding, too," she said. She walked to him, and turned her back to him, and lifted the hair from the nape of her neck. He reached for the zipper at the back of her dress, and gently lowered it.

3

It was October outside, but the drapes were drawn, and in the room it might have been any season. The bedclothes were rumpled, and a pillow was on the carpeted floor. Millie, in lavender tights and brassiere was applying lipstick at the mirror. In the bathroom, Frank was singing loudly. He sang badly off-key, and she could not recognize the tune.

"Frank?" she said.

"Mm?"

"Don't you think you should call her?"

Frank came out of the bathroom, a towel around his waist, his hair wet. He had been growing a mustache for the past month, and he wore it with supreme confidence.

"What, honey?" he said.

"Don't you think you should call Hope?"

"What for?"

"It's pretty late. She . . ."

"Hell with her," he said, and picked up his shorts and trousers, and went back into the bedroom again.

Millie put the cap on her lipstick, dropped it into the bag, and then picked up her hairbrush. Brushing out her hair, she said, "You still haven't told me why Mae closed the shop so suddenly?"

"I guess she just got tired of it," he said.

"Maybe she took a lover," Millie said.

"What?" Frank said, and came out of the bathroom in his shorts.

"I said maybe she . . ."

"I doubt that sincerely," Frank said.

"It's a possibility," Millie said, and shrugged.

"I doubt it."

"You forgot to say sincerely."

"I think she just got bored with selling antiques, that's all," he said, and stepped into his trousers and zipped up the fly.

"Probably the pitcher that did it," Millie said. "My returning the ironstone pitcher. Michael says that stores operating on a small volume . . ."

"Mae's shop wasn't Bloomingdale's," Frank said, "but I'm sure a refund on a pitcher that cost fifteen dollars . . ."

"Seventeen dollars."

". . . wouldn't drive her out of business. Anyway, why'd you return it?"

"I didn't like having a pitcher belonging to another woman."

"It didn't belong to her. The moment you bought it, it became yours."

"It still seemed like hers." Brushing her hair, evenly stroking it, she said, "Would you like to know why she sold the shop? I can tell you, if you'd like to know."

"Why'd she sell it?"

"Because of your trip last month."

"My trip?"

"Mmm. Your second honeymoon," Millie said.

"You mean the trip to Antigua?"

"Well, where *else* did you go last month?"

"That was not a second honeymoon," he said. "Have you seen my shirt? Where'd my shirt disappear to?"

"I meant to tell you, by the way, that September is the hurricane season down there. Why anyone would go to Antigua in September is beyond me."

Frank lifted the bedspread from one of the chairs; his shirt was not under it. "We had beautiful weather," he said.

"Then why didn't you come back with a tan? All you came back with was a mustache."

"I also came back with a tan. Now where the hell is that shirt?"

"Not a very good tan, Frank. Would you like to know why? Because it was a second honeymoon, that's why. It's a little difficult to get a tan when you're up in the room all day long."

"We were not up in the room all day long," he said, and got down on his knees and looked under the bed. "Now how did it get *there*?" he said, and reached under the bed.

"Then where were you?" Millie asked.

"In the water, most of the time."

"Suppose a shark had bitten off your leg?"

"There were no sharks," he said, and stood up, and shook out the shirt.

"A barracuda then. How could you have driven here to New Jersey with only one leg?"

"I'm back," he said, putting on the shirt, "and I still have both my legs, so obviously . . ."

"Yes, but you never once gave it a minute's thought, did you? When you were scuba diving down there."

"I was snorkeling."

"What's the difference?"

"Snorkeling is recreational. That's the only reason I do it. For recreation."

"Why'd you have to go all the way to Antigua to do it?"

"Mae wanted to go to Antigua."

"So naturally, you went. Never mind me."

"Millie, I was only gone for a lousy three weeks!"

"Twenty-four days, if we choose to be precise. And you never called me once," she said, and threw the hairbrush into her bag, and crossed the room to the clothes rack, and took her blouse from a wire hanger.

"I couldn't phone," he said. "We were on the beach most of the day."

"Didn't you ever come off the beach?" Millie asked, and put on the blouse.

"We came off the beach, yes," Frank said. "But there wasn't a phone in the room. The only phone was in the lobby."

"Then why didn't you go up to the lobby and call from there?" she said, buttoning the blouse.

"Because it took hours to get through to the States."

"Oh, then you *did* call the States," she said, and turned to face him.

"Yes, I called the office once to see how the new campaign was shaping up."

"But you couldn't call me," she said.

"Millie, this was a very isolated little hotel, with these small cottages on the beach, and . . ."

"Honeymoon cottages," she said.

"Suppose Mae had seen me making a phone call?"

"You could have told her you were calling the office to check on your brilliant campaign."

"I'd already called the office, and they'd told me my brilliant campaign was shaping up fine."

"I still think you could have called me, Frank. If you hadn't been so busy growing a mustache . . ."

"A man isn't busy growing a mustache. It grows all by itself."

"Yes, and there's a very definite connection, too. Between a mustache and sexuality."

"Take Michael, for example."

"Don't change the subject. If you hadn't been so involved with Mae, if you hadn't been enjoying your second honeymoon so much . . ."

"Millie, it was *not* . . ."

"Which, of course, is why she sold the damn shop ten minutes after you got back. She simply didn't need it anymore. She found her husband again."

"Millie, it was not a second honeymoon. And I don't think the Antigua trip was the reason Mae sold the shop. And I would have called you if it was at all possible, but it wasn't. Would you hand me my tie, please?"

"I still think you could have called," Millie said, and handed him the tie, and then said, "I went to bed with Paul while you were gone."

"What!" he said, dropping the tie. "Why the hell did you do that?"

"Oh, for recreation," she said airily.

He stared at her silently, and then picked up the tie, and turned to the mirror.

"I figured . . ."

"I'm not interested," he said.

"That's exactly what I figured. A man goes away for three weeks . . ."

"Twenty-four days."

"Yes, and doesn't even call the woman he professes to love so madly . . ."

"Yes, so the woman runs back to a two-bit sculptor she used to *screw* every Tuesday!" Frank shouted.

"Right!" she shouted back, and suddenly there was a hammering on the wall.

"Oh, *hell!*" Frank said. The hammering stopped. "You know what he does in there?" he asked Millie. "He's not at all interested in that frumpy little blonde he brings here every week. All he does is sit in there and wait for us to raise our voices so he can jump up on the bed and bang on the wall. You *hear* that, you fat bastard?" he shouted. The man next door immediately hammered on the wall again. Frank went to the wall and began banging on it himself. The hammering on the other side stopped at once. Satisfied, he went back to the mirror and began knotting his tie.

"It was awful with Paul," Millie said.

"Good."

"Do you know what he's into these days? Sculpting, I mean."

"Nipples, I would imagine," Frank said.

"Ears. His whole studio is full of these giant-sized ears."

"Let me know when he gets to the good part, will you?"

"These huge ears all over the place." She shook her head in wonder. "All the while we were making love, I had the feeling somebody was listening to us." She went to the clothes rack, took down her skirt, and stepped into it. "I don't know why I went there," she said. "Maybe I sensed what was about to happen."

The telephone rang. Frank went to it instantly, and picked up the receiver. "Hello?" he said. "Yes, this is Mr. McIntyre. Really?" he said. "Banging on the wall? No, I don't think so. Just a minute, please." He turned to Millie, and said, "Darling, were you banging on the wall?" Then, into the phone again, he said, "No, nobody here was banging on the wall. Maybe it's the plumbing. Have you had the plumbing checked lately? Well, that's what I would suggest. Goodbye." He hung up, went to the dresser again, scooped his change, keys, and wallet off the top of it, and put them into his pockets.

"Frank?" she said. "Do you think we're finished?"

"No," he said immediately.

"I think we are," she said.

"Millie," he said, "let's get a couple of things straight, okay?"

"Okay."

199

"Number one, the trip to Antigua was not a second honey-moon. The situation between Mae and me has not changed an iota."

"What's the situation?"

"Mae and I *love* each other, but we are not *in* love with each other."

"You're comfortable with each other, right?"

"Right."

"Just a pair of comfortable old bedroom slippers tucked under the bed, right?"

"Right."

"Then why didn't you come back with a tan?" Millie said.

"Millie, let's get a couple of things straight, okay?" he said.

"We already got the first thing straight," she said, "so what's the second thing?"

"The second thing is that I still feel the same way about you. I'll always feel the same way about you, in fact."

"That's very nice," she said. "How do you feel about me?"

"I'm in love with you."

"But you don't love me."

"It's the same thing, Millie. Being in love with someone and loving someone . . ."

"How come with me it's the *same* thing, but with Mae it's a totally *different* thing? A minute ago you were a pair of old bedroom slippers . . ."

"I've known Mae for twenty-two years," he said. "I've only known you for ten months."

"And twelve days."

"Who's counting?" Frank said.

"*I* am, damn it!" Millie said.

"I don't think you understand what I'm trying to . . ."

"I understand fine," Millie said, and walked to where she'd left her pumps near one of the easy chairs. Sitting, she said, "Mae's your wife, and I'm your Tuesday afternoon roll-in-the-hay."

"Millie, that isn't . . ."

"Look, Frank, you're Italian and you've got all these romantic notions about being in love, but actually I think what you really enjoy most about coming here is the idea that I'm some kind of whore or something."

"I have never thought of you as . . ."

"Have you ever thought of me as a *mother*, Frank?"

"A mother!"

"I have two children, you know. I have two adorable little girls that *I* made. *Me*. Personally."

"With a little help from Michael, I assume."

"What would you do if, with a little help from Michael, I got pregnant again? I can just imagine how *that* would sit with you. Big fat belly marching in here every week, what would *that* do to the image of the bimbo on the Via Margherita?"

"The what?"

"The Via Margherita. That's where Italian men keep their little pastries."

"I'm not an Italian man, I'm an American man."

"Right, you're Mr. McIntyre, right?"

"I'm Mr. Di Santangelo, but I don't have a bimbo on the Via Margherita, wherever the hell that may be. As a matter of fact, I don't have a bimbo *anywhere*."

"As a matter of fact, you have one right here in New Jersey," Millie said. She reached down for one of her pumps, and without looking up at him, slipped her foot into it and said, "Michael wants to have another baby." She put on the other shoe and only then looked up at him. "What should I do?" she asked.

"That's up to you and Michael, isn't it?"

"It's also up to you," she said.

"Why don't we arrange a meeting then? Three of us can discuss it, decide what we . . ."

"Do *you* want me to have a baby, Frank?"

"No," he said flatly.

"Why not?"

"I hate babies," he said.

"It wouldn't be your baby."

"I hate *anybody's* babies."

"How can a man who hates babies write a popcorn commercial with two little kids . . . ?"

"That has nothing to do with it. I hate popcorn, too."

"You'd never even *see* this baby," Millie said. "All I'm trying to find out is whether you like the idea of me *having* one, that's all."

"No, I don't like the idea."

"Why not?"

"I don't like the idea of your having another man's baby."

"Another man? He's my husband!"

"Anyway, what is this, a conspiracy or something? Is everybody in the whole *world* having a baby all of a sudden?"

"What?"

"Nothing," he said, and went immediately to the clothes rack, and took his jacket from its hanger.

"*Who's* having a baby all of a sudden?" she asked.

"Millions of women," Frank said. "Chinese women are having them right in the fields. As they plant the rice seedlings, they . . ."

"Never mind Chinese women, how many *American* women are having babies that you know of?"

"Right this minute, do you mean?"

"No, I mean nine months from last month when you and Mae were in Antigua working so hard on your suntans."

"Mae, do you mean?"

202

"Is Mae pregnant?"

"Who? Mae?"

"Mae. *Is* she?"

"Yes," he said.

"Which is why she ran out instantly to sell her little shop, right?"

"I don't know why . . ."

"Probably at Bloomingdale's this very minute, picking out a bassinette."

"Millie . . ."

"Knitting little booties in her spare time," she said, her voice rising, "papering the guest room with pictures of funny little animals! How could you *do* this to me, Frank?"

"To *you?*"

"Yes, to *me!*" she shouted. "Who the hell do you think?"

"Please lower your voice," he said. "If he bangs on the wall one more time, he'll put a hole through it."

Whispering, Millie said, "Didn't you once consider the possibility that . . ."

"What? Now I can't hear you at all."

In her normal speaking voice, but enunciating each and every word clearly and distinctly, Millie said, "Didn't you once consider the possibility that the thought of Mae having a baby might prove distressing to your lady friend on the Via Margherita?"

"Oh, cut it out with that Via Margherita stuff."

"Didn't you?"

"Do you know what you sound like, Millie?"

"What do I sound like?"

"A jealous wife."

"I suppose I do," she said. "But I'm *not* your wife, am I? I'm no more your wife than she is." She gestured toward the wall and the room next door. "To *him,* I mean. The man who bangs on the wall."

"Millie, I don't think you need equate us with a frumpy blonde and a fat old man."

"To *him*, she isn't a frumpy blonde," Millie said. "To him, she's all perfume and lace, the girl on the Via Margherita. All right to open these drapes now?" she asked.

"Sure," he said.

She pulled the drapes back on their rod. Sunlight splashed into the room. The day outside was clear and bright, the courtyard lined with the brilliant reds and oranges of autumn. She turned from the window, the sunlight behind her.

Frank looked at his watch. "We'd better get going," he said. "Hope's got a meeting scheduled for . . ."

"Just a few minutes more, Frank," she said. "I gave you plenty of time on the train, when we were just beginning. I think you can give me a few minutes now . . . when we're about to end."

"End?"

"Yes, what do you think we're talking about here?"

"Not ending, Millie."

"No? Then what?"

"I don't know. But two people can't simply *end* something after ten months together." He looked at his watch again. "Millie, really, we've got to go now, really. We'll talk about it tomorrow, okay? I'll call you in the morning . . ."

The telephone rang.

He looked at the phone, and then he looked at his watch again. The phone kept ringing, but he made no move to answer it. Millie went to it, and lifted the receiver, and said, "Hello?" and then listened, and then said, "No, I'm sorry, Mr. McIntyre isn't here." Gently, she replaced the receiver on the cradle. "The manager," she said.

"What did he want?"

"I don't know. The television's off, and neither of us is yelling, and no one's banging on the wall." She shrugged. "Maybe he just felt lonely, Frank, and wanted to say hello." She went to him. "The way we did, Frank."

They looked at each other. It seemed for a moment as though they would move again into each other's arms. But Millie turned away, and went to the dresser and picked up her bag.

"I think I'll tell Michael okay," she said.

"I think you already have," he said.

"Maybe so," she said.

She went to the door and threw back the slip bolt and opened the door wide. He came to her, and they paused before stepping out into the sunshine, and turned, and stared back into the room. Then, gently, he took her hand, and together they left the room, closing the door behind them.

The Intruder

David's mother took him with her to Paris the day after his eighth birthday, which was July the Fourth.

Paris was all lights. It was the best time he ever had in his life. Even if the business with the doorbell hadn't happened when they got back from Paris, he *still* would think of Paris as the best time he ever had. They were staying at a very nice hotel called the Raphäel on Avenue Kléber. Hardly anyone spoke English at the Raphäel because it was a very French hotel, and English was grating on the ears. David learned a lot there. He learned, for example, that when someone asked *"Quel temps fait-il?"* you did not always answer, *"Il fait beau,"* the way they did in Miss Canaday's class even if it was snowing. He told this to Miss Canaday when they got back from Paris, and she said, "David, I like to think of the weather as being *toujours beau, toujours beau.*" He used to speak to the concierge on the phone every morning. He would say, *"Bonjour, monsieur, quel temps fait-il, s'il vous plait?"* And the concierge would usually answer in a very solemn voice, *"Il pleut, mon petit monsieur."*

It rained a lot while they were in Paris.

He and his mother had a suite at the Raphäel, two bedrooms and a sort of living room with windows that opened onto a nice stone balcony. David used to go out on the balcony and stand with the pigeons when it wasn't raining. The reason they had a suite was that his mother was a buyer for a department store on Fifth Avenue, and they sent her over each year, sometimes twice a year, to study all the new fashions. What it amounted to was that the *store* was paying for the suite. David's father was account executive and vice-president of an advertising agency that had thirty-nine vice-presidents. The reason he did not go to Paris that summer was that he had to stay home in New York to make sure one of his accounts did not cancel. So David went instead, to keep her company. He wrote to his father every day they were in Paris.

Escargots were little snails, but they didn't really look like snails except for the shell, and they didn't taste like them at all. They tasted like garlic. David and his mother ate a lot of *escargots* in Paris. In fact, they ate a lot of everything in Paris. They used to spend most of their time eating. What they would do, his mother would leave a call with the desk for eight o'clock in the morning. The phone would ring, and David would jump out of bed and run into his mother's bedroom and ask her if he could talk to the concierge for a moment. *"Bonjour, monsieur,"* he would say. *"Quel temps fait-il, s'il vous plait?"* and the concierge would tell him what kind of day it was and then he would hand the phone back to his mother and lie in her arms while she ordered breakfast. Every morning, they had either melon or orange juice, and then croissants and coffee for his mother, and croissants and hot chocolate for David. The chocolate was very good; the room waiter told them it came from Switzerland. They would eat at a little table just inside the big windows that opened onto the stone balcony. His mother used to wear a very puffy white nylon robe over her nightgown. One morning a man in the building opposite waved at her and winked.

The salon showings used to start at ten on some mornings, it all depended, sometimes they were later. Some days there were no showings at all, and some days they would go to the showing at ten and then have lunch and go to another one at two, and then another one in the afternoon around cocktail time. His mother was a pretty important buyer, so she knew all the designers and the models and they used to go back and everybody would make a fuss over David. He didn't mind being kissed by the models, who all smelled very nice. Once, when he went back before a showing, two of the models were still in their brassieres. One of them said something in French (she said it very fast, not at all like Miss Canaday or the concierge) and the other models started laughing, and his mother laughed too and ran her hand over his head. He didn't know what was so funny; he'd seen a *hundred* brassieres in his lifetime.

For lunch they used to like the cheese place best; it was called Androuet, and it had about eight hundred cheeses you could choose from. Every now and then, they would go to a ritzy place on the Left Bank, but that was only when his mother was trying very hard to impress a designer, and then he was supposed to just keep his mouth shut and not say anything, just eat. They had the most fun when they were alone together. One night, on top of the Eiffel Tower, his mother ordered red wine for him. She held up her glass in a toast, and he clinked his glass against hers and saw that she was crying.

"What is it?" he said.

"Nothing," she answered. "Taste your wine, David. It's really lovely."

"No, what is it?" he insisted.

"I miss Daddy," she said.

The next day, he sent his father a card from Notre Dame. On the back he wrote, as a little joke, "Can you find Quasimodo?" He had read that in the spring in Classics Illustrated. His father wrote back and in his letter he sent a thing that he'd had one of his art directors work up. What it was, was a composite from the monster magazines, with very good type across the top saying, "Yes, *this* is Quasimodo! But where oh where is DAVID?"

The fourteenth of July, Bastille Day, fell on a Sunday and that was lucky to begin with because it meant there were no showings to attend. David woke up at eight o'clock, and then slept for another two hours in his mother's bed and then they had breakfast and she said, "David, how would you like to take a car and go out into the country for a picnic?" So that's what they did. They hired a car, and they drove out down by the Loire where all the French castles were, and they stopped by the river and had sausage and bread and cheese and red wine (His mother said it was okay for him to drink all the wine he wanted while they were in France) and they drove back to Paris at about seven in the evening, getting caught in the traffic around the Étoile. Later they stood on their little stone balcony and he held his mother's hand and they watched the fireworks exploding over the rooftops. He didn't think he would forget those fireworks as long as he lived.

The next week, they were back in New York.

The week after that, the doorbell started.

The building they lived in was on Park Avenue, and there were two apartments on their floor—their own and Mrs. Shavinsky's, who was an old lady in her seventies and very mean. Mrs. Shavinsky was the type who always said to David as he came off the elevator, "Wipe the mud off your shoes, young man," as though it were possible to get mud on your shoes in the city of New York. Mrs. Shavinsky wore hats and gloves all of the time, because she was originally from San Francisco. She was constantly telling the elevator operator, as if he cared, that in San Francisco the ladies all wore hats and gloves. Even though there were only those two apartments on the floor, there were four doors in the hallway because each apartment had two doors, one for people and the other for service. Their own main entrance door was on one side of the hall, and Mrs. Shavinsky's was on the other side. The two service doors were in a sort of alcove opposite the elevator. They hardly ever saw Mrs. Shavinsky (Except she always managed to be there when David got off the elevator, to tell him about his muddy shoes) until the business with the doorbell started, and then they practically lived in each others' apartments.

The first time the doorbell rang, it was two o'clock in the morning on July 29th, which was a Monday.

David's bedroom was right behind his mother's and when the doorbell rang, he sat up in bed thinking it was the telephone. In fact, he could hear his mother lifting the phone from the receiver alongside her bed, since she thought it was the phone, too. She said, "Hello," and then the ringing came again, from the front door, and there was a short puzzled silence. His mother put the phone back on its cradle and whispered, "Fred, you'd better get up."

"What?" David's father said.

"There's someone at the door."

"What?" he said again.

"There's someone at the door."

His father must have looked at the clock alongside the bed because David heard him whisper, "Don't be ridiculous, Lo. It's two o'clock in the morning." His mother's name was Lois, but everybody called her Lo except David's grandmother who called her Lois Ann, which was her full name.

"Someone just rang the doorbell," his mother said.

"I didn't hear anything," his father said.

"Fred, please see who it is, won't you?"

"All right, but I'm telling you I didn't hear anything."

The doorbell rang again at just that moment. In the next

bedroom, there was a sudden sharp silence. From the other end of the apartment, where the housekeeper slept, David heard her yelling, "Mister Ravitch, there is somebody at the door."

"I hear it, Helga, thank you," my father called, and then a light snapped on, and David heard him swearing as he got out of bed. David went to the doorway of his room just as his father passed by in his pajamas.

"What is it?" David whispered.

"Someone at the door," he said. "Go back to bed."

His father walked through the long corridor leading to the front door, stubbing his toe on something in the dark and mumbling about it, and then turning on the light in the entrance foyer.

"Who's there?" he said to the closed door.

Nobody answered.

"Is someone there?" he asked.

Again, there was no answer. From where David was standing at the end of the long hall, he heard his father sigh, and then heard the lock on the door being turned, and the door being opened. There was a moment's hesitation, and then his father closed the door again, and locked it, and began walking back to his bedroom.

"Who was it?" David asked.

"Nobody," his father answered. "Go back to sleep."

That was the first time with the doorbell.

The second time was two nights later, on a Wednesday, and also in the early morning, though not two o'clock. David must have been sleeping very soundly because he didn't even hear the doorbell ringing. The thing that woke him up was his mother's voice saying something to his father as he ran down the corridor to the front door. Helga had come out of her room and was standing in her pyjamas watching his father as he went to the door and unlocked it. David's mother was wearing the same white nylon puffy robe she used to wear when they were in Paris.

"Did they ring the doorbell again?" David asked her.

"Yes," she said, and just then his father opened the door.

"Who is it?" David's mother asked.

"There's no one here, Lo."

"But I heard the bell, didn't you?"

"Yes, I heard it."

"I heard it, too, Mister Ravitch," Helga said.

"I wonder," David's father said.

"What do you think?"

"Maybe someone rang it by mistake."

"Monday night, too."

"It's possible."

"And left without waiting for the door to open?"

"Maybe he was embarrassed. Maybe he realized his mistake and . . ."

"I don't know," David's mother said, and shrugged. "It all seems very peculiar." She turned to David and cupped his chin in her hand. "David, I want you to go back to bed. You look very sleepy."

"I'm not sleepy at all. We used to stay up much later than this in Paris."

"How you gonna keep 'em down on the farm?" his father said, and both his mother and Helga laughed. "Listen, Lo, I'd like to check this with the elevator operator."

"That's a good idea. Come, David, bed."

"Can't I just stay to see who it was?" David asked.

"There's probably some very simple explanation," his mother said.

The elevator operator was a man David had never seen before, about fifty years old, but with a hearing aid. David

knew most of the elevator men in the building, but he supposed this one always had the shift late at night, which is why
he'd never seen him before this. The man told his father his
name was Oscar, and asked him what the trouble was.

"Someone just rang our doorbell."

"Yes?"

"Yes. Did you take anyone up to our floor just now?"

"No, sir. Not since I came on, sir."

"And when was that?"

"I came on at midnight, sir."

"And you didn't take anyone up to the eleventh floor all
night?"

"No, sir."

"What is it?" David heard a voice ask, and he looked past
his father to the opposite end of the hallway where Mrs.
Shavinsky had opened her door and was looking out. "What's
all the noise about?" she said. "Do you realize what time it
is?" She was wearing a big flannel nightgown with red roses
strewn all over it, printed ones. Her hair was in curlers.

"I'm terribly sorry, Mrs. Shavinsky," David's father said.
"We didn't mean to awaken you."

"Yes, well you did," Mrs. Shavinsky said, as pleasant as
always. "What's going on?"

"Someone rang our bell," his mother said.

"Good morning, Mrs. Shavinsky," David said.

"Good morning, young man," Mrs. Shavinsky said. "It is
far past your bedtime."

"I know," David said. "We're up to catch the bell ringer."

"Did you say someone rang your bell?" Mrs. Shavinsky
asked, ignoring David and looking up at his mother.

"Yes. Monday night, and now again."

"Well, who was it?" Mrs. Shavinsky asked.

"That's what we don't know," David said. "That's why

we're all here in the hallway."

"It was probably some D-R-U-N-K," Mrs. Shavinsky said.

"No, it wasn't no drunk, ma'am," Oscar said. "I didn't take nobody up here."

"Then why would anyone want to ring your bell at three-thirty in the morning?" Mrs. Shavinsky asked, and no one could answer her.

Later, David's mother kissed his cheeks and the tip of his nose and his forehead and hugged him tight and tucked him in.

Mrs. Shavinsky told him about her demitasse cups the next day, and when he hinted that he didn't believe such a collection existed, she asked him to wipe off his feet and come into the apartment. The apartment smelled of emptiness, the way a lot of apartments smell when there is only one person living in them. She had her demitasse collection in a china closet in the dining room. David told her it must be fun to have a big dining room table like the one she had, and then he looked at her demitasse collection, which was really quite nice. She had about thirty-seven cups, he guessed. Four of them had gold insides. She said they were very valuable.

"How much do they cost?" he asked her.

"You should never ask anyone that," she said.

"Why not?"

"Because it is impolite."

"But you told me they were valuable, Mrs. Shavinsky."

"They are," she said.

"Then why is it impolite to ask how much they cost?"

"It's not only impolite," she said, "it's impertinent as well."

"I'm sorry, Mrs. Shavinsky," he said.

"They cost several thousand dollars," she said. Her voice lowered. "Do you think the bell ringer is after them?" she asked.

"After what, ma'am?" he said.

"After my demitasse cups?"

"I don't think so, ma'am," he said.

"Then why would he ring your bell at three-thirty in the morning?"

"I don't know, Mrs. Shavinsky, but it seems to me if he was after *your* cups he would ring *your* bell. Maybe he's after *our* cups."

"Do you have a valuable collection of demitasse cups?" Mrs. Shavinsky asked.

"No, ma'am."

"Then how, would you please tell me, could he be after *your* demitasse cups, if you do not even *own* demitasse cups?"

"I meant our coffee cups. In the kitchen."

"Why would he want those?" Mrs. Shavinsky asked.

"Maybe he likes big cups of coffee," David suggested, and shrugged.

Mrs. Shavinsky wasn't sure whether or not he was making fun of her, which he wasn't, so she kicked him out.

That night, the doorbell rang at one o'clock in the morning.

David was asleep, but his father was still awake and watching the news final on television. The doorbell rang and David's father leaped out of bed at the first ring and ran down the long corridor to the front door and pulled open the door without saying a word. There was no one there.

"Damn it!" he yelled, and woke up the whole house.

"What is it?" David's mother called.

"Damn it, there's no one here," his father said.

"What is it, Mister Ravitch?" Helga called from her bed-room.

"Oh, go to sleep, Helga," his father said.

David was awake by this time, but he knew better than to ask his father any silly questions. He just lay in bed watching the ceiling and realizing the doorbell had rung again, and his father had gone to answer it again, and again there was no one there. Through the wall separating his bedroom from his mother's, he heard his father going into the room and getting into bed, and then he heard his mother whisper, "Don't be upset."

"I *am* upset," his father whispered back.

"It's probably just someone's idea of a joke."

"Some joke."

"He'll grow tired of it."

"He's got Helga scared out of her wits."

"She'll survive."

"How the hell does he disappear so quickly?" his father whispered.

"I don't know. Try to get some sleep, darling."

"Mmm," his father said.

"There."

"Mmmmm."

While David was investigating the hallway the next day, Mrs. Shavinsky's black housekeeper came out with the gar-bage. Her name was Mary Vincent, but David was not sure whether Vincent was her last name or just part of her first name, the way "Ann" was part of his mother's "Lois Ann." What he was doing as Mary Vincent came out with the gar-bage was pacing off the number of steps from the stairway in the service alcove to the front doorbell.

"What are you doing, David?" Mary Vincent said.

"There are fifteen paces," he said. "How long do you think it would take to run fifteen paces from our door back to those steps?"

"I don't know. How long would it take?"

"Well, I don't know, Mary Vincent. But whoever is ringing the doorbell manages to disappear before we can open the door. If he doesn't use the elevator, he *must* use the steps, don't you think?"

"Unless this here's an inside job," Mary Vincent said.

"What does that mean? An inside job?"

"Somebody in the apartment."

"You mean somebody in *our* apartment?"

"Could be," Mary Vincent said, and shrugged.

"Well, that would mean just my family." David paused. "Or Helga."

"I didn't say nothing," Mary Vincent said.

"Why would Helga want to ring the doorbell in the middle of the night?"

"I didn't say nothing," Mary Vincent said again. "All I know is she was mighty angry while your mother and you was away in France and she had to stay here and work, anyway, without no kind of a vacation."

"But she is getting a vacation, Mary Vincent. Mother asked her if she wanted to take her vacation when we went away or in August sometime, and Helga said August."

"That ain't what she told me right here in this hallway, David."

"When was this?"

"When we was putting out the garbage."

"I mean *when*."

"When you and your mother was in France."

"Well, that sure sounds mighty strange to me," David said.

"It sure sounds mighty strange to me, too," Mary Vincent said, "that somebody would be ringing your doorbell in the middle of the night."

"I don't even see how Helga could manage it," David said.

"Her bedroom is right close to the service entrance, ain't it?"

"Yes, but . . ."

"Then what's to stop her getting out of bed, opening the back door, ringing the front doorbell, and then coming in again through the back door and right into her bed? What's to stop her, David?"

"Nothing, I guess. Only . . ."

"Only what?"

"Only why would she want to?"

"Spite, David. There's people in this world who do things only because it brings misery to others. Spite," Mary Vincent said, "plain and simple spite. If I was you, David, I would keep my eye on her." Mary Vincent laughed, and then said, "In fact, I would keep *both* my eyes on her."

David started keeping both his eyes on her that very night because the doorbell rang at exactly two-thirteen a.m. David had a watch that was waterproof and shock resistant which his grandfather gave him when he was seven years old. When he heard the doorbell ring, he jumped up in bed and turned on the light and looked at the watch, and it was two-thirteen A.M.

"There it is again," he heard his father say in the next room, but David was listening for sounds coming from the back door. He didn't hear anything. The doorbell rang again.

"Let him ring," his father said. "If he thinks I'm getting out of bed every night, he's crazy."

The doorbell rang again. David still hadn't heard a sound from Helga's room. He kept looking at the sweep hand of his watch. It was now two-fifteen.

"Are you just going to let it ring?" his mother whispered.

"Yep," his father said.

"All night?"

"If he *wants* to ring the damn thing all night, then I'll *let* him ring it all night."

"He'll wake up Mrs. Shavinsky."

"The hell with Mrs. Shavinsky."

"He'll wake up the whole building."

"Who cares?" David's father said, and his mother giggled, and the doorbell continued ringing. David still hadn't heard a peep from Helga.

"Mom?" he said.

"David? Are you awake?"

"Yes. Do you want me to see who's at the door?"

"You stay right in your bed," his father said.

"Someone's ringing the doorbell," David said.

"I hear it."

"Shouldn't we see who it is?"

"We know who it is. It's some nut who's got nothing better to do."

"Mom?"

"You heard your father."

"Are we just gonna let him ring the damn thing all night?" David asked.

"What?" his father said.

"Are we gonna let him ring the damn thing all . . . ?"

"I heard you the first time," his father said.

"Well, are we?"

"If he wants to. Go to sleep. He'll get tired soon enough."

The bell ringer didn't get tired soon enough. David kept watching the red sweep hand on his wristwatch; the bell ringer didn't get tired until two forty-seven A.M., which was a half-hour after he had first begun. In all that time, Helga hadn't said a word. It was almost as if she wasn't even in the house.

For the next two weeks, the doorbell rang almost every night at two in the morning or a little after. David's father let it ring each time, without getting out of bed to answer the door. Once, while the doorbell was ringing, David sneaked out of bed and went to the other end of the apartment, near the service entrance, to see if Helga was in her room. But the door to her bedroom was closed, and he couldn't tell whether she was there or not. The doorbell woke the entire family each time, but they simply pretended it wasn't ringing. Each time, David's mother would come into his bedroom after the doorbell had been ringing a while, to see if it had awakened him.

"David?" she would whisper.

"Yes, Mom."

"Are you awake?"

"Yes, Mom."

"You poor darling," she would say, and then she would sit on the edge of his bed and put her hand on his forehead, the way she would sometimes do when she thought he had a fever, though he certainly didn't have any fever. The doorbell would continue ringing and his mother would sit in her nightgown in the dark, her hand cool on his head. In a little while, she would kiss his closed eyes, and he would drift off to sleep, not knowing when she left him, not knowing when the doorbell stopped ringing.

This went on for two weeks. By the end of that time, David was getting used to waking up at two in the morning and getting used to his mother's visits each time the doorbell rang. He was beginning to think, though, that once Helga left on her vacation, the doorbell ringing would stop. He was beginning to think that Mary Vincent was right, that Helga was ringing the bell just out of spite, just to cause misery for others. But on August the twelfth, Helga went off, and that night at two o'clock the doorbell rang. It couldn't have been Helga because she had taken a plane that morning at Kennedy Airport, bound for Copenhagen where her parents lived.

The next day, David's father called the police.

It was David's guess that his father had suspected Helga, too, because he told the two detectives right away that it *couldn't* have been the housekeeper since she was in Denmark. That explained why he hadn't called the police up to now; he *had* thought it was Helga and had expected her to quit ringing the bell after a while. The two detectives didn't look anything like television policemen at all. One of them looked like Mr. Harriman who ran the candy store on Madison Avenue, and the other looked like Uncle Martin, David's father's brother. Mr. Harriman did most of the talking.

"When *did* your housekeeper leave?" he asked David's father.

"Yesterday morning."

"And you say the doorbell rang again last night?"

"Yes, it did."

"Who else lives on this floor?" Mr. Harriman asked.

"Mrs. Shavinsky and her housekeeper."

"Her name is Mary Vincent," David said.

"Thank you, son," Mr. Harriman said. "Would either Mrs. Shavinsky or her housekeeper have any reason to want to annoy you?"

"I don't think so," David's father said.

"He may be after Mrs. Shavinsky's demitasse cups," David said.

221

"What was that, son?" the one who looked like Uncle Martin asked.

"Mrs. Shavinsky's demitasse cups. They're worth several thousand dollars."

"If the intruder wanted *her* cups," Uncle Martin said, "why would he ring *your* doorbell?"

"That's just what I said to Mrs. Shavinsky."

"Is there anything you can do about this?" David's father asked the detectives. "Can you leave a man here?"

"Well, that'd be a little difficult, sir," Mr. Harriman said. "We're always short-handed, but especially in the summertime. I think you can understand . . ."

"Yes, but . . ."

"What we *can* do, of course, is to dust the hallway and the doorbell for fingerprints."

"Will that help?"

"If the intruder left any prints, why yes, it could help a great deal."

"And if he didn't leave any prints? If, for example, he was wearing gloves?"

"Why, then it wouldn't help at all, would it?"

"No, it wouldn't," David said.

"Mmm," Mr. Harriman said, and smiled at David the way some grownups smiled at him when they meant Shut up, kid.

"Well, if you can't leave a man here," his father said, "and if dusting or whatever you call it doesn't come up with any fingerprints, well . . . well, what are we supposed to do? Just let this person keep on ringing our doorbell forever?"

"I suppose you could spend a night sleeping in a chair near the door," Mr. Harriman said. "That might help."

"How?"

"You could open the door as soon as the bell rang."

"We never know when it's going to ring," David's father

said, "or even *if* it'll ring at all. There's no pattern to it."

"Well, perhaps you could spend a few nights sleeping by the door."

"I could spend a few *weeks* sleeping by the door," David's father said. "Or maybe even a few *months*."

"Well," Mr. Harriman said.

"Well," David's father said, and everybody was quiet.

"Mrs. Shavinsky thinks it's some drunk," David said.

"It might be, son," Uncle Martin said.

"He doesn't use the elevator."

"He probably comes up the service steps," Mr. Harriman said. "We'll talk to the elevator operators and ask them to keep an eye open. Though, you know, there's the possibility he comes down from the roof. I'll check and see if there's a lock on the roof door."

"Why would anyone be doing this?" David's father asked.

"The world is full of nuts," Mr. Harriman said. "This is something like calling up a stranger on the telephone, only this guy uses your doorbell."

"But how long will he continue bothering us?"

"Who knows?" Mr. Harriman said. "It can go on forever, or he can get tired next week. Who knows?"

"Well," David's father said.

"Well," Mr. Harriman said, and that was that.

That night, David's father slept on a blanket in the entrance hall, and the doorbell didn't ring. The next night, he slept in the bedroom, and the doorbell rang at two o'clock. The night after that, he slept in the bedroom again, but this time the doorbell didn't ring. At breakfast the next morning, he told David's mother there was no way to figure this damn thing out, but that night he slept just inside the entrance door again. David woke up with a nightmare at about one o'clock, and went into his mother's bedroom. He climbed into bed with her, and she held him in her arms and said, "What is it, darling?"

"I'm afraid," David said.

"Of what?"

"That he'll get Daddy."

"No one's going to get Daddy."

"Suppose Daddy opens the door, and he's standing there? Suppose he kills Daddy?"

"No one's going to kill Daddy. Daddy is very strong."

"Suppose. What would we do?"

"Don't worry about it. Nothing's going to happen to Daddy."

"I don't want anything to happen to Daddy."

She put him back in his own bed in a little while and he lay there and looked at his watch and wondered if the doorbell would ring that night. He was just falling asleep again when it went off. It went off with a long loud ring, and then a short sharp ring but by that time his father was on his feet, making a lot of noise and unlocking the door as quickly as he could and throwing the door open and running into the hallway. David lay in bed with his heart beating faster and faster, waiting for his father to come back. At last, he heard him close the door, and walk through the apartment to the bedroom.

"Did you see him?" David's mother asked.

"No. But I heard a door slamming."

"What do you mean?"

"As I was unlocking *our* door, just after the ringing, I heard a door slamming someplace."

"Probably the door leading to the service steps."

"Yes," David's father said. He paused. "Where's David? Is he asleep?"

"Yes. He had a bad dream a little while ago."

"Poor kid. What shall I do, honey? Do you think our

friend'll be back tonight?"

"I doubt it," David's mother said, and paused. Her voice through the bedroom wall sounded very funny when she spoke again. "Come here," she said.

That night was the last time the doorbell rang.

What had happened, David supposed, was that his father had frightened the intruder away. He had jumped to his feet at the first long ring and was already unlocking the door by the time the intruder had pressed the bell the second time, which was probably why the second ring had been so short. The intruder must have realized a trap had been set, so he ran for the service steps just as David's father unlocked the door. That was probably the sound his father had heard, the service steps door slamming behind the intruder as he ran away. David's father didn't get to see anyone by the time he rushed into the hallway, but he certainly must have scared whoever had been ringing the bell because that was the end of it.

In September, school started and Helga came back from Denmark with stories about everything she had done. David began thinking about Paris again only because Helga had just come back from Europe. He would lie in bed each night and think about Paris, and one night he suddenly got the idea. He began laughing, and then stuck his head under the pillow because he didn't want them to hear him in the bedroom next door. He kept laughing, though, under the pillow. It seemed to him that it would be a great joke. In fact, the more he thought about it, the funnier it seemed. He took his head out from under the pillow and listened. The apartment was very quiet. He threw back the covers, got out of bed, tiptoed to the door of his mother's bedroom, and peeked in. She was lying with his father's arms around her, the blanket down over her hip, sort of. David covered his mouth with his hand because he felt another laugh coming on, and then tiptoed to Helga's bedroom. Her door was closed. He could hear her heavy breathing behind it.

He went to the service door of the apartment.

Carefully, he unlocked the door without making a sound, trying his best not to laugh. Then he opened the door and peeked out into the service alcove. There wasn't a soul in sight. It seemed to him that he could almost hear the whole building breathing in its sleep. He picked up a milk bottle from where it was standing outside the service door, and used it to prop the door open, and then went out of the service alcove and into the area just outside the elevators. He listened to make sure the elevator wasn't coming up, and then he went to the front door.

He almost laughed again.

He listened.

He couldn't hear anything.

This was going to be a good joke.

He reached out for the doorbell.

He rang the bell once. He heard it ringing inside the apartment. What he was going to do was run right back through the service entrance and then pretend he didn't know what had happened, if he could keep a straight face. He was only going to ring the bell that once, as a joke. But somehow, standing there in the hallway with the building asleep all around him, he rang the bell again. And then, he didn't know why, he rang it again. And again. As he rang it, he could remember the phone ringing each morning at eight o'clock in the Raphäel, and running into his mother's bedroom and climbing into her bed to ask the concierge *Quel temps fait-il?* He kept ringing the bell and ringing it. He didn't even hear the front door when it opened. His father was in pyjamas, his mother was standing beside him in her nightgown.

"David!" she said. "What are you doing?"

David started to smile, half-expecting his mother to laugh, or run her hand over his head. But instead she was looking down at him with a very puzzled look on her face, and he decided not to smile because he had the feeling something terrible was going to happen, though he didn't know what. He ducked his head.

"I'm sorry," he said.

They were all quiet for a few minutes, and then his father said, "Why'd you ring the doorbell, David?"

"I don't know."

"Well, you rang it, didn't you?" his father said.

"Yes."

"Well, why?"

"I thought it would be a good joke."

"A *what?*" his father said.

"A joke."

"A joke? After all we went through last month? You thought it would be a joke to . . ."

"I didn't do it last month."

"I know that, but how could you . . ."

"This is the first time I ever rang it."

"I know that," his father said, and the hallway went silent.

"Why did you do it, David?" his mother asked.

He looked up at her, wanting to explain, but a hundred crazy things popped into his head instead. He wanted to say, Mom, do you remember the little stone balcony with the big windows where we used to have our breakfast every morning, do you remember the man who waved and winked at you? He wanted to say, Mom, do you remember the models kissing me at the salons and those two with their brassieres that time, the way you laughed, do you remember? Do you remember driving out to have a picnic lunch by the Loire on Bastille

Day, and the wild traffic around the Étoile that night when we drove back into the city, and the fireworks later, do you remember holding my hand on the little stone balcony outside our room?

"Why," she said again. "Why did you ring the doorbell, David?"

"I don't know," he said.

"You *must* have had a reason, David," his mother insisted.

"No, Mom," he said. "I didn't have any reason."

She kept looking at him.

His father sighed then and said, "Well, it's very late. Let's all get back to bed."

On the Sidewalk, Bleeding

The boy lay bleeding in the rain. He was sixteen years old, and he wore a bright purple silk jacket, and the lettering across the back of the jacket read THE ROYALS. The boy's name was Andy, and the name was delicately scripted in black thread on the front of the jacket, just over the heart. *Andy.*

He had been stabbed ten minutes ago. The knife had entered just below his rib cage and had been drawn across his body violently, tearing a wide gap in his flesh. He lay on the sidewalk with the March rain drilling his jacket and drilling his body and washing away the blood that poured from his open wound. He had known excruciating pain when the knife had torn across his body, and then sudden comparative relief when the blade was pulled away. He had heard the voice saying, "That's for you, Royal!" and then the sound of footsteps hurrying into the rain, and then he had fallen to the sidewalk, clutching his stomach, trying to stop the flow of blood.

He tried to yell for help, but he had no voice. He did not know why his voice had deserted him, or why the rain had become so suddenly fierce, or why there was an open hole in his body from which his life ran redly, steadily. It was 11:30 P.M., but he did not know the time.

There was another thing he did not know.

He did not know he was dying. He lay on the sidewalk, bleeding, and he thought only *That was a fierce rumble. They got me good that time,* but he did not know he was dying. He would have been frightened had he known. In his ignorance, he lay bleeding and wishing he could cry out for help, but there was no voice in his throat. There was only the bubbling of blood from between his lips whenever he opened his mouth to speak. He lay silent in his pain, waiting, waiting for someone to find him.

He could hear the sound of automobile tires hushed on the muzzle of rainswept streets, far away at the other end of the long alley. He lay with his face pressed to the sidewalk, and he could see the splash of neon far away at the other end of the alley, tinting the pavement red and green, slickly brilliant in the rain.

He wondered if Laura would be angry.

He had left the jump to get a package of cigarettes. He had told her he would be back in a few minutes, and then he had gone downstairs and found the candy store closed. He knew that Alfredo's on the next block would be open until at least two, and he had started through the alley, and that was when he'd been ambushed. He could hear the faint sound of music now, coming from a long, long way off, and he wondered if Laura was dancing, wondered if she had missed him yet. Maybe she thought he wasn't coming back. Maybe she thought he'd cut out for good. Maybe she'd already left the jump and gone home. He thought of her face, the brown eyes and the jet-black hair, and thinking of her he forgot his pain a little, forgot that blood was rushing from his body. Someday he would marry Laura. Someday he would marry her, and they would have a lot of kids, and then they would get out of the neighborhood. They would move to a clean project in the Bronx, or maybe they would move to Staten Island. When they were married, when they had kids. . . .

He heard footsteps at the other end of the alley, and he lifted his cheek from the sidewalk and looked into the darkness and tried to cry out, but again there was only a soft hissing bubble of blood on his mouth.

The man came down the alley. He had not seen Andy yet. He walked, and then stopped to lean against the brick of the building, and then walked again. He saw Andy then and came toward him, and he stood over him for a long time, the minutes ticking, ticking, watching him and not speaking.

Then he said, "What's a matter, buddy?"

Andy could not speak, and he could barely move. He lifted his face slightly and looked up at the man, and in the rainswept alley he smelled the sickening odor of alcohol and realized the man was drunk. He did not feel any particular panic. He did not know he was dying, and so he felt only mild disappointment that the man who had found him was drunk.

The man was smiling.

"Did you fall down, buddy?" he asked. "You must be as drunk as I am." He grinned, seemed to remember why he had entered the alley in the first place, and said, "Don' go way. I'll be ri' back."

The man lurched away. Andy heard his footsteps, and then the sound of the man colliding with a garbage can, and some mild swearing, and then the sound of the man urinating, lost in the steady wash of the rain. He waited for the man to come back.

It was 11:39.

When the man returned, he squatted alongside Andy. He studied him with drunken dignity.

"You gonna catch cold here," he said. "What's a matter? You like layin' in the wet?"

Andy could not answer. The man tried to focus his eyes on Andy's face. The rain spattered around them.

"You like a drink?"

Andy shook his head.

"I gotta bottle. Here," the man said. He pulled a pint

231

bottle from his inside jacket pocket. He uncapped it and extended it to Andy. Andy tried to move, but pain wrenched him back flat against the sidewalk.

"Take it," the man said. He kept watching Andy. "Take it." When Andy did not move, he said, "Nev' mind, I'll have one m'self." He tilted the bottle to his lips, and then wiped the back of his hand across his mouth. "You too young to be drinkin', anyway. Should be 'shamed of yourself, drunk an' layin' in a alley, all wet. Shame on you. I gotta good minda calla cop."

Andy nodded. Yes, he tried to say. Yes, call a cop. Please. Call one.

"Oh, you don' like that, huh?" the drunk said. "You don' wanna cop to fin' you all drunk an' wet in a alley, huh? Okay, buddy. This time you get off easy." He got to his feet. "This time you lucky," he said. He waved broadly at Andy, and then almost lost his footing.

"S'long, buddy," he said.

Wait, Andy thought. *Wait, please, I'm bleeding.*

"S'long," the drunk said again. "I see you aroun'," and then he staggered off up the alley.

Andy lay and thought: *Laura, Laura. Are you dancing?*

The couple came into the alley suddenly. They ran into the alley together, running from the rain, the boy holding the girl's elbow, the girl spreading a newspaper over her head to protect her hair. Andy lay crumpled against the pavement, and he watched them run into the alley laughing, and then duck into the doorway not ten feet from him.

"Man, what rain!" the boy said. "You could drown out there."

"I have to get home," the girl said. "It's late, Freddie. I have to get home."

"We got time," Freddie said. "Your people won't raise a

fuss if you're a little late. Not with this kind of weather."

"It's dark," the girl said, and she giggled.

"Yeah," the boy answered, his voice very low.

"Freddie . . . ?"

"Um?"

"You're . . . you're standing very close to me."

"Um."

There was a long silence. Then the girl said, "Oh," only that single word, and Andy knew she'd been kissed, and he suddenly hungered for Laura's mouth. It was then that he wondered if he would ever kiss Laura again. It was then that he wondered if he was dying.

No, he thought, I can't be dying, not from a little street rumble, not from just getting cut. Guys get cut all the time in rumbles. I can't be dying. No, that's stupid. That don't make any sense at all.

"You shouldn't," the girl said.

"Why not?"

"I don't know."

"Do you like it?"

"Yes."

"So?"

"I don't know."

"I love you, Angela," the boy said.

"I love you, too, Freddie," the girl said, and Andy listened and thought I love you, Laura. Laura, I think maybe I'm dying. Laura, this is stupid but I think maybe I'm dying. Laura, I think I'm dying!

He tried to speak. He tried to move. He tried to crawl toward the doorway where he could see the two figures in embrace. He tried to make a noise, a sound, and a grunt came from his lips, and then he tried again, and another grunt came, a low animal grunt of pain.

"What was that?" the girl said, suddenly alarmed, breaking away from the boy.

"I don't know," he answered.

"Go look, Freddie."

"No. Wait."

Andy moved his lips again. Again the sound came from him.

"Freddie!"

"What?"

"I'm scared."

"I'll go see," the boy said.

He stepped into the alley. He walked over to where Andy lay on the ground. He stood over him, watching him.

"You all right?" he asked.

"What is it?" Angela said from the doorway.

"Somebody's hurt," Freddie said.

"Let's get out of here," Angela said.

"No. Wait a minute." He knelt down beside Andy. "You cut?" he asked.

Andy nodded. The boy kept looking at him. He saw the lettering on the jacket then. THE ROYALS. He turned to Angela.

"He's a Royal," he said.

"Let's . . . what . . . what do you want to do, Freddie?"

"I don't know. I don't want to get mixed up in this. He's a Royal. We help him, and the Guardians'll be down on our necks. I don't want to get mixed up in this, Angela."

"Is he . . . is he hurt bad?"

"Yeah, it looks that way."

"What shall we do?"

"I don't know."

"We can't leave him here in the rain." Angela hesitated. "Can we?"

"If we get a cop, the Guardians'll find out who," Freddie said. "I don't know, Angela. I don't know."

Angela hesitated a long time before answering. Then she said, "I have to get home, Freddie. My people will begin to worry."

"Yeah," Freddie said. He looked at Andy again.

"You all right?" he asked. Andy lifted his face from the sidewalk, and his eyes said: *Please, please help me,* and maybe Freddie read what his eyes were saying, and maybe he didn't.

Behind him, Angela said, "Freddie, let's get out of here! Please!" There was urgency in her voice, urgency bordering on the edge of panic. Freddie stood up. He looked at Andy again, and then mumbled, "I'm sorry," and then he took Angela's arm and together they ran toward the neon splash at the other end of the alley.

Why, they're afraid of the Guardians, Andy thought in amazement. But why should they be? I wasn't afraid of the Guardians. I never turkeyed out of a rumble with the Guardians. I got heart. But I'm bleeding.

The rain was soothing somehow. It was a cold rain, but his body was hot all over, and the rain helped to cool him. He had always liked rain. He could remember sitting in Laura's house one time, the rain running down the windows, and just looking out over the street, watching the people running from the rain. That was when he'd first joined the Royals. He could remember how happy he was the Royals had taken him. The Royals and the Guardians, two of the biggest. He was a Royal. There had been meaning to the title.

Now, in the alley, with the cold rain washing his hot body, he wondered about the meaning. If he died, he was Andy. He was not a Royal. He was simply Andy, and he was dead. And he wondered suddenly if the Guardians who had ambushed him and knifed him had ever once realized he was Andy? Had they known that he was Andy, or had they simply known that he was a Royal wearing a purple silk jacket? Had they stabbed *him,* Andy, or had they only stabbed the jacket and the title, and what good was the title if you were dying?

I'm Andy, he screamed wordlessly. *For Christ's sake, I'm Andy!*

An old lady stopped at the other end of the alley. The garbage cans were stacked there, beating noisily in the rain. The old lady carried an umbrella with broken ribs, carried it with all the dignity of a queen. She stepped into the mouth of the alley, a shopping bag over one arm. She lifted the lids of the garbage cans delicately, and she did not hear Andy grunt because she was a little deaf and because the rain was beating a steady relentless tattoo on the cans. She had been searching and foraging for the better part of the night. Now she collected her string and her newspapers, and an old hat with a feather on it from one of the garbage cans, and a broken footstool from another of the cans. And then she delicately replaced the lids and lifted her umbrella high and walked out of the alley mouth with queenly dignity. She had worked swiftly and soundlessly, and now she was gone.

The alley looked very long now. He could see people passing at the other end of it, and he wondered who the people were, and he wondered if he would ever get to know them, wondered who it was on the Guardians who had stabbed him, who had plunged the knife into his body.

"That's for you, Royal!" the voice had said, and then the footsteps, his arms being released by the others, the fall to the pavement. "That's for you, Royal!" Even in his pain, even as he collapsed, there had been some sort of pride in knowing he was a Royal. Now there was no pride at all. With the rain beginning to chill him, with the blood pouring steadily between his fingers, he knew only a sort of dizziness, and within the giddy dizziness, he could only think: *I want to be Andy.*

It was not very much to ask of the world.

He watched the world passing at the other end of the alley. The world didn't know he was Andy. The world didn't know he was alive. He wanted to say, "Hey, I'm alive! Hey, look at me! I'm alive! Don't you know I'm alive? Don't you know I exist?"

He felt weak and very tired. He felt alone and wet and feverish and chilled, and he knew he was going to die now, and the knowledge made him suddenly sad. He was not frightened. For some reason, he was not frightened. He was only filled with an overwhelming sadness that his life would be over at sixteen. He felt all at once as if he had never done anything, never seen anything, never been anywhere. There were so many things to do, and he wondered why he'd never thought of them before, wondered why the rumbles and the jumps and the purple jacket had always seemed so important to him before, and now they seemed like such small things in a world he was missing, a world that was rushing past at the other end of the alley.

I don't want to die, he thought. *I haven't lived yet.*

It seemed very important to him that he take off the purple jacket. He was very close to dying, and when they found him, he did not want them to say, "Oh, it's a Royal." With great effort, he rolled over onto his back. He felt the pain tearing at his stomach when he moved, a pain he did not think was possible. But he wanted to take off the jacket. If he never did another thing, he wanted to take off the jacket. The jacket had only one meaning now, and that was a very simple meaning.

If he had not been wearing the jacket, he would not have been stabbed. The knife had not been plunged in hatred of Andy. The knife hated only the purple jacket. The jacket was a stupid meaningless thing that was robbing him of his life.

237

He wanted the jacket off his back. With an enormous loathing, he wanted the jacket off his back.

He lay struggling with the shiny wet material. His arms were heavy, and pain ripped fire across his body whenever he moved. But he squirmed and fought and twisted until one arm was free and then the other, and then he rolled away from the jacket and lay quite still, breathing heavily, listening to the sound of his breathing and the sound of the rain and thinking *Rain is sweet, I'm Andy.*

She found him in the alleyway a minute past midnight. She left the dance to look for him, and when she found him she knelt beside him and said, "Andy, it's me, Laura."

He did not answer her. She backed away from him, tears springing into her eyes, and then she ran from the alley hysterically and did not stop running until she found the cop.

And now, standing with the cop, she looked down at him, and the cop rose and said, "He's dead," and all the crying was out of her now. She stood in the rain and said nothing, looking at the dead boy on the pavement, and looking at the purple jacket that rested a foot away from his body.

The cop picked up the jacket and turned it over in his hands.

"A Royal, huh?" he said.

The rain seemed to beat more steadily now, more fiercely.

She looked at the cop and, very quietly, she said, "His name is Andy."

The cop slung the jacket over his arm. He took out his black pad, and he flipped it open to a blank page.

"A Royal," he said.

Then he began writing.

Afterword

Trying to pin down the stories in this collection is like trying to take a snapshot of a pit of vipers. Of the eleven stories in the book, only two of them were originally published under the Ed McBain pseudonym. "The Intruder" first appeared in *Ellery Queen's Mystery Magazine* in 1970. Barking at Butterflies, from which the collection takes its title, was first published in 1999. In fact, before May of 1956, when the first 87th Precinct novel was published, Ed McBain didn't exist.

You may wonder why there was a need for Ed McBain at all. By 1956, Evan Hunter was already a bestselling novelist. So why Ed McBain? Here's why. My publishers felt that if it became known that Evan Hunter was writing mystery novels, it would be damaging to my career as a "serious novelist," whatever that may be. I personally consider writing mysteries as serious an occupation as writing any other kind of fiction. But these were older, wiser men (I was not yet thirty at the time) and so I followed their advice. Besides they had given me a contract for only three books, and I never once suspected the series—with its renegade concept of a conglomerate cop hero in a mythical city—would ever capture the public imagination. The irony, of course, is that Ed McBain may now be better known around the world than Evan Hunter is.

Nine of the stories in this volume were published under my own name. Three of them have never before been published in the United States. Most beginning writers think that once a writer is published—and *The Blackboard Jungle* was an enormous success, mind you—the rest is sliding on ice. You send a new story to a magazine, it's automatically purchased and a check for $10,000 arrives in the mail the very next day. Sure. But no editor in the United States thought "Short Short Story" or "Motel" were good enough to publish in any magazine. (The most recent American rejection on "Motel" was in 1999.) Before now, "Short Short Story" was published only in Australia and Germany in 1978. "Motel's" first (and only) appearance was in the German edition of *Playboy* in 1978. "The Movie Star" was never published here, either. It first appeared in a British anthology in 1996, and has since been published in Holland and South Africa.

Of the published Evan Hunter stories in this volume (my publishing life hasn't been entirely one of rejection, abandonment and loss) "Uncle Jimbo's Marbles" first appeared in *Redbook* in 1963, "First Offense" in *Manhunt* in 1955, "On the Sidewalk, Bleeding" in that same magazine in 1957, "The Beheading" in a now defunct *Playboy* imitator called *Escapade* in 1965, and "The Birthday Party" in *Playboy* itself in 1967. Perhaps the short story that accounts for Evan Hunter still being here at all is "To Break the Wall." It first saw the light of day in an experimental magazine called *Discovery*, published in paperback format by Pocket Books, Inc. in 1953. You may recognize it as the penultimate chapter of *The Blackboard Jungle*.

Evan Hunter a.k.a. Ed McBain
Weston, CT